Great
Australian Girls

This book is dedicated to my Great Australian Girls:
Miss Kate Murphy
Lauren (Princess Lolly) Young
Lady Emma Reniewick
Rianna (Mademoiselle Lulu) Geason
& Rebecca Rose (Rosie) Geason
and my mother, Joan Geason

Great Australian Girls

Susan Geason

ABC
BOOKS

Published by ABC Books for the
AUSTRALIAN BROADCASTING CORPORATION
GPO Box 9994 Sydney NSW 2001

First published 1999

National Library of Australia
Cataloguing-in-Publication entry
Geason, Susan, 1946– .
  Great Australian girls : and the remarkable women they
  became

  Bibliography.
  Includes index.
  ISBN 0 7333 0758 2.

  1. Women – Australia – Biography – Juvenile literature. 2.
  Women – Australia – History – Juvenile literature. I.
  Australian Broadcasting Corporation. II. Title.

920.720994

Designed by Monkeyfish
Set in 12.5/16.5 Adobe Garamond by Asset Typesetting Pty Ltd, Sydney
Colour separations by Finsbury, Adelaide
Printed and bound in Australia by
Griffin Press, Adelaide.

5 4 3 2 1

Contents

Acknowledgments

For Alice Betteridge and Berta Reid — Valerie Thompson, Royal NSW Institute for Deaf & Blind Children; Nancy Bird, and Susan Stafford, Powerhouse Museum; Beverley, Joan and Ted Buckingham, and Jason King; Tamara Anna Cislowska and Neta Maughan; Fiona Coote; for May Gibbs — Maureen Walsh, Marian and Neil Shand, Robert Holden, and Tim Curnow, Curtis Brown (Australia) Pty Ltd; for Vida Goldstein — Janette Bomford; Evonne Goolagong Cawley; Lorrie Graham; Sonya Hartnett; for Marjorie Lawrence — Geoff Mathison, Winchelsea & District Historical Society; for Mary MacKillop — Claire Dunne, and Sr Marie Foale and Sr Moya Campbell, Sisters of St Joseph; Irene Moss; Linda Tritton McLean and Harold Tritton; Pat O'Shane; for Mary Reibey — Nance Irvine; for Henry Handel Richardson — Axel Clark; Louise and Rita Sauvage, and Karen McBrien; Heather Tetu, Matt Hughes, and Robin Lawrie, Circus Oz; Monique Truong, and Det. Snr Constables Garth Hazell and Julie Day, Cabramatta Police.

For listening to stories out of this book ad infinitum — Byron Addison, Carmel Bird, Ron Clarke, Frank Frost, Joan Geason, Neil McDonell, Tony Mitchell, Erna Nelson, Anthea O'Brien, Elizabeth Parker, David Peterson, Simon Taafe and Graeme Wiffen. For assistance with material and photographs — the staff of Kings Cross Library, Alan Davies and Kevin Leamon at the Mitchell Library, Jessie Street National Women's Library, staff at the Fairfax Photographic Library, and Jo Philp at the University of New England.

Thanks to the people at ABC Books, especially to Ali Lavau, who put so much thought, work and enthusiasm into editing this book. For thinking of the ABC, my agent, Fran Bryson, AMC (Australia) Pty Ltd. Also thanks to Alf Mappin.

Most specially, I want to thank the girls and women in this book for leading such extraordinary, stimulating and inspiring lives and for opening their memories, homes and photo albums to me.

Introduction

In many ways, the women selected for *Great Australian Girls* seem to have nothing in common. What could a convict girl transported for horse theft have in common with a champion tennis player or a trapeze artist? How could a pioneer aviator be compared with a musical prodigy?

Researching and writing these stories has given me some insights into what made these women great, what enabled them to achieve their goals. It has little to do with their backgrounds — some came from well-off families, others from humble beginnings — and a lot to do with their personal qualities. Qualities like courage and determination, the strength to face adversity and obstacles and still fight on. And something else all these women have in common — whether they're artists or athletes, pioneers or performers — is that they started doing their life's work, or began to achieve astonishing things, while they were still only girls.

The dreams of these women were vastly different, but whether their ambition was to sing opera in Paris or swim the fastest 100 metres in the world, they all shared two unshakeable convictions — one was a strong belief in themselves; the other was the belief that girls can do anything.

MARY HAYDOCK REIBEY 1777 — 1855

From convict to respected citizen

In 1791, fourteen-year-old Molly Haydock disguised herself as a boy and ran away from her home in Lancashire, England. Desperate for money, she stole a horse — and got caught. The crime changed her life forever. Transported to New South Wales as a convict, Molly reinvented herself again. As Mary Reibey, she became one of the richest and most respected women in the colony.

Mary (Molly) Haydock was born into a provincial family in the town of Bury-Blackburn, Lancashire, on 12 May 1777. Bury-Blackburn was a large town on the major coach routes to the industrial cities of Manchester and Liverpool. Her parents, James Haydock and Jane Law, belonged to England's agricultural middle class. Molly had a sister, Elizabeth, six years older. Before Molly was two, her parents had died, and the girls were taken in by their grandmother. They were looked after by a nurse and educated at the Blackburn Free Grammar School.

When Molly was thirteen and Eliza nineteen, Grandmother Law died. Eliza was either in service or married by this time, but Molly was left destitute. None of her relatives offered to take her in, so her only options were an orphanage or domestic service. Whatever Molly's fate, she hated it so much she ran away just after she turned fourteen. She set off south towards London, dressed in boy's clothing. Small and thin and covered by the loose smock, pantaloons and heavy boots of a farm labourer, Molly easily passed for a young boy. She called herself James Burrow, after a friend who had died two years before.

With no money to get herself to London, Molly became a vagabond, sleeping rough in haystacks and fields. When she couldn't scrounge food from farmers' wives, she stole it. It was a dangerous life. The roads were busy with travellers, tramps and highwaymen, many quite willing to pilfer a boy's last penny or steal his boots while he was sleeping.

Somehow, Molly survived for two months. Then, on her way south through Chester, she saw a mare in a field. Half-starved and desperate for money, she succumbed to temptation. Seizing the horse, she led it to a fence, climbed on and rode off. That evening, a young boy rode up to Robert Silvester's inn at Stafford, about 64 kilometres from Chester. The boy hailed the innkeeper and asked if he'd like to buy the mare. It belonged to his uncle, who lived outside of Chester, he said. The landlord was not interested. Undeterred, the boy hung about the stables till early the next morning, and tried to sell the horse to several other men.

Unfortunately for Molly, a passer-by saw the mare, suspected it was stolen, and seized her. The constable was called, and Molly was arrested. She was in very serious trouble. Horses were valuable possessions, indispensable to farmers, merchants and stage coachmen. Horse theft was a capital crime, punishable by death.

It was frighteningly easy to put your head in a noose in Molly's day. Two hundred and thirty-one offences attracted the death penalty — in theory, anyway. In fact, most offenders were transported to the colonies instead of being hanged. In the 1790s, that meant New South Wales, as America had stopped taking England's cast-offs after it won the War of Independence in 1776.

Molly was thrown into gaol in Stafford. Like all English gaols at that time, it was overcrowded, filthy and dangerous. The squalid conditions bred disease, despair and immorality. Men and women, some of them as young as Molly, were thrown in together, and no young female was safe from predatory men. Aware that a boy would be less vulnerable than a girl, Molly hung on to her disguise. In the milling chaos of the gaol she somehow managed to escape detection.

After six days in hell, Molly was taken before the Mayor. Afraid to reveal her identity, she remained stubbornly silent when he interrogated her. Then her worst nightmares came true — the Mayor found that James Burrow had a case to answer. Molly was bound over for trial at the Summer Assizes on 24 August 1791. Most girls would have broken at this point and called on their relatives for help, but Molly did not. She'd been rejected once before, when they'd refused to take her in after her grandmother's death. It was unlikely they'd come to her aid now that she'd been branded a common criminal.

So, as James Burrow, Molly Haydock was tried for the crime of feloniously stealing a bay mare to the value of ten pounds. Five witnesses testified against her. She was found guilty and sentenced to be hanged. Despite her shock and disbelief, Molly somehow kept her wits about her. While the wheels of justice ground on inexorably, she continued to pass as a boy in gaol. Finally, to her immense relief, she discovered she was not to be hanged. Because of James Burrow's extreme youth, the magistrate asked for the sentence to be commuted to transportation for seven years.

Some time in October, the inevitable occurred — Molly was found out. It happened when the convicts were being washed and deloused before boarding the convict ships. When James Burrow was forced to undress, the astonished guards saw that the prisoner wasn't actually a boy. The gaol buzzed with the story of the cross-dressing girl.

With her last defence gone, Molly gave in and contacted her family. In an attempt to free her, Molly's uncle, Adam Hope, organised an appeal. The appeal argued that an unidentified man had tricked Molly into holding a stolen horse for him. Though many of Blackburn's leading citizens signed the petition, attesting to Molly's good character, none of her other relatives stood up for her. To get Molly out, they would have to guarantee that she would behave herself for four years. Nobody was prepared to take the risk. After all, Molly Haydock was a proven liar and thief, who had spent the last few months in close contact with the dregs of English society.

The judge remained unmoved by the petition. Molly had received a fair trial. According to the evidence, she'd committed the crime alone and had acted with considerable cunning. Her family's refusal to vouch for her would certainly have influenced him. She had to be punished, both to reform her and to deter other potential horse thieves.

All avenues of escape exhausted, Molly boarded the *Royal Admiral*, and sailed from Gravesend on 27 April 1792. She was listed on the ship's muster as Mary Haddock — the clerk had probably misheard her Lancashire accent. About the size of a large ferry, the *Royal Admiral* housed 47 female convicts and 289 males. The women were each given a cloth petticoat, a coarse shift, a pair of stockings, 450 grams of soap, 112 grams of thread, six needles, a thimble and a pair of scissors. When they reached Botany Bay, they would be given cloth to sew.

The *Royal Admiral* was part of the second fleet of convict ships despatched to New South Wales. Unlike the first fleet, which was under the control of the intelligent and humane Captain Arthur Phillip, the second fleet had been turned over to private contractors. Determined to wring the maximum profit out of the enterprise, the contractors had often overcrowded the ships and cut rations to a minimum. But the toll in illness and death was so high that the public eventually demanded an end to the cruelty and exploitation.

Mary was fortunate enough to set sail after the system had been reformed. The *Royal Admiral* was one of the first ships contracted from the East India Company, and the voyage was well organised and properly provisioned. Even so, it was no pleasure cruise. The male convicts were housed in cramped conditions, sometimes in chains, and were not allowed on deck. Mary and the other women were allowed to mingle with the crew and other passengers on deck — those who would deign to talk to them, anyway — but conditions below were grim. The quarters were overcrowded, stinking of unwashed bodies and clothes, and plagued by rats and scuttling cockroaches. During storms, Mary found the voyage almost unbearable. With filthy seawater washing around the bunks, women vomited from seasickness and cried, afraid they were going to drown thousands of miles from anyone who knew or cared.

In 1792, New South Wales was the end of the earth. The distance was totally beyond Mary's imagination. If she hadn't run away from home, she could have expected to die in the town, perhaps even in the street, in which she was born. Now she wondered if she'd ever see her home, family and friends again. In fact, it would be 28 years before Mary would set foot on English soil once more.

Cooped up together, the women traded stories they'd heard about life in the colony. Mary learnt about the harsh conditions, the food shortages, the fierce natives, and strange animals that hopped on their hind legs. She also discovered that there were six times more men than women in her new home.

After a fast run across the Pacific, the *Royal Admiral* sailed through Sydney Heads on 7 October 1792. Mary had been on the ship for five months and ten days. The sight of dry land was exhilarating. She'd never seen anything like this magnificent harbour before. It was huge, with secluded inlets, sandy beaches, and heavily wooded headlands. The light was dazzling, bouncing off the dark blue water and making her squint. Someone cried out that there were big fish leaping alongside the ship, and a sailor told them they were dolphins. Too excited to take much in when they reached Port Jackson, Mary did not notice the *Britannia* moored nearby. The first mate of this East India Company store ship was Thomas Reibey, who was to become her husband.

Mary Haydock arrived in her new country clean, tidy and in good health. She sent up a prayer of thanks for her escape. Ten men and two women had died on the voyage and seventy-two men, eleven women and five children caught fever. So that the diseases would not spread to shore, Mary and the other convicts were all washed and given new clothes before disembarking.

After the prosperous towns of Lancashire, Sydney Town was a shock. It was tiny, with smelly mudflats at the water's edge. There were only a couple of streets, and rows of small brick huts lined either side of the cove. After a glimpse of the town, the convicts were taken to Parramatta to be assigned their duties. Along with all the other unattached women, Mary was paraded before a crowd of soldiers and settlers. The governor allowed the men to choose 'wives' to live with because he believed it would lead to marriage, thus turning these bad women into good citizens. Although this sounds like little more than slavery, it actually worked quite well. Many of the women were glad of the protection of a man and a roof over their heads. Marriages did take place, and people who came to the settlement later commented on how clean and healthy the colony's children were.

But Mary Haydock had no intention of becoming a slave to some drunken marine. She made herself look as small, young and plain as she could. To her relief, she was not selected. Instead, she was assigned to one of the sixteen women's huts on the western side of the cove. She shared the two rooms with nine other women, and came and went as she pleased. In return for her ration of one pound of rice and four pounds of salt pork a week, she made clothes. Mary was lucky. Later on, gaols were built and the convicts were locked up.

At seventeen, Mary walked proudly down the aisle of the first church in Sydney. It was September 1794, and she was marrying 25-year-old Thomas Reibey. Thomas Reibey had lived an exciting life. As a boy, he'd served as a midshipman on the East India Company's ship, the *Tannah*, during England's war with the French. When the French caught the ship and burned it to the waterline, he'd narrowly escaped death. Rescued by some Bengalis, he was taken to Entally, near Calcutta.

Mary had made an excellent choice in Tom Reibey. Not only was the marriage happy, it also turned into an efficient business partnership. Tom brought land, and experience in trading and shipping to the union. Mary brought ambition, brains and a capacity for hard work. Tom had no old-fashioned ideas about a woman's place being in the home. Perhaps because he was aware of the dangers of his occupation, he encouraged his wife to learn how to run the family business.

When Tom fell in love with Mary, he gave up his commission with the East India Company, and obtained a land grant of twenty hectares on the Hawkesbury River. Tom and Mary sailed up the river to their new home on Tom's sloop, the *Raven*. There they cut down wattle trees, mixed mud, and built a hut. It had earth floors, a thatched roof and a lean-to kitchen. Tom made their rough furniture out of the swamp mahogany and red cedar that grew on their land. They planted vegetables, maize and wheat, and kept pigs.

In this hut, at the age of nineteen, Mary gave birth to her first child, Thomas Junior, in 1796. He was followed by James in 1798, and George in 1801. Two years later, Tom and Mary were granted another forty hectares of land, and called it Reibeycroft. By this time Mary had been a free woman — an 'emancipist' — for four years.

Though the soil on the banks of the Hawkesbury was fertile, life there was hard. The settlement was isolated, and food had to be brought upriver by boat. Like most of the settlers, Tom and Mary had never farmed before. They had to learn by bitter experience. There were few animals, which meant little fertiliser, and their tools were primitive. It was hard to find good workers to help on the farm, and skilled tradesmen were scarce.

Life could also be dangerous on the Hawkesbury. Smuggling was rife, and some settlers set up illicit stills and sold sly grog to the convicts. There was drunkenness and fights, and some farmers let their properties fall into ruin. When the settlers drove the Aborigines off their traditional lands, the blacks fought back, and people on both sides were killed and injured.

At times nature itself seemed to turn against them. In their first year on the river, the wheat crop was badly damaged by blight. Then bushfires broke out when farmers burned off the wheat stubble. The following year, the Hawkesbury River flooded. Rising almost seven metres above its normal level, the swollen, muddy river swept away houses, barns, corn stacks and livestock. Many of the Reibeys' neighbours gave up in despair and fled back to Sydney.

None of this fazed the Reibeys — Mary had survived two English gaols and a convict ship, and Tom had fought off pirates near the coast of Sumatra and survived a war. When other farmers failed, they bought up the leases and expanded their holding. But Tom and Mary eventually realised they weren't cut out to be farmers, and that Tom was wasting all the experience and knowledge he'd gained from those years in the merchant navy. Leaving Mary to run the farm, he began transporting Hawkesbury grain and cedar to Sydney in the *Raven*.

The next step was moving to Sydney, where fortunes and reputations could be made. Tom had secured a grant of land on the edge of the harbour, at what is now Circular Quay. In 1804, when Mary was 27, they sold some land, leased out their other farms, and left the

Hawkesbury. In Sydney they opened a store with a timber yard and boat-building sheds at the back. Mary ran the store, and Tom began carrying coal and timber from Newcastle in the *Raven*. In order to expand the business, he took on a partner, an emancipist called Edward Wills.

After a time, the Reibeys moved to The Rocks, where Mary opened a general store. The Rocks had no running water or sewerage, but was well supplied with pubs, illegal grog shops, prostitutes and drunken sailors. Mary — who was small, but tough — thrived there. The couple now owned two shops and three small sloops.

Like most entrepreneurs, the Reibeys had their rough patches. Once they had to borrow money and mortgage three farms on the Hawkesbury to stay afloat. But they persevered and prospered. Before Mary had turned thirty, they had enough money to build Entally House, a fine residence with grain stores alongside. And Sydney was growing fast. By 1810 there were 12 000 people living in the city, all needing to be fed, housed and clothed. As well as using his vessels to carry wheat, sealskins and even convicts, Tom built the *Mercury* for trading with Fiji and the South-Sea Islands. He also captained his own ship to Calcutta and China, and brought back goods such as rice, cashmere shawls, china dinner sets, calico and sandalwood for Mary's store. While Tom was away, Mary took over the Sydney end of the business, as well as looking after her growing family.

These were the best years of Mary's life. A respectable

wife and mother with a loving husband and a thriving business, she could not have been more content. But in 1811, Tom died of a fever after a long illness. He was only 42. At 34 Mary was a widow. Not only did she have seven children to support — the youngest only fifteen months old — she also had three ships, several farms, shops, a hotel and a warehouse to run.

A less resourceful woman might have sold up and returned to England to be near her family, but Mary stayed. Sydney was her home now. Her future, and that of her children, lay here. Taking control of the business, Mary moved the family to George Street, and sent her fifteen-year-old son, Thomas Reibey Junior, off to sea on the *Mercury* to learn his father's job.

Now that she and her children were financially secure, Mary began planning her assault on Sydney society. Her children were growing up, and she began plotting to marry them well. One way of breaching the ruling class is to give money to its charities. By supporting the Anglican church, Mary met all the right people and got a name as a philanthropist. There was one serious obstacle to her ambition, however — her convict past. Mary's solution was simple: cover it up. Her reasoning? She'd committed the crime and paid the price, but she wasn't going to pay forever. Mary Reibey, former convict, began her disappearing act in 1806. In the census of that year, Mary appears as Mary C. Haddock, married with five children. In the 1828 census, Mary grew even bolder, and claimed she'd come to the colony 'free on the

Mariner in 1821'. All the best lies are partly true. Mary did enter Sydney on the *Mariner* in 1821, but that was on her return from a trip to England with her daughters. No matter how successful and respectable Mary Reibey became, the Molly Haydock who changed her identity and stole a horse was never far beneath the surface.

In 1816 Mary put almost all her property, including twelve farms on the Hawkesbury and a schooner, up for sale. The following year she bought another ship and applied for land grants in Van Diemen's Land (now Tasmania). Her two eldest sons were getting married, and she wanted them to set up a branch of the family business there. Thomas built a grand house, also called Entally, on 160 hectares of land at Hadspen, near what is now Launceston. From the Reibey wharves on the Tamar River, Thomas sailed as Master on his vessels to Port Jackson, taking cargos of Huon pine and bringing back coal and provisions. James and his wife settled on a property near Hobart.

In 1820, Mary decided it was time to return to the scene of the crime. The wealthy widow set out for England with her two eldest daughters — Celia, seventeen, and Eliza, fifteen — to visit relatives and meet business contacts. After a long sea voyage, the three women arrived ill in London, but soon revived sufficiently to start enjoying themselves. They went to the theatre, dances and teas, and the girls had their portraits painted. Mary swept to her business appointments in a hired hackney carriage.

From London they travelled by coach to Liverpool, Glasgow, Edinburgh, Manchester and, most importantly, Mary's old home town of Bury-Blackburn. Mary was anxious and nervous about the visit. In a diary she kept of the trip, she wrote: 'It is impossible to describe the sensations I felt when coming to the top of Dewen Street my native home and amongst my relatives and on entering my once Grandmothers House where I had been brought up, and to find it nearly the same as when I left nearly 29 years ago, all the same furniture and most of them standing in the same place as when I left but not one person I knew or knew me.'

This is plaintive, but not true. Mary visited relatives from both sides of her family and met her cousin Alice Hope, with whom she'd been corresponding. Alice was the daughter of the uncle and aunt who had got up the petition for Molly Haydock all those years ago. While she was in Bury-Blackburn, Mary had her daughters confirmed in the church she'd attended as a girl, and was reunited with her old nurse, now 82.

To improve her daughters' chances of an advantageous marriage, Mary enrolled them in a finishing school in Edinburgh. But they were colonial girls, used to sunshine, comfort and freedom, and they rebelled against the Scottish cold, discomfort and discipline. Within four months, Celia and Eliza were back in London with their mother. Before they embarked on the *Mariner* to return home, the Reibey women went on a monumental shopping spree. With them on the ship went twenty chests and packing cases, a grand carriage, and Lieutenant Thomas Thomson, who had fallen in love with Eliza. They had been away a year.

Over the ensuing years, the rest of Mary's children married and produced grandchildren. Mary was respectable and wealthy, but she suffered her share of misfortunes. She lost a clipper ship when convict labourers loading coal in Newcastle hijacked it and disappeared. Her daughter Eliza's husband was gaoled for embezzlement and had to be bailed out with Reibey money. And worst of all, five of Mary's seven children died before her.

Mary shared a house with Elizabeth until her daughter's marriage, then moved back to Entally House. In 1850, she bought land in Newtown — then a country retreat, now an inner-city suburb of Sydney — and built Reibey House. She died there in 1855 at the age of 78. She left behind the Reibey dynasty, a fortune, several landmark buildings in the centre of Sydney, and a rags-to-riches legend. Mary had laid the ghost of Molly Haydock, teenage horse thief, to rest and died a rich woman and a respected matriarch. Today there are seven streets in Sydney named after her.

LOUISA ATKINSON 1834 — 1872

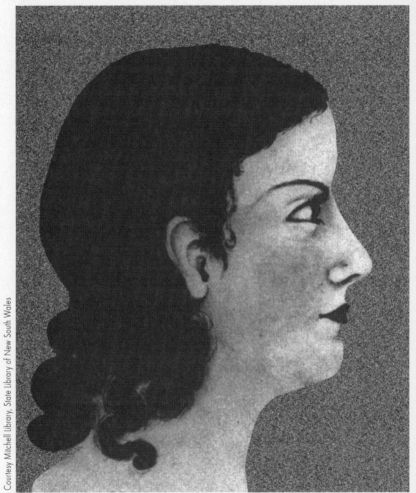

Botanist, artist, writer

As a child, Louisa Atkinson watched her widowed mother fight a six-year legal battle to keep her inheritance and her children. Determined to become financially independent, she prepared herself for a career in science. When she died at 37, she was one of the best-known botanists in New South Wales, as well as a successful writer and artist.

Louisa Atkinson was born in February 1834 in a stone homestead on a large property called Oldbury. Her father, James Atkinson, came from a farming family in Kent, and had immigrated to Australia in 1820. After working in the Colonial Secretary's office, he had received two land grants comprising 2000 acres. James was well respected in the colony, and had many influential friends. He was also a skilled farmer, who had written a book on agriculture. He turned Oldbury — situated in the Southern Highlands of New South Wales — into a model farm.

Louisa's mother, Charlotte Warner, had become engaged to James Atkinson on board a ship when he was returning from a trip to England. Charlotte, who was 29, was on her way to New South Wales to work as a governess. She had been forced to earn her own living after the death of her father, a barrister. Although he did not leave her any money, her father passed on to Charlotte his love of natural history. Charlotte loved 'botanising', or studying plants. Well-educated and independent, she chose to leave her family and embark on an adventure in the colonies.

Charlotte and James were married in 1827. Louisa was

their fourth, and last, child. Two months after her birth, James died. It was a catastrophe for his family. James had named Charlotte and three male friends as executors of his will. That meant his friends had legal power over the family money. Unfortunately, the executors disliked Charlotte, who was strong-minded and unyielding, and tried to use their power to control her. They had underestimated their friend's widow: she was not concerned with being liked, and she hated to be bullied.

Rather than lease the property and move to the city, Charlotte decided to manage Oldbury herself. It was a huge task for a woman, and dangerous, too. Most women would have been too frightened to ride out, as she did, with the convict labourers on long and difficult journeys to the property's out-stations. But Charlotte was brave and determined — and she needed to be. Law and order had broken down in the colony, and Oldbury was isolated. Gangs of escaped convicts and bushrangers roamed the countryside robbing stations and holding up travellers. One of Oldbury's convict labourers was murdered, and the station was robbed many times. Once Charlotte was held up by a gang of bushrangers who threatened to flog and shoot her.

Not surprisingly, Charlotte decided she needed protection. When Louisa was two, her mother married George Barton, the station manager at Oldbury. It was a disastrous choice. An unstable, violent alcoholic, Barton almost ruined the farm and Charlotte's life. The executors eventually terminated his lease and sold the livestock. Oldbury's prized flock of sheep had to be sold for a pittance in 1839.

After three years of hell with Barton, Charlotte fled, taking her children — five-year-old Louisa and her three older siblings. With their possessions loaded onto ox drays, they set out for the Atkinsons' cattle station at Budgong, near Nowra. The party included several convict servants, an Aborigine called Charley and a friend from England.

After crossing miles of rough, barren country, they reached the coastal escarpment, with its moist, dank rainforest. But to reach Budgong, they had first to conquer Meryla Pass. That meant coaxing the horses and bullocks down the rough steps that had been cut into the side of the steep and narrow track. One false step, and a child or an animal could be lost in one of the deep gullies on either side. During the dangerous descent, the children's pet koala, Maugie, managed to stampede the oxen and escape up a tree.

Though their new home was a primitive shack on the edge of wild, unexplored country, it must have seemed like a sanctuary after the violence and tension at Oldbury. These years in the bush were vitally important to Louisa Atkinson's development as a natural scientist. A skilled amateur botanist herself, Charlotte took advantage of the pristine bush at Sutton Forest and Budgong to teach her children how to observe and sketch plants and animals. She soon realised that Louisa was the most talented of them all.

Seven months later, the executors drove George Barton out of Oldbury, and the family returned home. But when Louisa was eight, she was uprooted again. Unable to run the huge property alone, Charlotte moved the family to Double Bay in Sydney. They found no peace there, however. James Atkinson's executors immediately launched a campaign of persecution against his widow. They cut off her funds and tried to take the children away, charging that she was an unfit mother. In those days a woman had no legal right to her own children; under the law, they belonged to their father. Charlotte had two choices: give in and lose her children, or fight. She hired lawyers and took her tormentors to court.

The court case dragged on for six years, bankrupting Charlotte and blighting the children's lives. But Charlotte kept the family together and instilled in her children a love of music, learning and nature. The older children went to school, but Louisa, who had been born with a heart defect, was considered too delicate. Instead, Charlotte taught her at home.

To pay the lawyers' bills, Charlotte had to sell off the family possessions one by one. When there was nothing of value left, she tried her hand at writing. Using the pen-name 'A Lady Long Resident in the Colony', she wrote down the adventure stories she'd been telling her own children for years. *A Mother's Offering to Her Children* was the first children's book published in the colony.

Eight years after James Atkinson's death, the will was finally settled. Charlotte had won. All his debts and legacies were paid, and she was given an allowance to raise and educate her children.

James Atkinson had left Oldbury to his son, James Junior, in his will. When James was fourteen the family returned to Sutton Forest so he could learn to become a farmer like his father. The house was dilapidated and the orchard had gone to rack and ruin, but it was home.

Louisa's childhood was traumatic, but she did not react by becoming rebellious or bitter. Despite her poor health, she was cheerful, vivacious and hard-working. Unlike her mother, who rubbed people up the wrong way, Louisa made friends easily. When she was twelve, Louisa was suddenly faced with a crisis. Charlotte stopped giving her lessons. Perhaps the years of struggle and conflict had exhausted her. This was Louisa's biggest test. Would she remain a half-educated 'lady', dabbling in botany and painting? Or would she fight to become a real scientist? Louisa had inherited her mother's determination: she decided to educate herself. She practised drawing, and studied birds and animals by dissecting them and treating their skins. In her botanical notebooks she recorded seasonal changes and the habits of birds and animals. She even taught herself taxidermy so she could preserve her specimens.

Charlotte's treatment at the hands of George Barton and the executors had a profound effect on Louisa. The lesson was plain: a woman without money and friends was at the mercy of men. Marriage was not the answer; her mother had married twice and had almost ended up destitute. A woman had to gain the skills and knowledge to earn her own living. And that's what Louisa did. At nineteen, she went looking for an audience for her ideas. She found it in a new magazine called the *Sydney Illustrated News*, which snapped up her nature notes and drawings. Her career as a botanical writer and artist was launched.

When Louisa turned 21, she came into a small inheritance — independence at last. She and Charlotte moved to Burwood in Sydney. As well as securing a monthly nature column in the *Sydney Illustrated News*, Louisa tried her hand at fiction. At 22 she wrote *Gertrude, the Emigrant: A Tale of Colonial Life*. It was the first novel written by an Australian-born woman. Though it was published under the pseudonym 'An Australian Lady', everybody in Sydney knew Louisa Atkinson was the author.

During their time in Burwood, Charlotte had had a house built at bushy Kurrajong Heights, north of the Bell's Line of Road at the foot of the Blue Mountains. She called the house Fernhurst. Below the house was a gully which came to be known as Miss Atkinson's Gully. Once they had moved out of the city, Louisa's health improved. She began making long, arduous and often hazardous treks into uncharted territory searching for new plants.

Her favourite travelling companion was Emma Selkirk, a doctor's wife with four step-children and two young children of her own. On horseback, with their long skirts hiked up like trousers, the two would pick their way up and down steep ravines, through dense forest and undergrowth. They trekked to the Grose Valley, Colo, Wiseman's Ferry and Mount Tomah. One of their favourite haunts was the fern gully at the Kurrajong waterfalls, where they discovered several new ferns. Louisa collected many smaller ferns and established them in her fernery at home. In this rugged mountain bushland she also observed, painted and described reptiles, insects and birds. Her colourful paintings of bellbirds, lyrebirds, honeyeaters, friar-birds and parrots are among her finest work.

Louisa described these adventures in 'A Voice from the Country,' the nature series she began writing for the *Sydney Morning Herald.* This newspaper column, which ran for more than eleven years, made her the first female journalist in the colony.

Louisa's deep knowledge of the bush turned her into an early conservationist. One hundred and fifty years ago she warned that tree felling was killing off large flocks of birds, that shooters were wiping out whole species of animals, and that land clearing was turning productive land into marshes. Nobody listened.

Although she was still young and untrained, Louisa was becoming famous in New South Wales for her botanic discoveries. Her name was also known in scientific circles overseas. Already several plants, including a type of mimosa, had been named after her. Through her friend William Woolls, she got to know the famous German botanist, Ferdinand von Mueller, who was in Australia to set up the Melbourne Botanical Gardens.

But in the 1860s Louisa had to give up her explorations. She'd contracted tuberculosis and the illness had recurred. Then her mother fell and broke her arm, dislocating her shoulder. The fall also affected Charlotte's spine, making her an invalid. Despite her own delicate health, Louisa, who was very close to her mother, took on all the heavy nursing. But eventually the women had to give in and return to Oldbury to live with Louisa's brother, James. After more than two years of suffering, Charlotte died there at the age of 71.

After Charlotte's death, Louisa returned to her scientific work. She took up exploring again and began work on her great project — an illustrated book on Australian natural history. In 1870, Louisa sent Ferdinand von Mueller the text and drawings for her book, hoping to get it published in Germany. She could not have chosen a worse time. That year war broke out between Prussia and France. In the ensuing upheaval, von Mueller was not able to find a publisher for the book, and Louisa's manuscript was lost.

Meanwhile, to everyone's surprise, at the age of 35 Louisa married James Snowden Calvert. Then 44, Calvert had led an adventurous and interesting life. As a twenty year old just out from England, he had joined the German explorer Ludwig Leichhardt on his first great Australian expedition. This epic 5000-kilometre trek started in the Darling Downs in Queensland and ended at Port Essington in the Northern Territory. But Calvert was badly wounded in a battle with Aborigines,

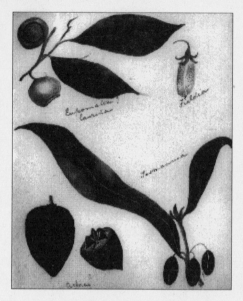

Tasmanian plants by Louisa Atkinson (known as Louisa Caroline Calvert)
Courtesy Mitchell Library, State Library of New South Wales

sustaining injuries which plagued him all his life. He gave up exploring and turned to farming and botany.

The couple set up house at Calvert's farm at Cavan, near Yass. They also bought a property at Nattai, thirteen kilometres from Berrima in the Southern Highlands, and began building a house. Here they planned to cultivate native plants and animals and try new methods of farming and grazing.

Charlotte Atkinson had discouraged her youngest daughter from marrying; she was afraid that Louisa — like her sister Emily, who had died in 1854 — would not survive childbirth. Louisa was willing to take the risk. At the age of 37 she became pregnant. At first it looked as if she had beaten the odds, but eighteen days after the birth of Louise Snowden Annie Calvert, Louisa died.

From her window, the bedridden Louisa would watch for her husband to come home. Then one day his horse galloped into the yard with its saddle empty. Louisa immediately concluded that James must be lying out in the bush, injured and alone — or worse, dead. The shock stopped her heart. James later returned on foot, unhurt, to find his wife had died. In an obituary, the *Sydney Morning Herald* lamented that Louisa was 'cut down like a flower in the midst of her days'.

After Louisa's death, James Calvert fell into a deep depression. He handed over baby Louise to his wife's family at Oldbury, and moved to the property at Nattai. But when Louise was two, he quarrelled with the Atkinsons, and took her away. They moved to Botany, in Sydney, where James became a virtual recluse. Raised by housekeepers, Louise had a miserable and lonely childhood. James Calvert died, probably of cholera, in 1884. Louise's guardian returned his twelve-year-old charge to her uncle and aunt at Oldbury. By this time, James Atkinson had lost most of his money through bad investments, and Oldbury was a dairy farm. Then James died in a fall from a horse the following year, and his wife could not afford to look after Louise. Her guardian arranged for her to live with the family of the Anglican minister at Sutton Forest. They were good to her, and she finally found some happiness.

The following year, Oldbury was sold. Many of

Louisa Atkinson's belongings were stored there. Sadly, nobody at Oldbury seemed aware of the importance of her botanical research. Her daughter was told to come and get anything she wanted before the auction. Only thirteen, and with no help from the family, Louise could only manage to salvage some letters, papers and drawings. Everything else, including numerous cases of stuffed birds and animals, was burned or destroyed. Fortunately for posterity, Louise treasured her mother's papers and handed them on to her own daughter.

Of the four children of Charlotte and James Atkinson, it was the youngest and weakest who left the greatest legacy. Frail and largely self-educated, she nonetheless made a name for herself as a botanist in a time when only exceptional and determined women could force their way into the scientific world. She was also our first woman journalist and novelist. Louisa Atkinson Calvert was greatly loved and admired — her early death was widely mourned. Although the greater part of her work has been lost, enough of her splendid drawings and nature notes have survived to show us how singular and talented she was.

MARY MACKILLOP 1842 – 1909

Australia's first saint?

*When Mary MacKillop was eight, she told her aunt that a beautiful lady
had visited her in the night. Her aunt believed the little girl had seen a
vision of Mary, the Mother of Christ. After a deeply religious, but traumatic
and poverty-stricken childhood, Mary MacKillop founded the first
Australian order of nuns at the age of 24. She is expected to be
our first Catholic saint.*

Mary MacKillop was born in Melbourne on 15 January
1842, the eldest of eight children. Her parents,
Alexander MacKillop and Flora MacDonald, had
immigrated separately to Australia from Scotland in the
late 1830s and married here. Alexander MacKillop had
quit the priesthood after eight years of study in Rome. In
Australia he found a job with a trading company, and by
the time Mary was born the MacKillops lived in a big
house in Fitzroy and owned land.

But when Mary was two, her father was declared
bankrupt after some reckless business deals. The house
was sold and the family left Melbourne. They lived off
relatives for a time before settling on a farm. Life was
hard in the MacKillop household. Alexander was
argumentative and impulsive, and could not seem to
hold down a job for long, while Flora never learnt to
cope with her big family or manage what little money
they had. As the eldest daughter, Mary had to help her
mother in the house and look after the babies.

The first inkling of Mary's religious calling came when
she was eight. She had lost both her beloved grandfather

and her baby brother, Alick, within sixteen months of each other. Deeply traumatised, she was sent off to Melbourne to stay with her aunt and uncle, the L'Estranges. One night, her aunt discovered her sitting up in bed, wide awake, in the middle of the night. Asked what was wrong, Mary said: 'A beautiful lady has been here, and told me she would be a mother to me always.' Mrs L'Estrange always believed that her niece had seen a vision of the Virgin Mary.

But mostly Mary was an ordinary girl. Flora, who was a fearless horsewoman, taught her to ride fast and well, and she loved playing at rounding up cattle on her pony. When the family had enough money to pay school fees, she and her sisters and brothers went to school; the rest of the time Alexander taught them at home. Mary soaked up English, Gaelic and simple mathematics. He also instructed her in the Catholic religion. As Mary learnt more, she began to wonder how her father could have dropped out of his studies for the priesthood. She came to believe she had to take his place in religious life. That meant becoming a nun — and Mary soon found an avenue for her religious work.

In 1851, when Mary was nine, gold was discovered in Victoria. Men rushed off to the goldfields, abandoning their wives and children. Forced to fend for themselves in primitive bush huts and filthy slum tenements, the women left behind either had to rely on charity or starve. When young Mary heard about their plight, she decided to devote her life to the poor, the sick and the homeless.

Mary MacKillop as a girl
Photograph used with permission of the Trustees of the Sisters of St Joseph

The MacKillops were soon threatened with homelessness themselves. When a dying friend asked Alexander to accompany him back to Scotland, he mortgaged the farm to his brother Peter and left the country. During the year he was away, Peter MacKillop evicted Flora and her children. Flora's brother Donald took them all in at his property near Plenty, a few kilometres away.

Their bad luck continued after Alexander's return. By the time Mary was fourteen, the MacKillops had to return to Melbourne penniless. Alexander found work, but was sacked for criticising the politician who gave him the job. Flora finally had to face the truth — she would never be able to rely on her husband to provide for her and the children. She opened a boarding house in Collingwood, but it proved too much for her to manage. Old enough to work now, Mary would have to become the family's breadwinner.

Her first job was with the L'Estranges, as a governess for their two children. Mary enjoyed the work, but the pay was too low. She looked around and found another job as a saleswoman in a stationery shop in Collins Street. The owners were kind, but Mary hated the job. It was humiliating being treated like a servant by rude customers, and it was not what she wanted to do. She should be in a convent, training to become a nun instead of wasting her time in a shop. Her cousins, the Camerons, gave her a way out. They asked her to teach their four children on their property at Penola, in South

Australia. About 160 kilometres from Portland and 12 kilometres from the Victorian border, Penola was the frontier. Undaunted, eighteen-year-old Mary packed her portmanteau, said a teary goodbye to Flora and the children, and took the Cobb and Co. coach to the very edge of civilisation. The tears soon dried; she was leaving behind the never-ending demands of her family and starting an adventure.

Penola was a shock after the green farmlands of Victoria and the comforts of Melbourne. Instead of proper houses, the townsfolk lived in bark, slab, log and weatherboard huts. A dray track served as a road. Though some squatters had become rich from running sheep, most of the small farmers in the district had to struggle to survive. When Mary asked about going to Mass, she discovered that an abandoned shop served as the Catholic church and the priest's home. There were only 1500 Catholics in the 52 000 square kilometre parish. The priest had to visit them on horseback.

In 1861, when Mary arrived, the parish priest was Father Julian Woods, a 28-year-old English Jesuit. A compelling man, Father Woods had been a journalist before joining the priesthood, and was an amateur geologist, botanist, scholar and writer. The governess and the priest clicked immediately. Father Woods became Mary's spiritual guide and friend, and encouraged her to become a nun. He dreamed about starting a new religious order, and saw in Mary the kind of woman he wanted in it. On his travels in France he'd come across an order of nuns who lived in poverty in the villages and taught basic skills to the peasant children. He was convinced that this was what South Australia needed.

An order is a community of men or women who share a desire to live their lives solely for God. Nuns promise to obey the Pope, who is head of the Catholic Church, and his delegates — that is, the cardinals, archbishops, bishops and priests. All the orders in Australia were run from abroad. Mary was galvanised by the idea. In those days, Australian Catholic children were taught by Irish and European nuns. Mary believed they would be better served by Australian nuns who understood their particular needs. But she had to bide her time. Until her sisters and brothers were old enough to work, she was trapped.

After two years, the Cameron children grew too old for a governess, and Mary had to return to Melbourne. Within weeks she was on the move again, this time to Portland, to teach the children of another branch of the Cameron family. But when she found out how spoiled and difficult the children were, she started looking around for a new job. In October 1863, Mary was offered a job in Portland's Catholic school. The following year, the rest of the family moved to Portland and her sister Annie joined her at the school.

In Portland, Mary and Flora took a lease on a big old guesthouse called Bay View House and turned it into a girls' boarding school. Flora MacKillop did the housework, Mary's sister Maggie taught the three boarders, and Mary and Annie helped out after finishing their duties at the other school. To prepare herself for her vocation, Mary spent long hours praying. One night she stayed so long in the local church she got locked in and had to sleep on a pew. She also turned down a marriage proposal in Portland — Mary MacKillop planned to be the bride of Christ, not the wife of a wealthy businessman.

For a time things went well, but with Alexander around the peace could not last. Sure enough, he took against the way Mary's headmaster treated her and demanded the man's dismissal. He won, but the town took sides and Mary was blamed. She had to leave Portland under a cloud. Unwittingly, Alexander had played into Father Woods' hands. To get his order started, he needed Mary in Penola. And now, just when the Catholic teacher in Penola was leaving to get married, Mary was available. But Father Woods' invitation did not extend to her trouble-making father. To fulfil her own ambition, Mary had to face a painful choice — God or family. After praying for guidance, she decided that the poor needed her more than the MacKillops did. It was time for her younger sisters and brothers to start looking after themselves.

The MacKillops split up. Flora stayed on in Portland with two of the boys, and Maggie went to live with Peter and Julia MacKillop on a property near Geelong. Alexander was despatched to one of his brother's properties near Hamilton, where he could do no more damage. He died there three years later, aged only 56. If Mary felt any guilt about her father's exile and lonely death, she never admitted it in public.

In 1865 the three older MacKillop girls set off to Penola to start their school. Mary was 24, Annie was17, and Lexie only 15. They started out teaching classes in their cottage and the local church. Later they moved into an old stable that their brother John renovated for them. In January 1866, with the opening of the first school of the Institute of Saint Joseph of the Sacred Heart, a new religious order was born in Australia. Two months later, Mary achieved her ambition of becoming a nun by dressing in a simple black gown and bonnet and signing her letters 'Mary, Sister of St Joseph'.

The audacity of Mary's actions shocked many Catholics — ordinary folk as well as priests. They made their disapproval known, but Mary ignored them. Because the church would never accept a woman as head of a religious order, Father Woods became the director of the Josephites, as they became known. He made all the decisions and drew up a set of rules which became the order's constitution. Mary and Father Woods had no trouble finding nuns for this new community. Many idealistic young women were attracted to the idea of serving the poor and living humbly. The Josephites soon began to make their mark. In 1867 Bishop Sheil invited them to Adelaide. There, on 15 August, Mary made her vows before Father Woods. To the traditional vows of obedience, chastity and poverty, she added another — to promote the love of Jesus Christ in the hearts of children.

The Josephite Sisters' lives were very basic. They lived two or three to a house, slept on straw beds and went out begging for food. Their habit, or uniform, was a traditional nineteenth-century nun's habit. It consisted of a black alpaca dress with a full skirt gathered at the waist (later, the dress would be brown), a small white starched bib which fitted snugly around the neck, and a black veil. The Sisters also wore a thick black leather belt buckled at the back, a crucifix and rosary beads. By 1869 there were 79 Sisters running 21 schools, some of them in isolated parts of the colony. The Josephites also looked after the sick, the old, the destitute, orphans and the imprisoned. They opened an orphanage, a refuge for women, and a crisis accommodation centre for women and children. But trouble was brewing. The Bishop had put Father Woods in charge of Catholic education in South Australia, and the priest began throwing his weight around and making enemies for himself and the Josephites among the parish priests.

Towards the end of the year, Mary took some of her Sisters to Brisbane to open a branch. They lived in an old pub, sweltered in the subtropical heat and fought off the mosquitoes. But inadvertently, Mary had blundered into an ancient power struggle in the church. The Bishop of Brisbane, James Quinn, belonged to a group of powerful Irish bishops who ran the church in Australia. They were at loggerheads with the Vatican in Rome about many religious matters. When they discovered that the Josephites wanted to run their order themselves and answer directly to Rome, they saw it as a challenge to their authority. They wanted to control the affairs of any religious order in their diocese or territory. Bishop Quinn set out to bend Mary to his will. Mary resisted.

Soon Mary had more pressing problems. A scandal had erupted in Adelaide. Two of her Sisters were claiming that they had been visited by the devil, and Father Woods believed them. After fires broke out in the convent, Mary tried to warn Father Woods that such shenanigans could damage the reputation of the order. She was afraid the Josephites would become known as religious cranks. When Father Woods ignored her advice, Mary retreated, not yet ready to challenge his authority. Powerless to intervene from Brisbane, she became depressed, bitter and angry about what was happening to the Josephites.

An even more serious threat arose in 1871 when a group of priests petitioned the Bishop of Adelaide to get rid of the 'incompetent' Josephite Sisters and their schools. Mary returned to Adelaide to defend her Sisters. All her worst fears were realised when the Bishop stepped in. He had decided to weed out the 'lazy and ignorant' nuns and to change the Josephites' constitution to make them more like other orders. Their convent was to be turned over to the Dominican nuns. Mary was devastated. These changes would take away all the Sisters' independence and force them to abandon the poor. She wrote to the Bishop begging him to reconsider, and threatening to leave the order if he did not. On 21 September 1871, the Bishop's adviser ordered Mary to leave Adelaide. When she refused, the Bishop threatened her with excommunication. This would mean she could no longer enter a church or practise her religion. Backed by her Sisters, Mary continued to defy him. At only 29, she was facing the toughest challenge of her life.

Worn down by the stress, Mary collapsed and took to her bed. The Bishop swept into the convent and called the trembling Sisters together. Mary was brought in and told to kneel before him. After scolding her for spiritual pride, he formally excommunicated her. Unwilling to stay in the order without Mary, some of the nuns asked to be allowed to leave. The Bishop refused. Shocked and incredulous, Mary left the convent. Living like a fugitive, she moved from house to house. She kept silent. God was testing her, she believed. If she endured, the order would survive. Within a week, most of the Sisters had been expelled or allowed to leave the order. With priests denouncing them from the pulpit, they tried to make new lives for themselves as governesses, servants or seamstresses. In November, the Dominicans took over their convent.

Fortunately, the dying Bishop lifted Mary's excommunication in March 1872. All the Sisters were accepted back into the order. But Father Woods was not forgiven. He was sacked as Director of the Josephites. Mary's ordeal was not over yet, though. In May, the Vatican initiated an inquiry into the affair. It appointed a new director for the Josephites and exonerated Mary. But there was no time to relax: Bishop Matthew Quinn, brother of the Bishop of Brisbane, was trying to take over the Josephites in Bathurst. Mary began to wonder if the bishops would ever leave her alone. When Father Woods wrote and told Mary that the only way to stop the bishops was to go to Rome and get the constitution approved, she realised he was right. It was a daunting prospect, though. Mary had never been out of Australia before. As there was only enough money for a one-way ticket for one person, she would have to travel alone. Donning ordinary clothes so she would not attract attention, and calling herself Mrs MacDonald, Mary left Adelaide on 28 March 1873 by ship. Six weeks later, she arrived in the holy city of Rome.

Clutching her letters of introduction, Mary began visiting Vatican officials to get her case heard. She found many supporters. One priest arranged a room for her in a French convent, and only two weeks after her arrival she was granted an audience with the Pope. In a letter to her mother, Mary called it, 'A day never to be forgotten, a day worth years of suffering.'

In December 1873, the Vatican's verdict came down. The good news was that the Josephites could continue to govern themselves. The bad news was that although individual nuns could live in poverty, the order had to own property and money. The Vatican ruled that the new constitution had to be tried out before being given final approval. Most importantly, the Australian bishops could not change the Josephites' constitution without permission from Rome.

Mary arrived back in Australia on Christmas Day 1874, bringing eight Irish girls for the order. She'd been away for two years. One hundred Sisters welcomed her home to the new Mother House in Kensington, Adelaide, and soon after Mary was elected Mother General — she was now head of the Josephites. It was time for Mary to have it out with the troublesome bishops. She went to Brisbane and confronted Bishop Quinn. He threatened to put the police onto Mary if she tried to enter the Josephite convent, but she stood her ground. Two months later the Bishop called a truce. When his brother refused to stop undermining the Josephites in Bathurst, Mary withdrew her Sisters from the town.

The constant conflict was starting to wear Mary and the order down. Sisters were leaving and it was getting harder to recruit new members. Tired and depressed, Mary became seriously ill. In a letter to one of the Sisters, she confessed: 'These things have crushed me to the heart and I have even dared to envy the dead. I stand utterly alone — I trust no human being now.'

As always, she rallied. In 1879 she withdrew her Sisters from Brisbane. Catholics in that city wrote angry letters to the paper and petitioned the bishop to keep the Josephites, but it was too late. The Josephites would not return to Queensland till the turn of the century, when the Bishop of Rockhampton invited them into his diocese. A period of calm followed. The order moved into New South Wales, and in 1881 Mary was again elected Mother General. Then a new round of troubles began. Bishop Reynolds set up a commission of inquiry into the Josephites' finances in Adelaide. It turned into a witch-hunt. The commissioners tried to prove that Mary, who'd been prescribed a nip of brandy at night to ease her headaches, was an alcoholic. They also accused her of using the order's money to buy furniture and clothing for her family and friends. As the Sisters had to swear an oath that they would never reveal what was said in the hearings, Mary was unaware of these allegations. When the Bishop tried to make some changes in the order after the inquiry, Mary protested. She was banished to Sydney. But the Vatican had been watching. In 1884 it held an inquiry of its own. Patrick Moran, the new Archbishop of Sydney, heard the evidence and absolved Mary from any suspicion of alcoholism or fraud. He also appointed Sister Bernard the Mother General, in an attempt to improve relations between the Josephites and the bishops.

Ignoring Rome, the Australian bishops voted in 1885 to place the Josephites under their control. Sixteen months later, Rome overturned their decision. The following year Patrick Moran, now a cardinal, returned from Rome with news that settled the issue once and for all. The Pope had officially recognised the Josephites as a religious order, with the right to govern themselves. The constitution was now untouchable. The Vatican also decreed that the Mother House move to Sydney and that Mother Bernard remain Mother General for another ten years. In the meantime, Mary had some personal issues to face — starting with the death of her mother. At Mary's urging, Flora had agreed to come to Sydney to help her daughter raise money for an orphanage. On

30 May 1886, the ship on which Flora was travelling struck a reef off the New South Wales coast and sank. All 76 passengers were drowned. Mary was overcome with grief and guilt. Three years later, Father Woods died. Mary was saddened. Though he had come perilously close to destroying the Josephites, the order would never have existed without him.

The worst of the Josephites' troubles was now over. By 1890 they had established schools and charitable homes all over Australia and New Zealand. Despite her rheumatism, Mary continued to travel to far-flung schools and convents, and visited New Zealand. And she could still kick up her heels and act like a highland lass. Once, when she was on her way to visit the Josephite orphanage at Kincumber on the central coast of New South Wales, her coach was held up at a flooded river. Instead of turning back, Mary mounted one of the horses and rode over to the other side.

In 1898, when Sister Bernard died suddenly, Mary found herself back in charge of the Josephites. But her health was beginning to fail. At sixty, on a trip to New Zealand, she suffered a stroke. It left her paralysed down the right side of her body, but her mind remained clear, and she learnt to walk with a stick. Her deputy, Sister La Merci, took on the bulk of the travelling and the day-to-day running of the order. After a second stroke, Mary was confined to a wheelchair. She still dictated letters to a typist and wrote with her left hand. Eventually gangrene took hold in Mary's paralysed leg, making her last months very painful. When the news spread that she was dying, many of her friends came to Sydney to say their farewells.

Mother Mary MacKillop died on 8 August 1909 at the age of 67. Cardinal Moran was with her. He said: 'I consider this day I have assisted at the deathbed of a saint.' She left behind 750 nuns teaching over 12 000 children in Josephite schools in Australia and New Zealand. The Requiem Mass for Mary — held at St Mary's in North Sydney — was packed, and the streets to the cemetery were lined with people. Her body now lies in the Memorial Chapel at Mount Street, North Sydney. Thousands of people have since made a pilgrimage there.

The move to canonise Mary MacKillop and make her a saint began in 1926. But when the old accusations about alcoholism resurfaced, the process was suspended. Then in 1951 Patrick Moran's report exonerating Mary was found and the case was reopened. In 1973 Rome gave her the title 'Servant of God'. In 1993 a miracle was attributed to Mary when a woman made an inexplicable recovery from leukemia after praying to her. Two years later the Pope gave Mary the title 'Blessed' Mary MacKillop. If the Vatican recognises one more miracle, she will be made a saint.

Mary MacKillop is revered in this country because she possessed qualities Australians admire. Everyone was equal in her eyes. She welcomed Sisters from all walks of life, and treated them all the same. Underdogs aroused her special sympathy — the down-and-out, the mentally ill, the homeless, unmarried mothers. Knowing that ignorance bred poverty and crime, she made sure that poor children got a free education. In a time when religious intolerance was rife, she had Protestant and Jewish friends and supporters. A feminist before the word was invented, she fought for the right of religious women to control their own affairs.

She was a born leader. When she set her heart on something — convincing a sinner to repent or persuading a rich woman to donate land for a convent in North Sydney — few could refuse her. She changed people's lives.

VIDA GOLDSTEIN 1869 — 1949

Suffragist, pacifist, social reformer

On her visits to the slums of Melbourne with her mother, the young Vida Goldstein saw poverty, malnutrition, illness and despair. When she realised that women and children suffered most, she decided to set about improving conditions for them. At a time when it took great courage for a woman even to speak in public, she became a social reformer, a suffragist who helped win the vote for women, and an anti-war activist.

Vida's mother, Isabella Hawkins, came from a wealthy but unhappy family in rural Victoria. Isabella's father was a violent alcoholic, who once assaulted her mother and tried to kill himself in a drunken rage. Isabella was orphaned at seventeen, and at eighteen married Lieutenant Jacob Goldstein.

Jacob Goldstein was the son of a Polish Jew who'd fled his homeland during the political upheavals of the 1830s and settled in Ireland. At nineteen, Jacob ran away to Australia and settled in Victoria. The Goldsteins were running a successful wholesale and general store in Portland when Vida was born in 1869. She was followed by Elsie, Lina and Selwyn.

In 1877 Jacob found a job as a draftsman in the Lands Department and the Goldsteins moved to Melbourne. Their youngest daughter, Aileen, was born there. With Jacob's salary and the money Isabella had brought to the marriage, the Goldsteins were well-off financially. From the outside they looked like any other prosperous middle-class family, but the Goldsteins were different. Instead of ignoring the plight of the poor and disadvantaged, they

The Goldstein children (l to r): Selwyn, Lina, Vida (standing), Elsie and Aileen
Courtesy National Library of Australia

committed themselves to social reform, both through charitable works and through changing the system which allowed such inequalities to exist.

Isabella had been profoundly affected by her mother's helplessness at the hands of her father. It convinced her that women must have equality under the law, that alcohol was evil, and that domestic violence had to be stopped. She became a feminist, a teetotaller and a pacifist. Jacob, though he did not practise the Jewish religion, was almost certainly influenced by the history of his people. In many countries in Europe, Jews had to live in ghettoes, were barred from most professions, and were at the mercy of gangs of anti-Semites.

The reforming passion of the Goldsteins was sorely needed in Australia in the 1870s. In the fetid slums of Melbourne people lived in rat-infested, crumbling houses with sewage flooding their backyards. Malnutrition was widespread, and polluted drinking water caused outbreaks of disease. There was no such thing as a social welfare system. The poor, the sick, the aged and widows had to rely on charity for help.

Isabella and Jacob believed that charity was not enough. People had to be prevented from falling into poverty in the first place. The best way of doing this was teaching them the skills to get jobs and look after themselves. For those who could not work, it meant setting up a system for distributing welfare where it was needed. These ideas were discussed passionately in the Goldstein household, and Vida drank it all in.

Fortunately for their daughters, Isabella and Jacob also held progressive ideas about education. They believed girls as well as boys should be taught to be useful and to contribute something to society. They hired governesses to teach their children at home, then sent them off to conventional high schools in their teens.

Vida was clever and precocious. At the age of ten, with her father's encouragement and help, she wrote her own autobiography. According to her governess, she was a conscientious child and a good influence on those around her. When she was fifteen, Vida was sent to Presbyterian Ladies College to finish her schooling. The principal said she was one of the most thoroughly grounded pupils he'd ever enrolled. Vida enjoyed school, and she was a good all-round student. She was also a perfectionist. In her matriculation year, she studied so hard she collapsed and was ill for days. This was an early warning of her single-mindedness and a tendency to drive herself to achieve.

After matriculating with good results, Vida followed her parents' example. She accompanied her mother on her rounds of the slums, dispensing food, clothing and medicine. But she also enjoyed herself like any teenage girl. She danced at balls, played billiards, tennis and the piano, shot clay pigeons, cycled energetically and rode horses. She had many suitors, but turned them all down.

Around this time Isabella and the children joined the Presbyterian Scots Church, probably because they admired the pastor, the progressive and controversial

Charles Strong. They supported Strong's campaign to clear the slums and improve conditions for prisoners in Victoria's jails. When Strong established his own church, the Australian Church, they followed him. Vida worked on many of Strong's charitable committees, learning how to organise and raise money.

In 1890 a nationwide economic depression began, and suddenly thousands of people were out of work. Charities could not keep up with the demand for their services. The Goldsteins were not immune from its effects. Jacob lost his job and his pension, and Vida and her sisters had to earn their own living.

One of the few professions open to women was teaching. Vida found a job at Toorak College, but soon left to open her own school in St Kilda with Elsie and Aileen. Here she was able to put some of her ideas on education into practice. The sisters made the school coeducational, with small classes and an emphasis on individual teaching. This put heavy demands on Vida's time, but she continued her charity work.

By now, Australian women were starting to demand equality under the law. In the late nineteenth century, husbands still controlled their wives' property, and could take their children away. Women were also barred from higher education and many occupations, so many widows and single women were doomed to poverty. And since women were not considered intelligent or responsible enough to vote, they could not change the system. Women's suffrage groups sprang up and began to campaign for the vote. Suffragists started collecting signatures for a petition, which was put to the Victorian Parliament in 1891, demanding the vote. Isabella and Vida helped collect the 33 000 signatures. They also joined the Victorian Women's Suffrage Society. At 23, Vida had taken the first step in a political career that would last thirty years.

This commitment to suffrage split the Goldstein family apart. Jacob Goldstein might have been progressive on some issues, but he did not believe in giving the vote to women. Isabella and Jacob became estranged. Though they continued to live in the same house, they stopped speaking to each other and were never reconciled.

Vida and Isabella were unmoved by Jacob's opposition. Unfortunately, the campaign for suffrage had ground to a halt. The legislation which would give Victorian women the vote needed to be passed by both houses of Parliament. It was stalled in the Upper House.

It was time, Vida decided, to find out exactly how the political system worked. This took some courage. Middle-class women were brought up to marry. The home was their sphere of influence. It was regarded as 'unwomanly' to try to break into male bastions of power. Vida didn't care. She haunted Parliament House, listening to debates which affected women and children and trying to persuade Members of Parliament to adopt her point of view. As Vida was tall, good-looking, articulate and witty, she got a sympathetic hearing, and managed to convert some MPs to her cause.

When the United Council for Women's Suffrage was established, Vida joined. This was a daring step. Suffragists were labelled agitators and extremists and accused of having loose morals. At a time when women did not speak in public, she was able to practise on a sympathetic audience. She quickly turned into an eloquent and persuasive speaker. When the Council's president, Annette Bear-Crawford, died in 1899, Vida succeeded her. It was a turning point for her. She closed down the school and devoted herself to political work. She also declared herself a pacifist, speaking out against sending Australian troops to South Africa to fight in the Boer War.

In 1900 Vida started a new career as a journalist and propagandist. She was appointed editor of a new monthly paper called the *Australian Women's Sphere*. Its mission was to air issues which affected women. Some of the articles Vida printed included stories about women who had succeeded in business and the professions, and profiles of leading Australian feminists, such as Rose Scott and Catherine Spence.

Australian women were not alone in wanting the vote. Huge suffrage campaigns were also being waged in England and the United States. In 1901 Vida found out that an International Women's Suffrage Conference was to be held in Washington the next year. Women's associations across the country got together and selected her as the Australian delegate, and launched an appeal to fund the trip. As Vida was now regarded as an authority on women's welfare, the Victorian government commissioned her to do some research in America.

At 33, Vida embarked on her first journey overseas. To her surprise, she found herself being treated as a distinguished visitor in the US. The conference organisers had arranged a whistlestop tour of the major cities for her. Nervous but excited, she set off on a train journey across the country, lecturing to enthusiastic women's groups. The trip was a triumph. Vida met Teddy Roosevelt, then President of the United States, and the legendary American feminists Susan Anthony and Elizabeth Cady Stanton, who were both still active in their eighties. As she travelled, she sent back reports on her impressions of America to the *Women's Sphere*.

Vida was away five months. By the time she returned in August 1902, Australian women had won the right to vote in federal elections. But first they had to be taught how to exercise this new right. To do this, a group of women set up the Women's Federal Political Association. Vida threw her weight behind it. As far as she was concerned, the next logical step in women's political journey was running for political office. She stunned the world by announcing that she would run for election to the Senate, representing Victoria as an independent candidate. This was revolutionary — no woman in the British Empire had ever contested a national election.

Vida threw herself into the 1903 federal election campaign. Yet despite the support of family, friends and fellow suffragists, she lost. It seemed that the people of

Victoria would not vote for a woman, particularly a woman without the backing of a political party. Between 1903 and 1917, she would run for federal parliament five times and lose every time.

The election defeat cast Vida into a crisis of anguish and self-doubt. She felt let down not only by the women she'd fought so hard to help, but even by her family. By now she'd had fallen out with her younger sister Lina, whose husband disapproved of Vida's political activities. On top of this, her newspaper was losing money and had to be closed down. She found solace in religion. Along with Isabella, Aileen and Elsie, she had joined the Christian Science Church, and she regarded it as the spiritual anchor for her social and political work. When she emerged from her depression, Vida decided to concentrate on campaigning to win Victorian women the right to vote in state elections.

It would take five more years of effort. After every other state in the Commonwealth, Victoria finally gave women the right to vote in 1908. The victory gave Vida a second wind. She started the *Woman Voter*, a monthly newsletter for the Women's Political Association which was designed to teach women how to use their vote wisely. In the pages of the newsletter, Vida campaigned vigorously against social problems such as selling girls into prostitution, violence against women and the high price of essential foods.

On the other side of the world, English women were still fighting for the right to vote, over forty years after the issue had first been raised in parliament. In 1908, 40 000 suffragists marched through the streets of London, then held a huge rally in Hyde Park. When they realised peaceful protest was never going to work, some women lost patience and began advocating civil disobedience. The Women's Social and Political Union, a militant group led by mother and daughter Emmeline and Christabel Pankhurst, led the charge. Calling themselves 'suffragettes', they smashed windows, defaced golf courses, set fires and marched in the streets.

They were arrested and thrown into jail with hardened criminals. When the women protested by going on hunger strikes, prison authorities retaliated by feeding them through tubes forced painfully down their throats. It was a political mistake: these women were respectable people's mothers, daughters and sisters, not common criminals. A huge public outcry ensued, and the government was compelled to stop the force-feeding.

Vida, who'd been following events in England, corresponded with the Pankhursts and wrote a newspaper article justifying their actions. In 1911 they invited her to London to participate in the campaign, which would culminate in a great procession on 17 June. Vida could not resist being part of history. In the procession, Vida was one of the leaders of the Australian women's contingent. Wearing purple, green and white ribbons, the suffragists marched five abreast. The crowd lining the streets stood ten deep. Onlookers were moved by the sight of the hundreds of women who'd been imprisoned, all clad in white.

After addressing an audience of 10 000 in London's Albert Hall, Vida embarked on a speaking tour of England. She met all the leading lights in the British women's movement, including the playwright George Bernard Shaw. She also visited her brother, Selwyn, who'd become an engineer. He'd moved his family to London after spending two years working in Mexico during the Mexican Revolution.

After five months away, Vida returned home determined to rally support for the English suffragettes. When she could not get the newspapers to print any of her articles on their plight, she ran them in the *Woman Voter*. But this was preaching to the converted. How could she get the message across to the public? She decided to sell the paper on the streets herself — something no woman had ever been seen doing before.

It was raining when Vida woke up on 5 August. She considered staying home, but her conscience got the better of her. She dressed, pinned a poster to the front of her skirt reading 'Votes for Women', and tucked a bundle of papers under one arm. Taking a deep breath, she ventured out and took up her position on the street. For hours she stood there, as people gaped, giggled, frowned and muttered disapproval. The next day Vida's picture appeared in the papers, poster and all. The suffragettes had got their publicity.

In 1914, Vida Goldstein found a new cause — peace.

When war broke out between the Allied powers (Britain, France, Russia and their allies) and the Central European Powers (Germany, Austria-Hungary and allies), Australia was expected to fight for the British Commonwealth. The country was seized with war fever. People attacked anything with a German name — neighbours, shops, even pianos. Rallies were held to recruit young men to fight.

As pacifists, the Goldstein women came out against the war, and were immediately branded pro-German. When Vida started publishing anti-war material in the *Woman Voter*, she was harassed by the police and military censors. Some pacifists were put under police surveillance and had their mail opened. Ordinary citizens, often women, sent white feathers — a symbol of cowardice — to men who failed to join up. Anti-war activists were covered in tar and feathers by soldiers.

The war fractured old alliances. The Women's Political Association split between those who were for and those who were against the war. To Vida's horror, the Pankhursts' group suspended the fight for the vote in order to support the English war effort. Vida immediately dissociated herself from the Pankhursts. In 1915, Vida established the Women's Peace Army to disseminate anti-war propaganda.

Two years into the war, the Australian government floated the idea of conscription, making it compulsory for young men to join up and fight. The country divided over the issue. To avoid conflict, the government decided to hold a referendum, a nationwide poll, to let the people decide. Before the voting took place, both sides swung into action to try to persuade the public to their view. Emotions ran high.

In the midst of this, on 12 January 1916, Isabella Goldstein died — six years after Jacob had died of a stroke. The poor lost a champion, and Vida lost her friend and mentor. Though she was grief-stricken, Vida once again drew comfort from her religion, which regarded death as a transformation rather than an end.

After her mother's death, Vida threw herself into her work and emerged as a major figure in the anti-conscription campaign. She addressed a crowd of about 30 000 at a meeting on 17 September, and on 4 October marched in a 40 000-strong procession organised by the trade unions. It was dangerous work. Soldiers vented their anger by disrupting marches, and at meetings on the banks of the Yarra they threw their opponents into the river.

For Vida, the high point of the anti-conscription campaign was the Women's No-Conscription Demonstration and Procession on 21 October. It was organised by her Women's Peace Army and Lizzie Wallace's United Women's No-Conscription Committee. Beginning at the Guild Hall, around 5000 women walked through the streets of Melbourne. Soldiers fell upon the marchers and tried to stop them. Before the soldiers were driven off, some women had their banners smashed in their faces, and one woman's finger was bitten off. The marchers were greeted by an ecstatic crowd of 80 000 at the Yarra Bank.

A week later, when the poll was held, Australia voted against conscription. Another referendum was held the following year, and it too was defeated.

The war ended in victory for the Allies in November 1918, but not without a terrible cost to Australia. Out of a population of almost five million, 63 000 were killed, and 152 000 wounded.

In May 1919, Vida went to Zurich, Switzerland to represent Australia at a Women's Peace Conference. She stayed on for three years. Now fifty years old, she was facing a crossroads in her life. She did not want to abandon the causes she believed in, but she had lost her faith in politics. She was obviously never going to win a seat in the Senate. Once again, she turned to her religion. From now on she would work through her Christian Science faith. She disbanded the Women's Political Association and closed down the *Woman Voter*. In 1922 she returned quietly to Australia to begin a new life as a Christian Science practitioner.

The Goldstein women became a united force again. Vida's rift with Lina had healed, and she moved into a flat with Aileen and the widowed Elsie. She and Aileen opened an office in the city, where they counselled people on religion, psychology and health according to Christian Science principles. Vida read, studied deeply and was influential in her church. She did not entirely give up on political action, and sometimes wrote letters to politicians and articles for the newspapers. But when World War II broke out in 1939, Vida campaigned for peace through prayer — no more marching in the streets chanting anti-war slogans.

In 1949, Vida Goldstein died, almost anonymously, at the age of eighty. She remained unknown for over twenty years, until, in the 1970s, a new wave of feminism swept across Australia. Angry at the way women's history had been ignored, feminists set about restoring the balance. Vida Goldstein was finally given the credit she deserved for her contribution to female suffrage, the welfare of women and children, and the cause of peace. In 1984, the Australian government named an electorate in Victoria after her, and in 1988 she was named one of the '200 People Who Made Australia Great' as part of the Bicentenary celebrations.

ETHEL (HENRY HANDEL) RICHARDSON
1870 – 1946

Writer

The decline and early death of Ethel Richardson's father filled her childhood with misery and horror. Fifty years later, as the novelist Henry Handel Richardson, she poured out her complex, contradictory feelings about her father and her early life into some of the greatest works in Australian literature.

An Irishman with a medical degree from the prestigious University of Edinburgh in Scotland, Walter Richardson came to Australia in 1852 for the gold rush. Three years later he married Mary Bailey, the daughter of a widow with ten children. Mary, who had immigrated from England with her sister and brother, was working as a children's nurse for a family who owned a hotel outside Geelong in Victoria.

It was a love match. Mary was much younger than Walter, poorly educated and from a different social class, but she was practical, competent and hard working. These qualities would stand her in good stead, for Walter was highly strung and erratic, had trouble sleeping, and fussed about his health.

Walter had come to Australia to recoup his family's fortunes, but he was also running from his past. In England he had narrowly escaped public disgrace when one of his patients died unnecessarily. And though he didn't know it then, he had contracted a disease which would eventually kill him.

Walter and Mary ran a store in Ballarat for a time, then Walter started practising medicine again. He made a reasonable living delivering babies, but in the 1860s he struck it rich through buying and selling gold shares. The hard times were over. Now Walter and Mary could afford a trip to Britain to visit their families. They stayed there for two years.

Fifteen years after their marriage, when they were living in the Melbourne suburb of Fitzroy, Mary Richardson gave birth to her first child on 3 January 1870. They named her Ethel Florence Lindesay Richardson. The baby girl was soon known as Ettie. A year later, Ada Lillian Lindesay, or Lil, was born.

When Ettie was three, the family set off overseas to visit relatives and do a grand tour of Europe. While they were away, Walter found out that his gold shares had crashed. He returned to Melbourne, leaving Mary to bring the girls home. Walter was far from broke, but he could no longer afford to be a gentleman of leisure. At the age of 49 he had to go back to work. It was the end of the opulent houses, grand trips, fine clothes and glittering dinners.

Ettie was five when her father lost his fortune. She was spoiled and precocious, and was already able to read and write. Whereas Lil was easygoing and sweet, Ettie was independent, troublesome, and a show-off. She had inherited her mother's temper, and the two often clashed. Mary had very firm ideas about how little girls should behave, but Ettie was determined to have her own way.

Ettie was skinny and dark, with straight hair and a bent nose. Lil was fair and pretty. By comparing Ettie

Mary, Ettie and
Lil Richardson, 1880
*Courtesy National Library
of Australia*

unfavourably with her sister, her parents gave her a complex about her looks. Her father made her feel even worse by trying to remove a dark red birthmark on her arm. All her life she hid the 'blemish' with long sleeves. Convinced that Lil was her mother's favourite, Ettie envied and resented her baby sister at first, but later in their turbulent childhood the two would become firm friends. Mary Richardson was class-conscious and worried about keeping up appearances. Although her beginnings had been humble, being the wife of a rich doctor had gone to her head and turned her into a snob. She wouldn't let the girls play with children who weren't 'good enough' for them. Thrown together, Ettie and Lil had to rely on each other for company and support, and they formed a close bond that would last all their lives.

After about a year in Fitzroy, the family moved to Hawthorn, where Walter had built a grand mansion before losing most of his money. He intended to practise medicine in the area. But Hawthorn had an established doctor already, and its small population could not support another one. Listening behind doors, an anxious Ettie overheard her parents arguing about money.

By now, Walter's health was failing. Once he'd been a distinguished doctor and businessman. Now he looked old before his time, and suffered from depression and insomnia. His daughter remembered him as a 'thin, stooped figure coming up the path, carrying a carpet-bagful of books' which was 'plainly too heavy for him'. Ettie's safe, secure world was beginning to fall apart.

To cut his losses, Walter rented out the Hawthorn house and abandoned his practice. He found an opening at Chiltern, where the doctor was retiring. Near Albury-Wodonga, Chiltern was the centre of a farming district, and serviced the Chiltern Valley Mine. The Richardsons' new life started well. Walter bought the best house in town and hired a governess for the girls, and soon he was a prominent figure in the small community.

Mary began teaching Ettie and Lil to play the piano, and it was immediately obvious that they both had an aptitude for music. Impressed by the Richardson girls' musical skills, the townsfolk invited them to play at church socials and teas. But Mary's airs and graces put people off. The girls were kept apart from the other children in town, and had a governess instead of attending the local school. They lived in a cocoon of their mother's making.

It was not long before Walter's practice began to fail. A drought was sending the farmers to the wall, and a flood at the mine put the men out of work. Few had money to spend on doctors. Walter became increasingly depressed, and fell ill. It was then that he started showing symptoms of 'paralysis of the insane'. He began to forget words, and sometimes lost his balance and staggered. People suspected he was an alcoholic. As well as behaving oddly, Walter was making medical mistakes. When he botched some children's vaccinations, he was accused of incompetence. It was another 36 years before doctors realised that paralysis of the insane was the final stage of syphilis. This disease, which Walter had probably contracted at university, can lie dormant for years after infection. It affects the heart and brain, and finally sends its victims mad. Until penicillin was discovered in the 1940s, it was fatal.

Ettie was seven now, and badly disturbed. Though she was too young to understand the reasons for their constant moves, she felt the tension in the household, and heard her parents arguing. To make matters worse, her father was sick all the time. To escape, Ettie invented a fantasy world. Chanting stories she made up, she would spend hours obsessively bouncing a ball up against the house. She walked in her sleep, and defied her governess.

Under a cloud of failure, the Richardsons moved again, this time to Queenscliff, on Port Phillip Bay. The seaside town was a great improvement on Chiltern. Walter was able to make a new start, and the girls were given more freedom. They learnt to swim and spent hours at the local baths. Mary also let them mix with other — carefully chosen — children. Walter was pleased to be close to Melbourne and its good bookshops, and brought home books such as *The Pilgrim's Progress* and *Robinson Crusoe*. He also read Walter Scott's novels to a captivated Ettie.

But once again Walter's odd behaviour made him a laughing-stock. He even tried to send a telegram to the Government Astronomer accusing the man of stealing his overcoat. Fortunately, the postmaster destroyed it. Ettie's feelings towards her father were complicated and confused. She hated him for embarrassing the family, and wished him dead. Then she'd feel guilty for such wickedness. At eight she was rebellious and angry and developed a severe facial twitch. People would laugh at her for 'making faces', but she couldn't help herself. Gentle Lil reacted by clinging to her mother.

The tension in the Richardson household reached breaking point. Walter was fast becoming an invalid, and Mary realised she would soon be a widow with two small children to support. How would they survive?

In June 1878 Walter Richardson was stripped of the

right to practise medicine. Faced with a choice between working or accepting charity, Mary chose work. She sought help from her influential friends. One came through for her, and she was promised a job as a postmistress at Koroit, in far south-western Victoria. She would receive 72 pounds a year plus free lodgings, firewood and kerosene. But first she had to prove she could master the skills.

While Mary was off learning how to work the telegraph, her two little girls had to look after Walter. When her father wandered away from home, it was Ettie's job to find him and fetch him home. She could feel people's eyes on her, pitying her and judging her father, and hated it. Realising she could not look after Walter and the girls while running a post office, Mary made one of the most difficult decisions of her life. She had Walter declared mentally unsound and he was committed to the government asylum at Yarra Bend. Ettie's father was officially insane.

Koroit would be Ettie's eighth home in eight years. The postmistress's house was poky and uncomfortable, with a tiny backyard. There wasn't even room for Ettie to bounce her ball. Mary brought in her orphaned niece, Gertrude, to help. Ettie was rude and insolent to Gertrude. A friend of the family described Ettie then as selfish and bad-tempered. Fortunately, Ettie had two distractions from her intolerable life — music and storytelling. She began writing poems and stories and read everything she could lay her hands on.

Walter Richardson came home to die when Ettie was nine. In *Myself When Young*, which was published two years after her death in 1946, she wrote: 'I can't say I grieved over his death. It came as rather a relief — Not till many years later when, with the help of old letters and diaries, I began to trace the shifting course of his life and the character behind it — did I grasp at least some of what he must have suffered, both for himself and for those dependent on him.'

When Ettie was ten her mother was promoted to the position of postmistress at Maldon, a much larger town than Koroit. It meant financial security at last, and a decent house with a big garden. Mary had also inherited some money from Walter's estate as well as the house in Hawthorn. In Maldon, Mary finally let her guard down, made friends in the town and let the girls play with other children. They went to parties and visited friends. With her newfound freedom to roam and play, Ettie became a tomboy, climbing trees and going on picnics.

After her father's death, Ettie's behaviour improved, and she lost her twitch. When she was thirteen, Mary sent her to board at one of the best schools in Australia — Presbyterian Ladies College in Melbourne. PLC prided itself on turning out useful girls, not socialites. In fact, after the University of Melbourne opened its doors to women in 1881, most of the female students came from PLC. But Ettie found it hard to fit in with the daughters of the rich and influential. She was an outsider from the start. Schoolmates and teachers saw her as a country bumpkin, and mocked her dowdy clothes and her looks. It was her manners that outraged them most, though. They found the new girl haughty, boastful and brash. They would soon cut her down to size.

'Lacking any form of restraint, I had sallied forth from home full of pep and assurance, not to say conceit; and teachers and schoolfellows alike felt it their duty to crush me,' she wrote in *Myself When Young*.

It wasn't all the school's fault. Ettie had no charm. She wasn't pretty, and she was pushy, relentless and irritating. She was also resilient, having been through experiences these well-bred girls could not imagine. After feeling crushed for the first year, she fought back. She caught up academically, and also won the headmaster's prize for tennis. Though she'd been praised for her musical skills in the country, at PLC she was far behind the other girls. She was sent back to practise scales. But eventually the school noticed that she had real talent.

At PLC an event occurred which shamed Ettie so much she would never explain it. Ettie could not bear being a nobody at the school, and decided to make the other girls sit up and take notice. One Sunday, after attending a service at St Peter's Anglican Church at Eastern Hill with some of her classmates, she told them a secret: she was having a romance with a clergyman! Ettie's saga held the other girls spellbound, but inevitably they discovered they'd been fooled, and they were outraged. Like her alter ego Laura Ramsbotham in *The*

Getting of Wisdom, which was published 25 years later, Ettie was labelled a liar and it stuck.

Although her affair with a clergyman had been pure fiction, it was at college that sixteen-year-old Ettie had her first real, not imaginary, love affair. The beloved was Constance Cochrane, a beautiful, rich and sophisticated older student. Connie would become the model for Evelyn Souttar in *The Getting of Wisdom*. In the novel, Henry Handel Richardson described their relationship: 'The attraction this girl had for me was so strong that few have surpassed it. Nor did it exist on my side only. The affinity was mutual; and that is harder to understand. For she was eighteen and grown-up, and I was but a skinny little half-grown.'

But what was a serious love affair for Ettie turned out to be a passing fancy for Constance, and the younger girl was left miserable. On top of this, Ettie had spent so much time mooning over Connie that she had neglected her studies. Her results in the school matriculation exams were disappointing. She did win the Senior Pianoforte Scholarship, however, and was the star of the half-yearly school concert. Though someone had written a hurtful poem about her in the school magazine, called 'The Genius of PLC', Ettie bounced back, and finally began to make friends. Her old fighting spirit returned. When she was not asked to join the school's literary club, she formed a rival club called the SSI — the Society for Suppressing Idiots.

In the university matriculation exams in December,

she performed creditably. At the end of year concert the school orchestra performed her composition, *The Sea-Fairies*, and she played the piano. Her performance was well reviewed in the newspapers.

After being told Ettie was musically gifted, Mary began to dream of a career as a concert pianist for her daughter. Encouraged by her mother and the school to think of herself as a musical 'genius', Ettie set her sights on studying music overseas. Mary Richardson began organising the family's affairs to get her there.

Luckily for Ettie, the mansion at Hawthorn sold for over 4000 pounds, a fortune at the time. Mary decided to spend the money on musical training for Ettie in Leipzig, Germany. Leipzig was considered to be one of the top musical cities in the world, famous for producing composers like Bach and Wagner.

On 3 August 1888 the Richardson women set off for England on the *Ormuz*. Connie came to see Ettie off. They intended to return in a year. As it turned out, Ettie and Lil came back to Australia only once, 25 years later. Ettie was then writing her famous trilogy of books about her father's life, and wanted to refresh her memory about her former home. Mary never returned.

At nineteen, Ettie was accepted as a private pupil of the renowned but formidable teacher Johannes Weidenbach. But before she was admitted to the Conservatorium of Music, she was made to practise humble finger exercises and scales for months to improve her technique.

Free of her shameful, complicated past, Ettie set about

reinventing herself in Leipzig. She learnt German, worked hard at her music and enjoyed life. She made friends with Martha Main, a Scottish cellist, and the girls regularly attended concerts at the Gewandhaus. Mary began inviting guests back to their apartment, and it soon became a meeting place for Leipzig's English-speaking community.

In the autumn of 1890, Ettie met George Robertson, a tall, bespectacled Scottish scholar. George was a scientist who'd abandoned science for literature. By introducing her to European literature, George had a profound influence on Ettie's education. But as her horizons widened, she began to get bored with piano practice.

Ettie and George's relationship seems to have been based on shared intellectual interests rather than passion. Ettie tended to reserve her most passionate feelings for women. But in Ettie's day a girl needed a husband because it was almost impossible for women to make a decent living. Most women would not have regarded George as a good catch. He had no money and few prospects. But he encouraged Ettie in her interests and stood up for her. He was also the opposite of her eccentric, restless, risk-taking father. Ettie had no intention of repeating her mother's mistake.

Meanwhile, Ettie's musical career was on the rocks before it had even begun. At the Conservatorium Ettie realised that she would never become a concert pianist. She was not as technically skilled as the European students, and she had become very anxious about performing in public. When she and George became engaged, she abandoned her music studies altogether.

Leaving George in Leipzig to finish his PhD, the Richardsons went to England. But Ettie found life there dreary and dispiriting after Germany. She and Mary fought incessantly. What would Ettie do with her life now? Rather than teach music, she tried her hand at journalism, but quickly found it did not pay. Helped by George, who had studied Scandinavian languages, she translated a Danish novel from its German version into English. *Niels Lyhne*, written by the poet and botanist Jens Peter Jacobsen, had taken Europe by storm, and made a huge impression on Ettie. To her delight, it found a publisher.

Mary Richardson began talking of returning to Australia, but her daughters had other ideas. Instead they moved back to Germany — this time to Munich — where Lil began studying violin. But Ettie was still at a loose end. In desperation, Mary gave her and George 300 pounds so they could afford to get married. In 1895, they were wed in considerable style in Dublin, Walter Richardson's native city.

In Munich, George concentrated on reading, writing and editing, and Ettie was asked to translate another Norwegian novel, under the name of Ethel Robertson. Then, in 1896, George secured a position in the English faculty at the university in Strasbourg. Ettie was restless, though. Both her translations had been well received, but she was dissatisfied. She longed to be an artist herself, not just the translator of someone else's work. George encouraged her, suggesting she use her experiences in Leipzig as the basis of a novel about a musician who fails to make good. She began writing it on 26 October 1896. The novel was *Maurice Guest*.

She had barely begun when Lil summoned her to Munich. Mary was very ill. She died on 26 November. There was no sense of relief this time. Despite their constant battles, Ettie had always relied on Mary's love and support. For the rest of her life, Ettie would wrestle with her conflicting feelings about her mother.

When George was appointed the first Professor of German Language and Literature at the University of London in 1903, the Robertsons moved back to England. This marked an extraordinary change in Ettie's life. She and George had led an active social life in Germany, but now she became a recluse. Her earlier dislike of being 'stared at' on the concert stage had hardened into a phobia. With a supportive husband, no children, no social obligations, and little responsibility, Ettie was free to shut herself in her study to write — and to come to terms with the demons of her past.

Maurice Guest, which featured the pen-name Henry Handel Richardson for the first time — probably because it was easier for men to find publishers in those days — appeared in 1908. The reviews were varied. *The Getting of Wisdom*, based on her years at Presbyterian Ladies College, was published in 1910. It has become a classic of childhood autobiography.

It was around this time that Henry Handel Richardson at last felt capable of examining her father's life and turning it into fiction. She embarked on her major work, the three novels that make up *The Fortunes of Richard Mahony*. The trilogy, which drew on her father's experiences as an immigrant in colonial Australia, would take twenty years to research and write. Its source was the love letters her parents had written to each other before their marriage. Ettie had read them at the age of seventeen, and had been greatly moved.

George and Ettie lived a quiet life in London until George died in 1933. After his death, Ettie moved to the tranquillity and solitude of Sussex, in the company of her housekeeper and friend, Olga Roncoroni. She remained there till her death in 1946.

Henry Handel Richardson once remarked that 'an artist has all his material before he is ten years old'. She spoke from knowledge. By that age, Ettie Richardson had been through an unusual amount of emotional trauma and instability, and spent most of her adult life making sense of that childhood and conquering those old fears. The result was great art.

MAY GIBBS 1877 — 1969

Artist, writer, myth-maker

Staying with her young cousins in the West Australian bush, the teenage May Gibbs told them stories about the little people she imagined lived there — not old-world fairies, but Australian bush creatures and plants brought to life. As an adult, May wrote these stories down and illustrated them in some of our best-loved children's books. Her vision coloured the imaginations of generations of Australian children.

Cecilia May Gibbs was not born in Australia, but immigrated from Surrey in England with her family in 1881, when she was four. Her mother, Cecilia Rogers — Cecie — had met and fallen in love with May's father, Herbert Gibbs, on the train travelling back and forth from London. Cecie attended the Slade School of Art there, and Herbert worked at the General Post Office. Their first child, Bertie, was born in 1875, and their second, May, in 1877.

The Gibbs had farmed for generations, and Herbert's brother George yearned to run a big property. A friend, Captain Teasdel, had selected land at Franklin Harbour in South Australia and had been writing glowing reports home. The colony was offering large tracts of free land to anyone brave or foolish enough to try to farm them. George wanted Herbert to go to South Australia with him. Six years after his marriage, Herbert finally gave in.

When May came down with measles, her mother postponed her voyage. Herbert and George went on ahead, arriving in Port Adelaide on 1 June 1881. They then set off for Franklin Harbour and the 1120-hectare property Captain Teasdel had selected for them. A boat took them to Wallaroo on Spencer Gulf, where they had to hire a fisherman to take them the last 72 kilometres to Franklin Harbour. After wading through the mud and mangroves, they walked the ten kilometres to Captain Teasdel's station. Instead of the prosperous farm Teasdel had described in his letters, they found his family living in a primitive house with tin walls and a hessian roof, surrounded by a rough bush fence. What had they let themselves in for? At least the sheep looked healthy. While they waited for their own gear to arrive, the brothers worked on Teasdel's farm.

Cecie meanwhile had discovered she was pregnant again. Calculating that she could have the baby in South Australia if she left immediately, she set sail in July 1881. May enjoyed the voyage immensely. She learned some sea shanties from the sailors and entertained the passengers with them in the evenings. But nature did not cooperate with Cecie. The ship was becalmed for two weeks, and baby Ivan was born at sea. Three weeks later the ship docked.

In Adelaide, Cecie found that the next boat to Franklin Harbour did not leave for a month. Clutching her two small children, the baby and her bags, she found lodgings and waited. The trip to Franklin Harbour was long and arduous, ending with a jolting journey by horse and cart. Her heart sank when she saw the two-roomed slab hut and her thin, weather-beaten husband and brother-in-law. She realised straight away the project was doomed. Other settlers were still living in tents after five years and had not made any money yet. How could the Gibbs do any better?

To add to the settlers' suffering, drought set in. Water had to be carted from two kilometres away. It was so scarce Cecie had to bathe baby Ivan in a teacup of the precious liquid. May's red curls became so dusty her mother cut them off. They both cried. Cecie soon convinced Herbert to cut his losses and leave Franklin Harbour before it broke his spirit. She took the children back to Adelaide on the next boat. Herbert and George followed when they'd disposed of the property. The night they left, Herbert wrote 'Failure at Franklin' in his diary.

Back in Adelaide Herbert got a job as a draftsman with the Lands Department and the family lived in an old cottage in Norwood. Bertie went to school, but Cecie instructed May during the day and her father read with her in the evenings. He also began taking her walking in the bush with him to sketch. It was the beginning of a close and sympathetic relationship between them.

In Adelaide George and Herbert became friends with Dr Henry Harvey and Mr John Young, both English immigrants. They also dreamed of owning a property. When the Stirling Estate in Western Australia was advertised, the foursome formed the Harvey, Young, Gibbs Pastoral Company and bought 5200 hectares. The Gibbs moved to Western Australia to run it. The Harvey, as this farm was called, already had an elegant homestead built by Governor Stirling. It also boasted orchards, a river running through, and views to the Indian Ocean. After Franklin Harbour, it was paradise.

As there was no school within riding distance, Cecie tutored the children at home and taught them music. She read to them from her favourite children's books — *Brer Rabbit, Through the Looking Glass, Little Women* and the *Boy's Own Annuals*. May imitated her mother and acquired a beautiful speaking voice. Having to make their own fun, the families in the district took turns holding musical evenings. May loved performing, and announced at eight that she wanted to be an actor.

When May was nine, she was given a pony for her birthday. Her world opened up. Mounted on Brownie, she started visiting other stations and farms and exploring her surroundings. Everything she saw on these journeys — the trees and flowers, and the small, scurrying animals and insects — lodged in her fertile imagination like seeds. Later they blossomed as characters in her stories.

But when May was ten, her idyllic country childhood came to an end. The Harvey was not making any money, and the Gibbs brothers had to leave. George bought another property, married and stayed on. Herbert and Cecie decided to try their luck closer to Perth. May was heartbroken — the two years at The Harvey had been the happiest of her life.

Unable to relinquish his dream of owning a farm, Herbert Gibbs took up four hectares of land at Butler's Swamp. Halfway between Perth and Fremantle and close to the water, it is now the suburb of Claremont. He built a sailboat, *The Gadfly*, and liked to sail the family to Fremantle. May learnt to sail, and would later use this knowledge of boats in her stories. Herbert loved to paint and draw, and was a skilled cartoonist. He encouraged May to draw and quickly saw that she had talent. Copying his political cartoons, she produced some comical scenes of the Gibbs household. When she was twelve, one of her drawings of children preparing for Christmas appeared in the *WA Bulletin*. It was her first published work.

But another change was in the wind. The Gibbs finally had to abandon their dream of owning a farm. Butler's Swamp wasn't doing well, and Cecie thought it was time the children went to a proper school. They moved to the city. Herbert once again found a job as a draftsman at the Lands Department and the family bought The Dune, a large, rambling house across the Swan River. They were quickly absorbed into Perth's social and artistic circles. At thirteen, May joined the Wilgie Club, a group to encourage young artists that her father had helped establish.

In Perth, May attended a real school, Miss Best's, for the first and last time. After only a term Cecie withdrew her. The Gibbs had been instrumental in setting up a musical group, and Cecie needed May to help her with the housework and the new baby, Harold, so she could rehearse her singing.

May didn't mind leaving school. Home was much

more fun. In her teens The Dune became a meeting place for musicians and artists, and there was always something going on. May played the violin well, and sometimes sang in the chorus, but she much preferred designing and painting sets and acting as art director for productions. She took over her father's studio at home and he taught her to use watercolours, then oil paints. For her holidays, May escaped to Australind, her Uncle George and Aunt Ellen's property at The Harvey. There she would tell her cousins stories, instruct them in bush lore and help with their lessons. But May had her troubles. Cecie liked to control her, and they often fought. And when she was sixteen, her eighteen-year-old brother, Bertie, died from rheumatic fever.

In the early 1890s, the gold rushes brought people to Western Australia, and Perth began turning into a real city. By 1897, when May was twenty, it even had its own public art gallery, and May began to study art. As a twenty-year-old art student, red-headed May was small, and considered herself plain. Gregarious and outspoken, she had a cutting wit. But at an age when most girls were getting engaged, she showed no interest in romance or domestic life.

She was a talented artist. Recognising this, her teachers urged her to go to England to continue her studies. After some resistance, Herbert and Cecie gave in. After all, women in Western Australia had the vote now, and ideas about what they could and could not do were changing. On 21 February 1900, at 23, the budding artist set sail for England, accompanied by her mother and her cousin, Daisy Rogers.

In London May was accepted at a prestigious art school, the Cope and Nichol. With May settled in, Cecie returned to Australia. May lived with her mother's family in Surrey and commuted by train six days a week, sketching seven hours a day. It was exhausting, but stimulating. At her teachers' suggestion, she also enrolled in night classes at the Chelsea Polytechnic Institute. That meant moving to Chelsea and looking after herself. May was never very good at that, particularly at cooking, and soon became run down. London was cold, damp and polluted. By the end of 1901 May's health had deteriorated, and she was suffering from recurrent chills. Concerned, her parents persuaded her to return home.

Back in Perth, May was soon restless and found fault with everything Australian. She missed London and her art classes. And if she didn't want Perth, it didn't want her either. She had no luck breaking into newspaper illustrating. It was only when Herbert pulled some strings that she got a job on a magazine drawing cartoons.

Around this time, May became interested in children's art. She started experimenting, adapting nursery rhymes to Australian settings. She also wrote a story, *John Dory, His Story*, about a local fish. When it did not find a publisher, May decided she was wasting her time in Perth. She went back to London, again with Daisy Rogers. The cousins moved back into May's old digs in Chelsea and May enrolled at the Chelsea Polytechnic and at Mr Henry

Blackburn's School for Black and White Artists in Westminster. She was soon back to her ten-hour days, devoting her evenings to life drawing with models. She passed the Polytechnic course with flying colours, but the term at Blackburn turned out to be more important for the career she wanted — illustrating for newspapers.

Unable to find work after she graduated, May became depressed and disillusioned — all those years of work and sacrifice for nothing. When Cecie arrived to put Harold into an English school in 1905, May could not bear the thought of putting up with her mother, and fled home. This time Perth was much more welcoming. The editor of the *Western Mail* newspaper commissioned her to illustrate the front page of the Christmas issue, and it was a huge success. May suddenly found herself in demand. Financially secure at last, she could finally try her hand at another book. But after spending months writing and illustrating a children's book called *Mimie and Wog*, she could not find a publisher.

At 32, apart from her inability to get her books published, May's life was going well. But in 1909 her confidence and pride took a severe jolt. For the first time in five years, she was not asked to do the Christmas page of the *Western Mail*. Worse, her successor was a young woman, Ida S. Rentoul, a children's artist who was making a name for herself with exquisite drawings of fairies. Rather than face the curiosity and the sympathy, May returned to England. She told friends she was going to look for a publisher for her books.

Cecie accompanied her daughter again, this time settling her into an exclusive boarding house. She hoped the good food and comfortable surroundings would prevent May from again becoming run down and ill. It proved too expensive for May, though, and she quickly moved into cheaper lodgings. To make matters worse, she had no luck selling her books to an English publisher. They were not interested in stories featuring Australia's strange plants and wildlife. May finally gave in and turned *Mimie and Wog* into an English tale. Published as *About Us* in London and New York — though not in Australia — it featured a little girl lost among the chimney pots of London. After getting herself an agent, May finally obtained work illustrating books for the publisher George Harrap & Company. It was a start.

In May's rooming house lived a girl called Rene Heames, a telephonist. Unlike May, who was not interested in politics, Rene was a socialist and a feminist. Despite their differences, they became lifelong friends. But once again May's health let her down and she succumbed to bronchitis. When Cecie found out, she swept in from Perth like the Fremantle Doctor to fetch her daughter home. After a series of battles, a compromise was reached: May would return, but not to Western Australia. She and Rene would move to Sydney. After 36 years, May felt that she was finally getting out from under Cecie's thumb.

In Sydney, May blossomed. She and Rene found a flat

in Neutral Bay and shared it with another friend, Rachel Matthews. May also rented a little studio high in Bridge Street and took the ferry into the city every day to work. When she missed the bush too badly, she caught the train to Blackheath in the Blue Mountains. As Australia's first professionally trained children's book illustrator, May found work immediately. She was commissioned to do book and magazine covers, and started a long and lucrative relationship with the Department of Education. Generations of Australian children got to know May Gibbs though her drawings in the *Primary Reader* and the *School Magazine*.

The characters who were to make May Gibbs immortal — Bib and Bub, the gumnut babies — were about to be born. They started life as two funny little animals peeping over the top of a gumleaf on a bookmark. Later they popped up in *The Magic Button* written by Ethel Turner, then Australia's most popular children's writer. The next creatures to spring from May's pen were wattle babies, flannel flower babies and Christmas bell babies. Within a year, the bush babies had become part of Australian culture. But May was busy writing as well. Two books — *Gum-Nut Babies* and *Gum-Blossom Babies* — appeared just in time for Christmas 1916. They were an instant hit.

At forty, May had a successful career and two close women friends. What more could she want? In 1918 she visited her parents in Perth, and found what she'd been missing — a husband. She'd finally fallen in love, with an

Irishman called James Ossoli (J.O.) Kelly, a family friend. Years later, May admitted that 'The day I first met J.O., I thought, "There's the man I'm going to marry."' J.O. was well dressed, well spoken and cultured. He'd immigrated in 1889 and had tried farming and prospecting for gold, with no success. When May met him he was a clerk in the Wheat Scheme Office.

Refreshed and relaxed, May returned to Sydney and began work on what would be the most important book of her career — *Tales of Snugglepot and Cuddlepie*. She dedicated the book to her parents. It introduced characters that still thrill children today — Little Ragged Blossom, Mr Lizard and villains like Mr Snake and the Bad Banksia Men. Everybody loved May's books, and she became a minor celebrity.

At Christmas, May returned to Perth, and at Easter 1919 she and J.O. were married quietly in a registry office. The couple returned to Sydney, where May would continue to write and paint, and J.O. would act as her business manager. It was not destined to be an intimate relationship, however. After six weeks, the couple moved into a flat in Neutral Bay with Rene and Rachel. It was an odd arrangement, but J.O. took it in his stride and christened the household 'May Gibbs & Associates'. With her domestic affairs under control, May settled back to work and produced *The Little Ragged Blossom* and *More about Snugglepot and Cuddlepie* in 1920.

May's new husband might have been an elegant companion to escort her to concerts and exhibitions, but

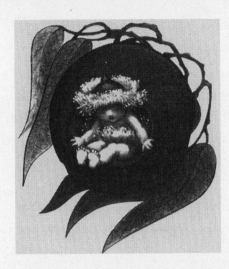

Little Ragged Blossom
*Mitchell Library, State Library
of New South Wales.
Courtesy Curtis Brown
(Aust) Pty Ltd, Sydney*

as a business manager he was less than ideal. He hated haggling with publishers even more than May did, so she was forced to do it herself. This sometimes caused trouble when May became too demanding. By now, she had developed a keen business sense, and began using her characters on postcards, calendars, handkerchiefs and even babies' bootees.

By her late forties, May Gibbs had published eight children's books, some of them destined to become classics. But when the last two Snugglepot and Cuddlepie stories did not sell well, May returned to her bush babies, Bib and Bub. She turned them into cartoon characters and started drawing a comic strip for the *Sunday News.* The strip was soon appearing in newspapers in other states and New Zealand. She also started a comic strip for another paper, featuring Tiggy Touchwood, a princess who'd been turned into a pig.

May's home life was as unconventional as ever. She and J.O. were seldom alone. They even took friends along on holidays. May had become disenchanted with her husband. While she slaved away at her cartoons and illustrations, he lived a leisurely life. He was a good friend, and he had improved her social life, but he was no support to her. Now that Rene had married and moved to Bombala, May had only herself to rely on — although there was always her mother.

In 1924, Herbert and Cecie arrived for a long visit. Cecie saw that May was earning all the money and that her husband had no idea how to manage it for her. They didn't even own a house. May had to have a house of her own, Cecie decided. She found a block of land at No. 5 Wallaringa Avenue, Neutral Bay and talked May into buying it. May's new house, a Spanish-style villa, was built on a steep slope running down to the harbour. It was painted yellow, with blue shutters. There was a big gum tree in the yard and a swimming pool at the bottom of the garden. May's studio had exquisite harbour views. She called the house Nutcote, and spent the rest of her life there.

Still in need of the occasional escape to the bush, May bought a second-hand car and learnt to drive so she could get out into the country more easily. Then, in the 1930s, her comfortable life was threatened by the Great Depression. She wasn't the only one to suffer. People had no money for food, let alone books. First her fees were cut, then her cartoons temporarily disappeared from the Sydney papers altogether. To add to her worries, J.O.'s health began to decline.

In 1933, they sailed to Perth to visit Cecie and Herbert for the last time. The following year, depressed and exhausted, May called on Rene for help. Widowed now, Rene came to Sydney to look after J.O. In August 1939, just before the outbreak of World War II, May's husband died. Shortly before her own death, May wrote: 'He and I were such tremendous pals. Always immaculately dressed, quite unconscious of himself, beautifully spoken and friends with everybody.'

Widowed at 62, May worked hard at her drawing and created a splendid garden as recreation. To prevent her becoming too isolated, her solicitor found tenants for the little flat attached to her house. In October 1940 her father died, and five months later, her mother. May wondered if things would ever improve. But then, because books could not be imported with a war on, the demand for Australian material increased. At Rene's urging, May wrote a new book, *Scotty in Gumnutland*, based on the exploits of her beloved Scottish terriers. When it sold well, her publishers released *The Complete Adventures of Snugglepot and Cuddlepie*. In 1943 she wrote a sequel to Scotty — *Mr and Mrs Bear and Friends*.

When Rene died in the early 1950s, May was devastated. After her father, Rene was the person closest to May's heart. From then on, she stayed close to home.

Passengers on the ferry to Kurraba Wharf would catch a glimpse of her in the backyard of Nutcote, gardening in her enormous sunhat. But still she worked. She wrote two more books and, nearing eighty, was still producing a Bib and Bub comic strip every week for the *Sun-Herald* newspaper.

After a stroke, May retired in 1967. She was ninety. Though she had very little money, she was too proud to apply for the old age pension. Hearing about her plight, the Commonwealth Literary Fund gave her a pension instead. When Cecilia May Gibbs died in November 1969, she made sure that children would continue to benefit from her life's work. She left her copyright and book royalties to the NSW Society for Crippled Children and the Spastic Centre of New South Wales. She left Nutcote to UNICEF, the United Nations' fund for children.

May Gibbs was the first Australian artist to turn our strange and wonderful animals and plants into characters and put them in stories. She felt that Australian children deserved their own folktales, not those imported from another culture. She was also a visionary. Her creations helped shape the imaginations of generations of Australian children, and forever changed the way we see our world. Who can walk through the bush without seeing Snugglepot and Cuddlepie, the gumnut babies, or even the fearsome Bad Banksia Men, out of the corner of their eye?

ALICE BETTERIDGE 1901 — 1966

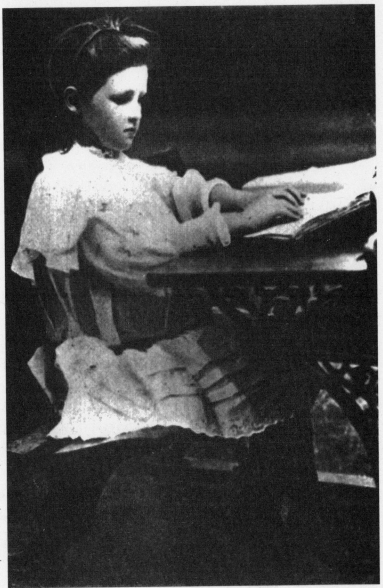

Into the light

When Alice Betteridge, a seven-year-old blind and deaf girl, made the connection between the pattern her teacher was tapping out on her palm and the shoes she hated wearing, she discovered language. She went on to learn to 'speak' and read, and led an active and useful life.

Alice Betteridge was born in 1901 in the tiny settlement of Sawyer's Gully in the Hunter Valley. Her parents were country battlers. Her father, George, had been a saddler, but now worked on farms or selling wine. Emily, her mother, was a practical, kind and intelligent woman who stayed home to raise their fourteen children. Alice was their second living child — one had been stillborn. As a baby, she was clever and quick, with a sunny nature. But when she was two, disaster struck.

One day, after eating a green banana, skin and all, Alice became violently ill. She developed a very high temperature and terrible pains. At first, her mother thought the banana was to blame. But when Alice grew worse during the night, Emily became alarmed and called in the doctor. After he'd examined the patient, he gave them the devastating news: their little girl had meningitis. Meningitis — which occurs when the membrane covering the brain becomes inflamed — was often fatal. There was no treatment for it at the time.

For days Emily hovered over Alice's bed, bathing her to bring down the fever and trying to keep her warm and dry. Her mother's devotion probably saved Alice's life, but as she began to recover, Emily realised what the illness had done to her daughter. When she held a candle or lamp close to Alice's eyes, the child did not blink. When her name was called, she didn't answer. Alice was deaf and blind.

Alice could say two words when she recovered — 'Mum' and 'banas' (bananas). But she soon forgot these, and could communicate only by touch. She recognised members of her family by their smell. Unable to express herself, she was often frightened, confused and frustrated.

Emily and George did their best, but they could not find a way to communicate with Alice. This made it very difficult to teach her anything. She could not be properly toilet-trained, and had no shame or modesty. It looked as if Alice would remain a helpless child, dependent on her family as long as she lived.

When Emily was expecting her fifth child, she realised it was time to get help for Alice. The hard work and stress of looking after her daughter along with her other children had exhausted her. Emily had heard about the Royal New South Wales Institute for Deaf and Blind Children in Sydney. Maybe its teachers could break through the wall of silence surrounding Alice.

Emily had probably also heard about Helen Keller, a deaf and blind American girl. Helen had been taught to read and speak by Annie Sullivan, a gifted teacher. Annie had succeeded so well that Helen had gone on to complete a university degree. In 1903 they'd written a book about Helen's life, and had become world famous.

The decision to take four-year-old Alice to the Institute was a painful one for Emily Betteridge. Alice would lose the family she'd grown up with, and the only safe place she knew. She would be left with strangers in a strange place. While this might sound cruel, at the beginning of the century children like Alice often ended up in institutions for the mentally ill. She was lucky her parents were loving and enlightened.

Alice had never been away from home before, and didn't understand what was happening to her. First there was the flurry of packing and leaving, then the trip by horse and buggy to Maitland. At the train station, there were new scents and sensations, like the acrid smell of coal dust, the heat of the steam engine, the jolt of departure and the long, lulling motion of the train.

When all the travelling ceased, Alice found herself surrounded by new people. Strange hands touched her, and there was a strange bed and unfamiliar food. But most frightening of all was the realisation that her mother had gone away and left her.

The arrival of Alice was traumatic for the Institute, too. They'd never admitted anyone this young before, and they'd never taken on a child who could neither hear nor see. The experiment was not a success. Alice's teachers soon discovered she was too young to respond to lessons, and sent her home after three months. Emily was told to bring Alice back in two years, when she might be mature enough to adjust to the discipline.

In fact, her family waited till Alice was seven before

they returned her to the Institute. This time she stayed. Except for holidays, she did not live with her family again for twenty years.

Though they'd invited her back, the directors of the Institute were not confident that much could be done for Alice. They decided to put her in the Blind School with Roberta Reid, rather than in the Deaf School. Berta Reid had joined the Institute after graduating from the University of Sydney. In those days, very few teachers in schools for the deaf and blind had degrees, and Berta was appointed principal of the Blind School and its thirteen pupils when she was only twenty. It was a demanding job, but Berta was determined to make her mark.

As well as teaching two grades together and supervising staff, Berta was given responsibility for Alice. Because she was so busy, Berta had to work with Alice outside normal school hours. She was immediately charmed by the little blue-eyed blonde, and they formed a lifelong bond. Alice would later praise Berta Reid for 'slaving' over her.

Berta was rather severe, but fair. She was not the sort to show affection, but it was clear she cared deeply about her pupils. In return, they loved and admired her. In later years, the girls remembered that she would come into the dormitory when she was on night duty and read to them. None of the other teachers bothered.

Educating Alice was a formidable task. Berta couldn't ask for advice, because nobody in Australia had ever attempted to teach a blind and deaf child. As a first step,

Alice Betteridge and
Roberta Reid
*Courtesy Royal NSW
Institute for Deaf
& Blind Children*

she set about winning Alice's trust and affection. Initially, Alice simply wandered around the schoolroom and playground in a daze. Where was she? Who were all these people? Where was her family? Berta would watch the little girl scrabbling in the grass in the playground, trying to build up a picture of her surroundings.

To teach Alice to communicate, Berta had to make her understand that objects had names. She gave Alice a doll, but the girl didn't know how to play with it. Which object could Alice recognise? The answer was totally unexpected: a shoe. At home Alice had gone barefoot, but now people kept putting shoes and socks on her. She had no idea what shoes were for; she only knew that they were hot and they pinched. She would immediately take them off. Those hated shoes were Berta's inspiration.

This is how Alice remembered it. One day, a hand took one of hers, put it on the hard object she hated, and tapped a pattern on her hand. This happened many times. What was this hand trying to tell her? Then at last she understood. She reached out, took Berta's hand, and copied the taps on her palm. Then she touched the shoe. This was the most important moment in Alice's life, and probably in Berta's too. They had broken through. Alice had discovered language.

Up till then, no one had any idea if Alice was intelligent or dull-witted. It soon became evident that Alice was very smart. Language unleashed years of pent-up curiosity. After shoe, she learnt 'doll', then 'sock', then 'teacher', and then 'Alice'. Her first verb was 'tell'. She asked everybody their name, then asked the names of all the objects in her world. Soon she could ask for 'milk' instead of going thirsty. In a few months, she knew 200 nouns and several verbs, including 'run', 'jump', and 'laugh', and could use them in sentences.

Sometimes Alice's language was odd, but the meaning was clear. When someone accidentally jabbed her with a knitting needle, Alice 'spoke' onto the offender's hand: 'Don't sharp in my bones!' And once, when made to stand in the corner of the classroom for misbehaving, she signed furiously: 'Naughty teacher! Naughty teacher!'

Next Berta introduced Alice to braille, so she could begin to read. Braille — which consists of raised dots which make up words — is difficult to master, but Alice picked it up quickly. She began reading her way through the school library.

With words, Alice began to use her imagination, learnt how to play and found a best friend. She also discovered a taste for music. When another girl, Nellie, played the piano, Alice would sit on the floor touching the piano to pick up the vibrations and rhythm. When Nellie stopped, Alice would get up, put her friend's hands back on the keys, then return to her listening post.

Though she was not allowed outside the gates, Alice made her way confidently around the school and grounds. She learnt to swim, and went on school excursions to places like the Australian Museum.

When Alice was ten, the school inspector visited. He was amazed at her progress. Using braille, she could read and write almost as well as the best sighted children her age, he reported. She could also count and add, sew, make dolls and dress them, and do bead work.

Alice didn't dwell on the pain and difficulties in her life, but she did admit later that she'd suffered some severe traumas. The worst was the realisation that she was the only one among her friends who could neither see nor hear. For many years she'd assumed everybody was like her. It was a brutal shock, and it took her a long time to recover.

Over the years, Alice became a role model for other children at the Blind School. Though she was more handicapped than any of them, she learnt to wash and dress herself, wash her underclothes and keep her room tidy. Her embroidery and knitting won prizes at agricultural shows in Sydney and the Hunter Valley, and she typed her own letters to dozens of penfriends.

Despite the miracle Alice and Berta had wrought, they were still unknown outside the school. The Institute did not want to publicise individual students. But when a new director was appointed, he overturned this rule. The Institute was always short of money, and he guessed that Alice's story would tug at the heartstrings of the public and bring in donations. Berta disapproved. She thought it would invade Alice's privacy and exploit her. She was overruled.

Soon articles about Alice began appearing in newspapers and magazines. After Alice had featured in the *School Magazine*, almost every child in New South Wales knew about the ten-year-old deaf and blind girl who had miraculously learnt to read.

In 1920, Alice graduated dux of the Blind School. Because she was such an inspiration to the other students, she was asked to stay on by the directors. But after nine years, she grew tired of living like a child and left the school to lead her own life. She went home to the family farm to live with her parents and four of her brothers and sisters.

For someone less independent and adventurous than

Alice, that would have been the end of the story. But Alice wanted what other women took for granted — marriage and her own home. At the age of 37 she married Will Chapman, one of her penfriends. Will had been blind and deaf since he'd been injured in an accident with a pitchfork at the age of 21. Though her mother was against the marriage, Alice refused to budge.

The newlyweds lived together at the Blackburn Institute for the Deaf in Melbourne, where Will worked in a sheltered workshop. They bought furniture and saved for a home of their own, but this was one dream that was not destined to come true for Alice.

In 1948, Helen Keller visited Australia on a fundraising trip. The Institute invited Alice to Sydney to meet her American counterpart, and paid her airfare. Berta, who had retired by now, chipped in and bought Alice a new suit so she'd look her best when she was presented to the famous author and lecturer. It was a moving meeting between two women who had made history. Impressed with Alice's story, Helen Keller offered to sponsor her to go the United States for more advanced teaching, but Alice declined. She was too old now, and she did not want to leave her husband.

Alice's elation at meeting her idol was short-lived. Three weeks after her return to Melbourne, Will died suddenly of a heart attack. Alice retreated to Maitland, and stayed with her widowed mother for several months. The newspapers got hold of the story, and money flowed in from the public to buy Alice a house. Alice, who was proud of her independence, was appalled. She turned all the money over to the Royal Blind Society, who were in the process of building Helen Keller House, a hostel for blind women in the Sydney suburb of Woollahra. When the hostel was finished, Alice moved in.

Alice settled into her life in Sydney and began writing her autobiography, but she died in August 1966 before finishing it. When her sister Doris and sister-in-law Ivy went to the hostel to claim her belongings, the manuscript was gone. It was a great loss. Only after Alice's death did Berta break her long silence. At the beginning, she admitted, she'd despaired of ever getting through to Alice. The breakthrough, when it came, was the greatest thrill of her life.

In 1990, the Special School for Multi-Handicapped Blind Children in North Rocks, Sydney, was renamed the Alice Betteridge School. Two years later, the Royal NSW Institute for Deaf and Blind Children opened a pre-school for deaf children and the hearing children of deaf parents. They named it the Roberta Reid Centre.

Alice Betteridge triumphed over her deafness and blindness. She could not have done it without parents who loved her enough to want the best for her. Neither could she have done it without the care and skill of Roberta Reid. But more than anything it was Alice's own intelligence and determination that enabled her to persevere and get the most out of life.

MARJORIE LAWRENCE 1907 — 1979

Opera singer

When she was eighteen, Marjorie Lawrence ran away from her family's farm to take singing lessons in Melbourne. After winning the singing competition at the Geelong Eisteddfod, she was able to realise her dream of going to Paris to study singing. Once in Paris, she sang her way to a brilliant career in the major opera houses of Europe and America in the 1930s.

Marjorie Lawrence was born in 1907 on a farm near Dean's Marsh, Victoria. The youngest of Elizabeth and William Lawrence's five children, Marjorie had an older sister, Eileen, and three older brothers, Lindesay, Ted and Cyril.

Elizabeth died when Marjorie was two, and her widowed Grandmother Lawrence, who was alone now in the family homestead at Penny Royal, took her in. Julia Lawrence had moved her seven children to Penny Royal from the family inn at Geelong when her husband became an invalid. They cleared the scrub, felled the huge trees to build a house, and sowed crops. In later life, Marjorie liked to think she'd inherited her grandmother's strength and her ability to carry on in the face of adversity.

When the old lady died, Marjorie had to return home. Treated like a princess at Penny Royal, Marjorie crashed to earth back at the family farm. Housekeepers came and went, and the children ran riot while their father was out working the land.

The Lawrences were musical. Bill Lawrence played a one-string fiddle and the concertina at barn dances, and

Elizabeth had played the organ at the church. Marjorie started taking piano lessons very young, her music teacher driving the fourteen kilometres from Birregurra in a horse-drawn buggy. She made her first singing appearance at five, singing 'Push the Pram for Baby' at a Sunday School concert in the Anglican church in Dean's Marsh. It was a sign of things to come.

The children's involvement in music grew when a new pastor arrived at the church. The Reverend Alex Pearce, who had trained prize-winning choirs in other parishes, set about building a choir in Dean's Marsh. Lindesay Lawrence became the choir baritone, Ted a tenor and Cyril a boy soprano. But the most exciting find was Marjorie Lawrence. Discovering that her voice was phenomenally powerful and had an extraordinary range, Pearce took over her training. Soon he had her singing Bach cantatas and oratorios by Handel, Steiner and Mendelssohn.

When she wasn't singing, Marjorie was an ordinary hard-working farm girl who had to milk the cows, move sheep from paddocks and feed the pigs. A tomboy, she'd learnt to ride horses at seven, and had to be dragged away from catching tadpoles to go to choir practice. Her favourite pastime was riding bareback across the hills in the moonlight, singing at the top of her voice. When neighbours heard the 'Hallelujah Chorus' from Handel's *Messiah* echoing across the paddocks, they knew Marjorie Lawrence was passing by.

Marjorie was eleven when the Australian troops

returned from World War I. Reverend Pearce organised a series of concerts around the district to welcome home the returned servicemen. This gave the Lawrence children an opportunity to display their talents. People started calling Marjorie 'our little Melba', after Dame Nellie Melba, the internationally celebrated Australian opera singer.

By the time Marjorie was fourteen, Bill Lawrence was doing well enough to buy 400 hectares outside the prosperous town of Winchelsea. He built a handsome homestead about five kilometres from town. It was in Winchelsea that the idea which would change Marjorie's life was born. In town one day collecting the groceries, she heard the sound of piano music, and tracked it down to a caravan in the local park. Peering inside the door, she discovered that the caravan was a mobile furniture display. Its owner, a stout, pleasant-looking man, was playing a pianola — a mechanical piano — to attract customers. He beckoned her in and played a ballad, and Marjorie began to sing. A crowd quickly gathered. The concerts ended when someone told her father what she was up to, but by then the pianola man had convinced her she should go to Paris to learn singing.

Marjorie began to plan. She would need professional lessons before Paris, and that meant going to Melbourne. When she broached the subject with her father, however, he exploded. No daughter of his was going on the stage. Knowing it was useless to fight, Marjorie decided to wait until she was eighteen and legally an adult. Then she could do as she pleased. In the meantime, she saved her money and spent hours listening to her Clara Butt and Nellie Melba records. She also took sewing lessons so she could support herself while she studied singing.

There was still the problem of choosing a teacher. Marjorie found the answer in a newspaper story. John Brownlee, an Australian who'd become one of the leading baritones at the Paris Opera, had returned to Australia. He spoke highly of his Australian teacher, Ivor Boustead, who had a studio in Melbourne. It was all beginning to come together. But Marjorie needed allies. She confided in her older sister, Eileen, who'd left school at fourteen and taken over running the household. Eileen promised to give her little sister her savings. Marjorie also confided in Cyril, her favourite brother and biggest fan. Cyril immediately said he'd go to Melbourne with her. A cousin in the city promised to put them up for a week. Eighteen at last, Marjorie was on her way.

At the crack of dawn one morning, Marjorie and Cyril crept from the farm with their suitcases. Rather than risk waking their father by taking the car, they walked the five kilometres into town to the railway station.

Once in Melbourne, Marjorie quickly wangled an audition with Ivor Boustead. The influential teacher told her she had one of the best natural voices he'd heard. If she got a job, he'd take her on as a student. The next day, Marjorie started work as a finisher in a clothing factory. Working from 8 a.m. till 5 p.m. each day in total silence, she sewed buttons on frocks. Twice a week she took lessons with Ivor Boustead in her lunch break. Cyril, who'd found a job selling insurance, helped pay for these.

This arrangement didn't last long. The boss caught Marjorie creeping in late from a singing lesson and sacked her on the spot. Marjorie gave up on factory work and got a job as a domestic in a private home. In return for bed, board and the use of the piano, she paid five shillings and did all the rough housework. The five shillings came from Eileen, who was saving it out of her housekeeping money. Unfortunately, Bill Lawrence discovered what Eileen was doing and stopped the money. So the resourceful Marjorie advertised for a job that paid her a salary of seven shillings, and ended up working in a boarding house. She landed the job by charming the landlady with a heart-rending version of a sentimental Irish song.

Marjorie was twenty now, and Ivor Boustead believed she was ready to sing in public. The fastest route to fame was winning the Geelong Eisteddfod, the most important musical competition in Victoria. It paid a big cash prize and the publicity brought the winner lucrative singing engagements. It was a daunting task, though. To be grand champion, Marjorie would have to sing in at least twelve separate events, including the hard-fought opera aria, and win them all. How would she ever get the time to prepare?

Ivor Boustead came to the rescue. He wrote to Bill Lawrence assuring him Marjorie had real talent, and asking if she could come home until the Eisteddfod. Her father agreed, on one condition — if Marjorie failed at Geelong, she had to abandon her dream of a singing career. Relieved, Marjorie went home. Every day she got up at five to milk the cows, and twice a week caught the 7 a.m. train to Melbourne for singing lessons.

Aware that she'd staked her future on this one contest, Marjorie was nervous. But she loved performing, and at her first appearance wowed the judges with 'Annie Laurie'. They awarded her first prize. She went on to win everything else, including the highly prized aria competition.

Wearing her unfashionable home-made clothes, an elated Marjorie went onstage to receive her prize. It was the most exciting moment of her life. Now anything seemed possible. The judges predicted a rosy future for the unknown singer, and the next morning she woke to find her face all over the newspapers. Proven wrong, her father changed his attitude and shouted a round of beers in the Winchelsea pub.

Back in Melbourne, Marjorie sang for John Brownlee. Echoing the pianola man, he advised her to go to Paris. He would arrange for her to train with Madame Cecile Gilly, the wife of his former teacher, Dinh Gilly. He also talked Bill Lawrence into footing the bill. To help raise the money, Marjorie sang in a series of public performances.

Five months after winning the Eisteddfod, 21-year-old Marjorie Lawrence left Australia. As the boat pulled out of the dock she sang 'Turn Ye to Me', and family and friends on shore responded with 'God Be With You Till We Meet Again'. Marjorie had mixed feelings. Though she desperately wanted to go to Paris, it meant leaving everything she knew and loved. That night she cried herself to sleep. A romance with a handsome Englishman on the ship soon cheered her up, though.

Marjorie arrived in Paris at the end of the 'Roaring Twenties', when the city was in the midst of a literary and artistic revival. The minute she'd checked into her hotel, she ran out to look at the magnificent Paris Opera House. The sight sobered her. Had she aimed too high? Could a farm girl from Winchelsea ever expect to sing in such a place?

The first hurdle was surviving Madame Gilly's audition. The famous singing coach agreed to teach Miss Lawrence to sing. She was impressed with the voice, but felt that the Australian girl needed education and social polish. Marjorie was despatched to live with the Grodets, a cultured family who had fallen on hard times and took in foreign students.

At Madame Gilly's it was back to basics, doing weeks of humbling scales and exercises. At the Grodets, Marjorie learnt French and became assimilated into the family and into Parisian life. The Grodet's daughter Mimi became her best friend, and Marjorie and Henri, the son, fell in love.

After a year of hard work, Madame Gilly arranged an audition for Marjorie with Phillipe Goubert, Conductor of the Paris Opera and Director of the Conservatoire. To her joy, Marjorie was engaged to sing in a concert — not the opera yet, but a foot in the door. Then the unthinkable happened: Marjorie's father died. She forgot their differences, and was overcome with grief and guilt. Now she thought about how hard it must have been for her father to raise five children alone after their mother's death.

Shortly after, the monthly bank-drafts from Australia stopped coming. Cyril wrote and gave her the bad news. Lindesay, who was now head of the family, had decided that they'd spent enough money on Marjorie's singing. If she hadn't learnt to sing in two years, she never would. Marjorie was stunned. Just as all the years of hard work and preparation were about to pay off, it looked as if she'd have to return home, defeated.

But her friends were not going to let that happen. The Grodets and Madame Gilly told her not to worry about paying for board or lessons. She could pay them back when she started making a living out of singing. Henri worked extra hours at the knitting mill to pay for some of her lessons.

Marjorie was 23 when she won her first opera role, as Elizabeth in Wagner's *Tannhaüser* with the Monte Carlo Opera. The morning after her opera debut in Monte Carlo, Marjorie and Mimi Grodet scoured the papers for the reviews. They were excellent. And at the Opera House she found a letter of congratulations from her heroine, the English opera singer Dame Clara Butt. Offers came in from the Paris Opera and the Opera Comique.

In 1933, at the age of 26, Marjorie made her debut at

the Paris Opera as Ortrud in Wagner's *Lohengrin*. By the end of the year, she had sung 33 major roles at the Paris Opera. The Aussie tomboy had arrived. She paid off her debts and took an elegant seven-room apartment with a view down the boulevard to the Opera House. The Grodet's maid moved in to look after her. It was a long way from Dean's Marsh.

The following year, Cyril arrived in Paris. Until her marriage seven years later, Cyril and Mimi were the most important members of Marjorie's entourage, and travelled everywhere with her. Henri was left behind. As Marjorie's reputation grew, the offers flooded in — from the New York Metropolitan

Marjorie Lawrence, from the farm (l) to the stage (r)
Courtesy Winchelsea & District Historical Society

Opera House (the Met), the Vienna Staatsoper and Covent Garden in London. The lure of America proved irresistible. In 1935, Marjorie took a leave of absence from the Paris Opera and went to New York to sing at the Met. With Cyril and Mimi, she moved into the Ansonia, a hotel for musicians in the middle of the Broadway district.

Marjorie quickly made her mark at the Met, not only for her voice, but for her striking good looks and athleticism. She caused a sensation in *Die Walkürie* (*The Valkyrie*) as the only Brunnhilde in history to ride a real horse into real flames the way Wagner had intended. Over the next six years she commuted between the Paris Opera and the Met.

But war was looming. Just beating the outbreak of World War II, Marjorie returned to Australia for her first concert tour. It was exciting, but frightening, too. Australians demanded high standards of visiting musicians, and they liked cutting down tall poppies. She needn't have worried. The media fêted her, and a huge crowd welcomed her on her arrival at Melbourne's Spencer Street Station. Most of her country relations were at the public reception.

Two hundred people on horseback met her motorcade outside Winchelsea, led by a family friend carrying an Australian flag. A ball was held for her at the Globe Theatre, followed the next night by a sell-out concert. 'That Winchelsea concert was as important to me as a human being, if not as a professional artist, as my debut in Monte Carlo or my first appearance in Paris [or] New York,' she wrote ten years later. But the joy was mixed with sadness — her father was not there to welcome her, and her brother Lindesay had sold the family farm.

By 1940 critics were predicting that Marjorie Lawrence would become one of the century's greatest dramatic sopranos. The world was at her feet. She'd sung the most sublime operas ever written in the great opera houses of the world. She'd given recitals in many countries and sung solos with famous orchestras in Europe and America. Marjorie wanted more than professional success, however. In March 1941, in a quiet, secret ceremony, she married Tom King, a young American doctor. Tom was tall, handsome and easygoing, but no push-over. He refused to abandon his medical career and become 'Mr Marjorie Lawrence'. Fortunately, Tom agreed to accompany Marjorie to Mexico City in June and treat it as a honeymoon.

After they'd been in Mexico City for a couple of days, Marjorie started complaining of terrible headaches and pains in her back. The locals told her it was altitude sickness. In great pain, she soldiered on, but during the rehearsal of *Die Walküre* for the new Mexican National Opera, she collapsed on stage. When she regained consciousness, she could not move.

By the end of that first day, Marjorie was paralysed from shoulder to toe. She had a searing fever, her body ached, and she vomited all night. The doctors at the American Hospital told Tom his wife had a particularly severe case of poliomyelitis. Until a vaccine was developed in 1954, epidemics of polio swept the world. The disease paralysed its victims' limbs and sometimes killed them. If Marjorie hadn't been so physically fit, she would probably have died. Tom decided her best chance for recovery was at a hospital in Hot Springs, Arkansas. The American Embassy helped him organise a flight, and Marjorie was carried on board on a stretcher. A nightmare journey followed: the flight to Texas, a three-day train journey to Arkansas, and a forty-kilometre ambulance ride.

The hot mineral baths at Hot Springs relieved some of Marjorie's physical pain, but her emotions were in turmoil. Would she ever sing again? Would she even be able to walk? When Tom finally told her she had polio, she was devastated. When she stopped improving, they left the hospital and found an apartment in a stone house on the 200-hectare Harmony Hills Ranch outside Hot Springs.

At that time, Sister Elizabeth Kenny, an Australian bush nurse, was getting amazing results rehabilitating polio victims at the Minneapolis University Hospital. Sister Kenny's revolutionary method included muscle exercises underwater, and keeping the patient moving. She agreed to treat Marjorie. In Minneapolis, Sister Kenny and her helpers laid hot packs on Marjorie's limbs and back, and put her through an exercise regimen. Her body began to come back to life. Tom learnt the treatment so he could help.

Meanwhile, the music world waited for news. Thousands of letters poured in. The Met wanted to know if their diva would be able to sing the next season. Realising she wasn't going to get better quickly, if at all, Marjorie succumbed to despair and insisted on leaving the hospital. The Kings rented an apartment in Sister Kenny's building, and Tom took over most of the treatment.

Gradually her state of mind improved. What if she could still sing? Propped up against cushions at the piano, she tried to sing *Tristan und Isolde*. Though her breathing was impaired by the damage to her chest and diaphragm muscles, her voice was still there. She began practising. As her muscles grew stronger, she sang longer and her voice became steadier and more powerful.

After three months of treatment with Sister Kenny, the Kings moved to Miami for the sun and the sea and to be near Tom's family. Marjorie learnt to crawl into the water to bathe, and began to help run the household. That Christmas, Tom persuaded her to sing at the Christmas service at his family church. It was seven months since her collapse in Mexico City, and Marjorie could still not sit up without help, but she found the courage to perform. It was a huge success, and she began to work towards a comeback.

'Again I was Marjorie Lawrence the singer and I was on my way back—back to the Metropolitan, the Paris Opera, Covent Garden, Carnegie Hall. There was a long way to go. The journey had only begun — but it had begun.'

There was another reason for singing again. The Kings were broke. Marjorie's medical expenses were high, and Tom had given up work to look after her. As soon as she could sit upright without props and had some movement back, Marjorie started looking for work. She talked her way onto radio and sang at charity benefits for the Red Cross and the Metropolitan Opera Guild. When offers started to come in, Marjorie hired an agent. After a successful recital at the New York Town Hall she began dreaming about singing opera again.

While Marjorie Lawrence was fighting her personal battle against polio, the world had been at war. Marjorie wanted to make her contribution, despite her disability. In 1944 she toured the south-west Pacific entertaining the Allied troops. After the war she toured Britain — where she sang for the Royal family — as well as Occupied Germany, the Netherlands and France. In 1945, she was awarded the Legion of Honour in Paris for her war work and for services to French music. She also visited the Grodets, including Henri, who had spent two years in a prisoner-of-war camp. At the end of the war she was invited back to do a concert tour of Britain.

By 1947 Marjorie could walk with the aid of crutches, and once again sang at the Met and the Paris Opera. After a moving platform was designed for her, she was able to sing the title role in Richard Strauss's *Elektra* standing. But though she had recovered her voice and some of her mobility, she was never again offered starring roles.

In 1948 Marjorie Lawrence wrote *Interrupted Melody*,

her life story, which was later made into an Oscar-winning film. She retired from the stage in 1952, and the Kings moved to Harmony Hills Ranch, which they now owned. Rather than let all that hard work, knowledge and skill go to waste, Marjorie built a second career teaching voice studies in American universities. She made a last trip to Australia in 1976, and the following year was awarded a CBE. She died in 1979.

Marjorie Lawrence's extraordinary talent, drive and belief in herself propelled her from a farm in Victoria to the opera houses of Europe and America. She overcame family opposition, lack of money and an inadequate education to master the most difficult opera roles and gain acceptance in the tough French musical world. In a career spanning only nine years, she established herself as one of the two finest dramatic sopranos Australia has ever produced. Polio shattered her body and her dream, but not her spirit. She fought back to sing again.

NANCY BIRD 1915 —

Pioneer pilot

When Nancy Bird was fourteen, some pilots brought their planes to Wingham, in rural New South Wales, to give joy-rides and exhibitions of trick flying. Nancy took two joy-flights and paid the pilot extra to do some loops and rolls for her. That was the day she decided to learn to fly. She got her pilot's licence at seventeen, and at nineteen became the first Australian woman to make a living from flying.

Nancy Bird was born in October 1915 in Kew, a tiny timber and dairy town on the mid-north coast of New South Wales. Her parents, William (Ted) and Fanny, owned a store there. Nancy was the second of five children.

Soon after Nancy's birth, the family moved to nearby Kendall, but when Nancy was six, the Birds moved to Sydney so the children could attend private schools. Ted found work as a builder, but when the Great Depression ruined Australia's economy — and people could no longer afford to pay rent, let alone buy new houses — he returned to shopkeeping in the country to support his family. Leaving Fanny and the children at home in the seaside suburb of Manly, he opened a store at Mount George, a tiny settlement on the Manning River near Wingham.

Nancy attended several schools on the northern beaches. She did not do well academically because her mother often kept her home to help. 'I was the practical one,' she says. 'I was one who put out the nappies and cooked the potatoes.' So it was Nancy, rather than her older sister Gwen, who was taken out of school and sent to Mount George to keep house for her father and help in the store. Nancy didn't mind leaving — she didn't like school much anyway.

Ted Bird ran a general store. 'My father stocked everything from a needle to an anchor, and if he didn't have it, he'd get it in,' Nancy recalls. He also had an interest in a sawmill, and trucked cream from the local dairy farms to the Wingham Butter Factory. For one pound a week, Nancy did the books and the banking, served in the store, scrubbed floors and cooked the meals on a wood-burning stove. As there was no running water and no bathroom, her day started with a cold wash in a basin on top of a packing case. For fun, she could listen to their two 78-rpm records on a portable gramophone — 'You Forgot Your Gloves' is permanently etched in her memory — or attend the occasional dance in the School of Arts hall.

The world opened up when Nancy taught herself to ride. On Sundays she would gallop out over the hills to visit friends on far-flung farms. Occasionally, when an Australian National Airways Avro 10 passed overhead on its way to Brisbane, she fantasised about flying *above* the trees and mountains instead of riding through them.

Flying was in its infancy then. Unlike today, when travelling by air is safer than travelling on the road, it was dangerous. Planes were flimsy — they were made of fabric and wood, and their spars, or wing supports, were stuck together with glue which became brittle in temperatures over 40°C. Running into bad weather could be fatal, but the only weather reports pilots had were telegrams sent in by oil company employees working in the mountains. As there were no airstrips, pilots had to land their aircraft in paddocks, and when they crashed were often injured or killed.

Because mass air travel was still in the future, there was little work for pilots. When they needed money, they would go barnstorming — touring the countryside giving demonstrations of trick flying and taking people on joy-flights. When Nancy was fourteen, an air pageant came to Wingham, a large town 21 kilometres from Mount George. Her father let her go into town on the cream truck to see it, and she finally fulfilled her dream of flying, taking not one but two joy-flights in a shiny new Gypsy Moth. She liked it so much she paid the pilot an extra hard-earned pound to do some aerobatics while she was in the passenger seat.

After that exhilarating day in Wingham, Nancy decided she was going to learn to fly. People tried to discourage her, but she had one staunch ally, a friend called George Campbell. A shy boy who used to ride an enormous draughthorse bareback over the paddocks, George had learned to fly at Mascot while on holiday in Sydney. It was George who told Nancy about Frank Swoffer's book, *Learning to Fly*. She got hold of a copy and started swotting up on technical terms such as lift, drag and angles of incidence. Every spare penny went into a savings account for flying lessons. The next time she went to Sydney to visit her mother, Nancy took the tram out to Mascot airport and made an appointment for a trial instructional flight.

At the Aero Club at Mascot, she was interviewed by Captain Leggett. He had trained Millicent Bryant, the first woman to obtain a pilot's licence in Australia. To Nancy's consternation, Leggett offered her a cigarette. Always game, she accepted it — 'I thought he would think I was older if I took it.' When Nancy asked him where she could buy a helmet, the Captain told her to visit Miss Martin's shop in the Strand Arcade. There she was measured up for a leather flying helmet, which had to be custom-made because she was so small, and proudly purchased a leather coat and goggles. Nancy was fully kitted out as a pilot now — all she needed was to learn to fly. So she went back to the country to grow up and save enough money for lessons. That year, Amy Johnson flew from London to Darwin in nineteen days, proving to the world that women could fly.

Three years later, when Nancy was seventeen, Charles Kingsford Smith and Pat Hall barnstormed Australia. One of Australia's most famous fliers, Smithy had made history in 1928 when he was the first person to fly across the Pacific, and again in 1930, when he became the first man to circumnavigate the globe by plane. Nancy turned up in Wingham in her flying gear, hoping for a lesson. But when she saw how big the planes were, she settled for a joy flight in the legendary *Southern Cross*. She confided her ambitions to Smithy, who was about to open a flying school in Sydney, and he offered to train her. Nancy couldn't believe her luck.

At seventeen, with 200 pounds saved, Nancy announced she was off to Sydney to become a pilot. Her father objected strenuously. He told her she'd be wasting her hard-earned money, that he couldn't afford to look after a crippled daughter, and that it would kill her mother if anything happened to her. He was also worried about losing a good worker. Arguments raged, but Nancy refused to budge. After three years of planning and saving, nothing was going to stop her now. Her sisters had to take turns helping their father in the shop.

In 1933, Nancy moved back to Manly. Every day she would take the ferry to Circular Quay, catch a tram to Mascot, and walk the last mile to the airport for her flying lessons. 'I was the first pupil to turn up when Kingsford Smith opened the doors of his flying school at Mascot on 11 August 1933.' Smithy gave her the first lessons, but when he left to attempt the England–Australia record, she was handed over to Pat Hall, his Chief Instructor.

Nancy quickly discovered that flying posed problems for females, especially small ones. For a start, she had to sit on a pile of cushions to see out the windscreen. And women's clothes were all wrong. To prevent the propeller blowing her dress up over her head, she designed herself a uniform that was a cross between knickerbockers and plus-fours. It was made of linen in summer and tweed in winter. With it she teamed long socks and flat shoes, and wore her hair in a bun at the nape of her neck. At a time when respectable women did not wear trousers, this was a daring costume. People who saw her on her way to the airport in her flying gear would gape at the red-headed teenager striding along the road in knickerbockers.

Once Nancy started to get the hang of flying, she set about learning how to maintain planes as well. A pilot who made a forced landing in an isolated spot risked death if she could not do simple repairs, she realised. Nancy hung around the hangars watching what the engineers did. Smithy's Chief Engineer thought he could put her off engineering by giving her the dirty jobs, like scraping carbon off the big spark plugs on the *Southern Cross* with her hands covered in dirty black petrol, but she persevered. She also learnt how to inspect the spars for cracks and sew up inspection cuts in the wings.

As part of her training, Nancy started taking passengers up. She also flew with other pilots as often as she could and learnt from them. To the delight of her little brothers and their friends, she would sometimes fly over the family's home in Manly. As a cross-country flying exercise, she hired a plane and flew with an instructor to the first Canberra Air Pageant in 1933. On another long-distance exercise, she flew in formation with a pilot from Sydney to King Island in the Bass Strait. They became lost in the Riverina district, and had to land in a wheat field to ask directions from a farmer. When they got lost again over the Bass Strait, they had to turn back and land on the beach at Apollo Bay. When she was not flying, Nancy hung around the Aero Club with the other trainees and pilots. She would watch the serious pilots at the big table swapping stories and long to be one of them.

In September 1933, still just seventeen, Nancy obtained her pilot's licence — Number 1150. She immediately set about studying for her commercial pilot's licence. Most pilots flew for fun and adventure, but Nancy was determined to make a living out of it. She built up her flying hours and took courses in the classroom. To practise for the hour's blind flying and the half-hour solo night flying tests, she did advanced training at the Aero Club. She passed her examinations, and at nineteen became the youngest woman in the British Empire to get a commercial licence.

But by then her money had run out. 'People thought I was a wealthy woman because I was flying a plane, but I didn't have two bob to rub together,' she recalls. She would have to get a job. But in those days there were few openings in aviation for men, and none for women. What would she do? She found the answer in a newspaper called *Country Life*, while reading a story about her own exploits. Noticing a list of forthcoming country shows and race meetings, Nancy decided to try barnstorming. A woman had never done it before, but she was confident. All she needed was an aircraft and a co-pilot. Her great-aunt came to the rescue with 200 pounds, and her father, who'd changed his mind about her flying, matched the gift. With this windfall, Nancy bought a Gypsy Moth and christened it *Vincere* — meaning 'to conquer'. Peg McKillop, who had trained with the Aero Club and had also spent long hours learning to fix planes, agreed to join her. As Peg was well-off and flew only for fun, she agreed to accompany Nancy on the tour without payment.

In 1935 Nancy and Peg set out on the First Ladies' Flying Tour of Australia. Sometimes they lived comfortably in the homes of Peg's country friends; otherwise they stayed in country pubs, often with communal bathrooms and outdoor lavatories. Travelling west from Inverell, Nancy flew over the outback for the first time. She fell under the spell of the vast open spaces and endless skies. At Narromine she met Tom Perry, the wealthy grazier who had built the airport. Perry let fliers use the airport for free, and often helped out pilots who needed money. He told Nancy she would need a new plane to make a go of commercial flying. She had no idea how she could raise that much money — or pay it back, for that matter — but the idea took root.

In Dubbo, Nancy met the Reverend Stanley Drummond and his wife Lucy. Drummond had started up the Far West Children's Health Scheme. It arranged for outback children with trachoma — an eye disease caused by dust and leading to blindness — to go to Sydney for treatment. Drummond also organised holidays at Manly for children who'd never seen the sea, and ran a baby health service. Nursing sisters were sent out by car to help mothers living beyond the reach of the government's clinics. But the cars got bogged or broke down on the bad roads, and it sometimes took days to get to isolated homesteads. Drummond thought aeroplanes might be the answer. Would Nancy be interested in flying the nurse on her rounds?

Nancy certainly would. After a second barnstorming tour, she accepted a six-month trial with the Scheme. Based in Bourke, she was paid a 200-pound retainer, and guaranteed 200 pounds more in charter flights a year. This contract wrote Nancy's name into Australian aviation history, as it made the nineteen-year-old flier the first woman in the country to operate an aircraft commercially. When Nancy asked Tom Perry's advice about buying a new plane, he told her to go to his bank in Narromine — they'd lend her the money. It was not till later that Nancy discovered he had guaranteed the loan which enabled her to buy an expensive new Leopard Moth. It was while she was in Sydney picking up the new plane that Nancy heard that the *Lady Southern Cross* had disappeared over Rangoon in Burma on a flight from England to Australia. Smithy and his co-pilot Tommy Pethybridge were never seen again.

In Bourke, Nancy moved into Fitzgerald's Hotel, and had a hangar built to protect the plane's wooden frame from the harsh outback sun. She soon realised what she was in for. Flying a single-engine plane with no radio over hundreds of sparsely settled, waterless kilometres took all the courage and stamina she possessed. The cabin heated up like an oven. Willie-willies blew up out of nowhere. Sometimes she could use road maps as guides, but on many flights there were not even roads or railway lines to navigate by. Her only navigation tools were her compass and a watch, which she used to calculate how many kilometres she had travelled.

There was plenty of charter work at first. As well as her baby clinic work, Nancy flew patients to hospital in emergencies — an early version of today's Air Ambulance. When the Bulloo River flooded and cut off Thargomindah, she flew in supplies. As the local post-master was also the correspondent for the *Courier Mail*, Nancy's adventures made it into the Brisbane newspaper.

One of the highlights of Nancy's stay in Bourke was the arrival of John Kingsford Smith, Smithy's nephew. John was shooting a film for Cinesound called *Angel of the Outback*, about the Aerial Clinic. He filmed Nancy and the nursing sister, Sister Silver, taking off on an errand of mercy, and on the release of the film Nancy briefly became a star.

Nancy's trial with the Scheme was a success, and her contract was renewed. But life in Bourke was hard and lonely. She had few friends her own age, and the locals were stand-offish. They didn't know that Nancy was deep in debt and wearing her sister's old clothes; instead, they suspected she was a rich girl playing at being a pilot. They were also a little scandalised by a girl pilot who wore shorts to work on her plane and lived away from her family.

After nine months in Bourke, the government withdrew its subsidy to the Scheme, which could then no longer afford to pay Nancy's retainer. That left charter flights. After some thought, Nancy decided to give it a try. She also decided to leave Bourke and move north to Charleville, where there was a Qantas engineer at the aerodrome. 'There were no engineers and no other flying people to talk to in Bourke. Out west you depended on other fliers to learn your trade. I used to go to Charleville, and when the mail plane came in from Singapore, it was like the world coming inside.'

At 21, Nancy took a room at Harry Corones' Hotel in Charleville with all the Qantas airmail pilots, and began to enjoy life again. In December that year she entered the Brisbane to Adelaide Race via Sydney and Melbourne and beat the four other competitors by one minute to take out the Ladies' Trophy. She also posted the fastest time between Melbourne and Adelaide. But when drought set in, graziers could no longer afford to fly about the country buying sheep, and Nancy's business declined. To cut expenses, she moved to Cunnamulla, where she'd been offered free accommodation. She found enough work to get by, but her enthusiasm for outback flying was waning fast. The uncertainty, the gruelling conditions and her financial insecurity were making her worried and anxious.

Back in Sydney after flying a passenger to the city, Nancy realised it was time to give up outback flying. She did not want to go back to the bush. 'I was recoiling from going back to the isolation, the heat and dust, and the worry about engine problems and finances. I never wanted to fly again.'

It was a difficult decision, but after three years in the bush, Nancy was disillusioned. She came to the conclusion that there was no future for women as pilots. But though she'd decided to give up flying, she was reluctant to leave the aviation industry. She'd put too much time, hard work and sacrifice into flying to throw it all away. Passenger air travel was becoming more popular — perhaps she could find a job in administration or catering.

Nancy had become famous for her intrepid mercy flights in the outback. The news that she was giving up flying spread quickly. Women's groups tried to get the subsidy reinstated so she could go back to the Far West Children's Health Scheme, but were unsuccessful. Then KLM, the Dutch airline which had opened up an Australia-Indonesia route, stepped in with an offer. They would fly her to Europe to study civil aviation developments and bring her knowledge back to Australia. Nancy sold her plane and paid off her debts. All she had from three years in the outback was the 400 pounds she'd started with.

At the age of 23, Nancy set off to see the world. KLM flew her to Amsterdam, where the press made a fuss of the attractive young outback pilot. Realising Nancy was a splendid advertisement for their airline and air travel, KLM opened doors all over Europe. In thirteen months Nancy travelled 72 000 kilometres and visited 25 countries as the guest of KLM, Lufthansa and other airlines. She was treated like a VIP, introduced to famous aviators, and wined and dined by airline and oil company executives. She met German flying aces in Berlin, spent Christmas Day in Sweden, attended the May Day Parade and the Bolshoi Ballet in Moscow, and was presented at Buckingham Palace in London before setting sail for the United States, travelling steerage on the luxury liner, the *Queen Mary*. She was rescued from her cramped, noisy quarters each night by an oil executive, who took her to dinner in first class, where she hobnobbed with the rich and famous.

When Nancy arrived in New York, she didn't know anybody, so she contacted Betty Gillies, the president of the Ninety-Nines — the Women Pilots Organisation of America — which she'd joined the year before. Betty took Nancy under her wing, even presenting her to Eleanor Roosevelt, the President's wife, who was so impressed she wrote a newspaper column about the Australian flier.

But with war imminent, Nancy realised it was time to go home, and booked a cheap passage on the *Monterey*. By Hawaii she could no longer stand the racket in her cabin from the propellers, and wired home for money to move to the upper deck. This decision changed her life. By the time the ship reached Fiji, she had fallen in love with Charles Walton, an English textile importer returning to Australia after a trip home. They were married in December 1939, and had two children — Annemarie (Tweed) and John.

For a period during the war, Nancy was commandant of the Women's Air Training Corps. Its volunteers worked at the Air Force recruiting centre and finance office, and acted as drivers for Air Force personnel. Out of it grew the Women's Auxiliary Australian Air Force. After the war she devoted herself to her family, but did not completely relinquish her links with flying. Remembering how hard it had been for her as a young pilot to get in touch with other women fliers, she organised a gathering in 1949, and out of this the Australian Women Pilots' Association was born. Nancy was elected its first president. The Association brought many old hands back into flying. Nancy, who'd let her licence expire during the war because of the shortage of aviation fuel, obtained her student pilot's licence so she could fly as a co-pilot.

In 1958, about to travel to the US and wanting to be able to fly with the Ninety-Nines, Nancy took lessons and got back her old pilot's licence — Number 1150. Once in the States, she decided to compete in the Powder Puff Derby, an annual cross-country race organised and flown by women pilots. At first, the difficulties seemed insurmountable, but Nancy overcame them one by one. She hired a Cessna 172 and learnt to fly it. Training in San Diego, she obtained an international pilot's licence and a national aeronautics licence, and passed an exam on American air law. Finally, her old friend Betty Gillies found her an American co-pilot.

The first-ever overseas entrant in the Derby, Nancy

did Australia proud, completing the journey in 16 hours and 39 minutes, coming in fifth. Her zest for flying renewed, she flew in another Derby in 1961 and was a passenger in 1976. In 1966 she competed in the Ansett Air Race, a re-enactment of the legendary 1936 Brisbane to Adelaide air race. She was the only pilot to compete in both races. That same year, Nancy received an OBE — the Order of the British Empire.

In 1990, at 75, Nancy wrote her autobiography, *My God! It's a Woman.* She has since made another career for herself as a lecturer on the history of flight, and is patron of the Women Pilots' Association. In 1998 the Nancy Bird Walton Terminal, a terminal at Bourke Airport, was named after her.

Nancy Bird's name turned out to be her destiny — all she ever wanted to do was fly. After two years of training, she took on one of the toughest flying jobs in the country and succeeded, becoming famous for her skill and daring in dangerous conditions. Though she would not have called herself a feminist, she proved that a woman could fly as well as any man. Sadly, Nancy was born too early. It would be 41 years before a major Australian airline would hire a woman pilot, and then only after a court case. These days, a girl with Nancy's determination could captain a passenger airliner, fly an Air Force bomber, or even go into space.

LINDA TRITTON MCLEAN 1917 –

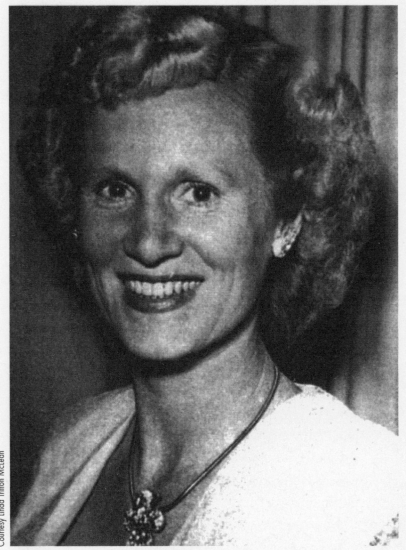

Child of the Depression

During the Great Depression, thirteen-year-old Linda Tritton helped her mother feed and bind the sores of two starving little girls at a bush camp. It was her political awakening. Six years later, stuck in a squalid labour camp with two small children, she began agitating for better conditions for the workers and their families. It would become a lifelong commitment.

Linda was the fourth child of Duke Tritton and Caroline Goodman, known as Dot. There would eventually be seven girls and three boys in the Tritton family. Duke and Dot had married when Duke was working in Mudgee, Dot's home town. When Linda was born in 1917, the Trittons moved to Sydney to seek work and a good education for their children.

Linda's mother and father had grown up the hard way. Duke had left school at thirteen. At nineteen, he took to the road, working his way around New South Wales. Dot's mother had died when she was nine. Her father, a salesman, took her and his two other young children with him in his horse-drawn van as he travelled the countryside. Believing it would be good for Dot to live in a family, her father handed her over to a woman with six sons. But the woman didn't want a daughter, she wanted a servant. Little Dot ended up scrubbing the floors, doing the washing in the copper and ironing with a heavy old flat iron. She was brutally punished for any mistakes. When one of the boys abused her, Dot ran away. She was quickly found and returned to her foster mother. One of her rescuers was suspicious, though. He followed Dot, and caught 'the missus' chasing her with a stockwhip. Appalled, the man took Dot home to his family and sent her to school until her father returned and collected her.

Dot and Duke Tritton were proud, hard-working battlers. Dot was a good housekeeper and an expert dressmaker, and her children were always clean, well fed and well dressed. They lived in dilapidated rented houses until Duke saved enough money to build their own home in Punchbowl, on the western outskirts of Sydney. There was no money for luxuries, but Dot could usually find a few pennies to send the kids to the Saturday matinee at the movies.

When Linda was twelve, her oldest sister, Dorrie, married a man named Chris, and the young couple moved into the family home to save money for a place of their own. Their timing could not have been worse. It was 1929, and the Great Depression was beginning.

This catastrophic international financial crash would last till the middle of the 1930s. It would throw men out of work and break up families. Tenants were evicted from slum houses with their pitiful piles of belongings. Some found refuge in makeshift camps; others took to the road, working in exchange for a bite to eat.

Before the Depression, Duke Tritton had been a driver on a timber truck. But when the timber workers' wages were cut and their hours increased, their union called a national strike. Several mills were burned down.

The only picture of Linda Tritton as a child
Courtesy Linda Tritton McLean

The owners brought in unemployed men as 'scab' or non-union labour, and the strike was defeated. Duke was sacked for refusing to break the strike.

Life went on. Dorrie and Chris had a daughter, Fay, shortly before Chris lost his job as a cabinet-maker. Another of Linda's sisters, Dulcie, married Vic, a painter, and they had a daughter called Patricia. They rented the house next door.

For a time the Trittons kept going, living on their savings and their wits. They ate fruit and vegetables grown in the backyard, and eggs from their hens. Dot made jam and pickles and sold them door to door, pushing a baby and a toddler in a pram. She also made a little money through her sewing, until people could no longer afford to buy clothes.

As the months wore on, Duke was forced onto the dole, which was thirty-two shillings and fourpence worth of food coupons. Unemployed families were also supposed to get two parcels of clothes a year, but most only got one, and even then the clothes and shoes might not fit. Mostly they relied on charity handouts. At the time, the basic wage was four pounds, fourteen shillings and sixpence. The basic wage was regarded as the lowest amount necessary for a worker to support a family, but it was almost three times as much as the dole.

One of the hardest things to give up, for the kids, was the Saturday matinee at the pictures. Dot told them the fourpence entry fee would buy a loaf of bread. People on the dole simply had to go without.

Dulcie's husband Vic scraped together enough money to buy a horse and cart, and delivered Dot's jam for a small commission. Linda's sister Jean gave rides on the horse and cart for a penny. The kids also brought home melons and vegetables they found growing at the tip, and sold flowers. Linda and her brother Harold (Habbie) collected horse manure and sold it to gardeners for sixpence a load.

But eventually the hens were eaten and there was no money to buy seeds and plants for the garden. As the Depression showed no signs of letting up, Duke and Dot decided to go back to Mudgee. Maybe Duke could make a little money digging for gold, and there was always fencing work in the country.

Dot and Duke set off in a borrowed truck with some furniture and the three youngest children — Audrey, Colin and Shirley. Habbie, Audrey and Linda, now thirteen, had to travel alone on the overnight train. The two married daughters, Dorrie and Dulcie, and fifteen-year-old Jean stayed in the family home to try to pay off the mortgage. Thinking they'd soon be back, Dot and Duke left their good furniture in Sydney. They were away four years.

The Trittons set up their new home on a travelling stock reserve by a creek at Mt Knowles, a goldmining district. The reserves were set aside for farmers to rest and water the cattle and sheep they were driving to the saleyards. The drovers were friendly, but the cattle bellowed all night and damaged their hut. One even forced its way into the kitchen. But some of the destitute families who camped at the reserve were more destructive than the cattle. Often Dot would have to clean up the filth and garbage they left behind.

A couple of hundred yards from a creek Duke and Dot built three huts — two for sleeping and one for cooking and eating. They were made of bush timber, with canvas and corn-bag sides and stringybark roofs. The kitchen hut was clay and stone with a corrugated iron fireplace. The beds were camp stretchers made from saplings and corn bags. Duke built a lavatory some way from the house, and they bathed in the creek in summer and in a tin tub in front of the fire in winter.

Although they'd arrived in the middle of winter, Duke immediately started panning for gold in the freezing creek. Linda was saddened by the sight of her father's hands, blue with cold, leeches hanging from every finger.

The real treasure in the family was Dot Tritton, who was smart and resourceful. She'd grown up on farms and knew how to live off the land. She taught the kids how to trap rabbits and catch yabbies, and knew what bush tucker to feed the family to keep them healthy. To give them iron, Dot boiled up stinging nettles, which tasted like strong spinach. Instead of cabbage, she used a weed called 'fat hen' and boiled up 'bird dock' to make pies. Watercress grew by the creek, and in season there were mushrooms, and blackberries and quinces for jam.

Dot cooked the meals over an open fireplace in half a kerosene tin with a wire handle. They practically lived on stew, sometimes consisting only of vegetables and rice. Sometimes Dot went without food to feed the babies and to keep Duke strong enough to work. If they had flour, Dot would make dumplings with golden syrup. Bread was always damper, Johnny Cake (a flat damper) or fried scones. When things got really bad, they had to make do with bread and dripping.

'We'd go for a long walk up the bush and eat berries,' says Linda. 'I found out later they were called Geebung berries. They were bitter horrible things, but Mum told us to eat them because they were nutritious.'

There was no money for store-bought clothes. Dot made the kids' clothes from calico flour bags. 'Try as she might, the brand name refused to wash out, and we would be wearing garments with Golden Gate Flour, Gulgong, firmly imprinted on them,' recalls Linda. 'Apart from bloomers, petticoats, night clothes or shirts, these bags also served as pillow cases or tea towels as our linen supply became depleted.'

Woollen jumpers were unpicked and knitted into squares to make patchwork quilts. Dot also made bush rugs — known as Wagga rugs — out of corn bags by covering them with scraps of material to make them colourful and warm.

In the meantime, things were getting tougher in Sydney. Dorrie and Chris had to go on the dole. At sixteen, Jean also got the dole, but could only keep it as long as she lived away from home. Deciding they'd be better off with the family, Dulcie and Vic headed for Mt

Knowles. Dulcie and the baby took the train, but Vic and Fred, Linda's cousin, walked all the way to the Hunter Valley. Fred arrived barefoot; his boots had disintegrated.

Unable to pay the mortgage any more, the Trittons lost their precious house in Punchbowl. With only eighteen months to go on the loan, the bank repossessed it. All Dot and Duke's treasured furniture was given away to friends and relatives. Jean retreated to Mt Knowles. Dulcie and Vic went to live with Vic's parents a few miles outside Lithgow. When Dot had two more children — Donald and Mavis — the family grew even bigger.

To get to school, thirteen-year-old Linda, eleven-year-old Habbie and eight-year-old Audrey had to walk more than five kilometres to Havilah over unpaved roads. The worst part was crossing the creek in winter wearing only canvas sandshoes, which was all they could afford. When the toes of the shoes wore out, their feet froze. Sometimes, on very cold mornings, Dot gave in to their pleading and let them stay at home. Eventually, she gave up and let them all quit school. Linda's formal education ended just before she turned fourteen, and Habbie's when he was almost twelve. But they kept up their reading and tried to help the little ones with their lessons.

To pass the time, the kids went mountain climbing or walked along the train line to Mt Knowles to meet the mail train. Sometimes the train drivers would toss them magazines and newspapers to read. They entertained themselves with singsongs, accompanied by an instrument made from a kerosene tin with a broom handle and wire strings attached.

To collect the dole, Duke had to walk fourteen kilometres into Mudgee. When Linda and Habbie tagged along, Duke would regale them with tales of his days on the road as a swaggie, and the shearers' strike in Queensland. He taught them never to look down on anyone, but never to look up to anyone either.

Linda quickly discovered that not everyone believed in equality. Many people who'd kept their jobs despised those who'd lost theirs, and called them 'bludgers' for taking the dole. The Trittons experienced this contempt first-hand. Few of the farmers who passed Duke, Linda and Habbie on that long walk to Mudgee offered the trio a lift in their carts. One farmer refused them milk for the baby because he needed it for his pigs.

Once a farmer cheated Linda's father out of his wages for two weeks' fencing. Instead of money, he gave Duke a load of pumpkins, and threatened to report him to the dole office for working if he complained. The Trittons ate pumpkin three times a day. Nobody grumbled. Even the youngest children sensed that their parents were close to breaking point.

When she turned fourteen, Linda was old enough to work. She found a job with a large family as a live-in help. For seven shillings and sixpence a week, she toiled fifteen hours a day, cooking, scrubbing floors, ironing and looking after six children. She wasn't even fed properly. Her first meal was half a sausage, half a potato and a small spoonful of cabbage. When she got back late from a weekend off, she was sacked and cheated out of a week's pay. Another woman tried to pay her for two weeks' work with some cast-off clothes.

Linda met her future husband when she was sixteen, and he was seventeen. Frank Wilkins was fair, blue-eyed and handsome. He also had steady work fencing, ploughing, and burr-cutting on farms. Linda married Frank when she was seventeen, with just a small family wedding. They couldn't afford a honeymoon, and moved into an extension built onto the Trittons' hut. Because Frank had a job, Linda could at last walk into a shop and pay cash for food, instead of trading the hated coupons. The good fortune didn't last, though. Frank was soon on the dole. It was 1934; the Depression was still in full swing.

Linda gave birth to her first child, a daughter called Judith, before her eighteenth birthday. She suddenly felt very young and alone. With no money and a baby, she suddenly realised what a burden Dot had borne. The future looked frightening.

But they were finally able to escape from Mt Knowles. After years of applications, Duke Tritton was given a land grant at Cullenbone, halfway between Mudgee and Gulgong. With Frank's help, Duke built a new house with three big bedrooms, a kitchen-cum-parlour and a verandah. They still had only the bare necessities, but it was a step up from the stock reserve. Dulcie, Vic and their children moved in, along with Linda, Frank and

Judith. Linda's mother-in-law helped out with seeds, milk and eggs, and the loan of a cow.

The farm did not do well that first year, but Habbie got a job droving sheep and cattle and Duke found some relief work as a labourer. Then one day, Linda's brother Don and her niece Patricia rushed up to the house with some coins they'd found while digging under a pepper tree. It was a stash of gold sovereigns and half-sovereigns. Dot took the coins to town and exchanged them for forty pounds at the bank. It was like winning the lottery. Dot bought a horse, sulky and harness, a milking cow, some second-hand furniture, blankets and curtain material. For the first time, everyone had their own toothbrush and comb.

In 1936, Linda's son Barry was born. When he was five months old, Frank and Duke were offered relief work on the notorious 'Sandy Hollow' line. This was a government project to build a railway line from Sandy Hollow, near Muswellbrook in the Hunter Valley, to Maryvale, south of Dubbo. Everyone was ecstatic — long-term employment at last. Linda and the children accompanied Frank, but Duke left Dot and the rest of the family on the farm.

Linda took all her worldly possessions with her. All their clothes fitted into one suitcase. She packed one pair of sheets, two pillow cases, a pair of towels and two tea-towels made of flour bags, two blankets and a Wagga rug made by Dot as a wedding present. She also had two old saucepans, a battered frying pan, a billy can for a kettle and a camp oven. A galvanised tub would serve as a bath and wash tub. Linda had never been separated from her mother before, and grieved. But she was also elated — Frank and Duke would be off the dole, working for a living again.

The government had made Sandy Hollow sound basic but livable. The reality was very different. The sight that confronted Linda was rows of tight-packed tents on a patch of clay. Pulling back the flap of her tent, she discovered rough dirt floors, open fireplaces for cooking and heat, and no beds. Duke came to the rescue by cobbling together some bush beds, and they scrounged a wooden box to make a cot for Barry. Another upturned box was used as a table.

When Linda set out to explore the campsite the next day, all her worst fears were confirmed. The communal lavatory was filthy. Excrement and garbage lay in piles between the tents. The children were friendly, but dirty and neglected. Many had lice, sores, and infected eyes from conjunctivitis. Their mothers seemed depressed and apathetic.

Worse was to come. When it rained, the dirt floors of the tents turned into a quagmire. Linda had to cook dinner on a smouldering fire with water swirling around her ankles. There was no privacy, and the carousing of drunken men kept them awake on payday. Some men beat their wives.

But Linda was a Tritton. Instead of sinking into apathy, she set out to change things. She had inherited

Dot's energy and fighting spirit, and her father's sense of justice. These qualities would be sorely needed during the next year and a half on the Sandy Hollow line.

Knowing that dirt caused disease, Linda made a birch-brush broom and cleaned up, dumping the rubbish well away from the camp. The other mothers watched her suspiciously, then some pitched in and helped. She treated the kids' sores with Dot's ointment, washed their infected eyes out with boracic acid, and doused their heads with kerosene to kill the lice. Following Linda's example, some of the mothers started bathing their kids in the river. But despite Linda's best efforts to create a more hygienic environment, gastroenteritis swept through the camp. After she led a delegation of angry women to confront the manager, a new cesspit was dug farther from camp and garbage drums were provided.

For Linda, the sense of time wasted, of dreadful boredom, was worse than the physical hardship. Having little in common with the other women, she had no one to talk to. To fill the time, she taught some of the children to knit, then tried to teach the younger children to read and write. Reading was her main solace.

Meanwhile, Duke and Frank were laying the railway tracks. The work was back-breaking. There was no machinery, so all the heavy work was done with picks and shovels. Many of the men had never done this kind of work before, and the overseers bullied them mercilessly. They could not fight back; if you threw in a relief job, you could not get the dole. In Linda's eyes, the men on the Sandy Hollow line were the nearest thing to slave labourers since the convicts.

Frank was a labourer, a navvy, while Duke was a 'powder monkey'. Linda worried about them ceaselessly. Duke earned good money because his job was dangerous. He set the charges of explosives to blast out the heavy rock. During the blasting, the men had to dodge the falling rocks.

The worst eighteen months of Linda's life ended when war broke out in 1939. The Sandy Hollow line was abandoned. Linda and Frank moved back to Sydney, and Frank joined the army. Their daughter Diane was born in 1941. When Frank went away to war, Linda found a job as a bus conductor. That meant she could afford little luxuries like hot water, thick towels and scented soap. But by the end of the war, Frank and Linda's marriage had fallen apart. At the age of 33, Linda married Pat McLean, a friend of Habbie's. This marriage was happy, and they had three sons.

Linda Tritton came from a generation whose lives were blighted by the Great Depression. Dot and Duke's courage, determination and skill ensured that the Tritton family survived, but the costs were high. They lost their home, had to live on charity, and the younger children missed out on a decent education. The experience taught Linda Tritton compassion for people worse off than herself, but it also convinced her that individual kindness was not enough. She decided that the only way to ensure that the Depression did not happen again was to agitate for change. Her children received the education she missed so they would never be subjected to the squalor, injustice and indignity she experienced on the Sandy Hollow line. And when she realised that young people in the affluent 1950s and 60s were ignorant about the Depression, she wrote a book — *Pumpkin Pie and Faded Sandshoes* — to make them understand just what life was like on the dole.

DAWN FRASER 1937 –

Detail of photograph by Sandy Edwards

Swimming legend

A scruffy kid from a poor suburb of Sydney, Dawn Fraser was a gifted swimmer who had so much natural talent she didn't need to train to win races. But at seventeen, Dawn got the shock of her life. She swam badly and missed selection for the Vancouver Empire Games. Dawn had to decide if she was committed to swimming. She began to train seriously, and became a sporting legend.

Dawn Fraser was born in September 1937 in the Fraser's rented semi-detached house in Birchgrove Road, Balmain. She was the youngest of eight children. A working-class suburb near Sydney's docks, Balmain was tough, clannish and close-knit. The Frasers were battlers. Her father Ken, a gentle Scotsman, worked at the Cockatoo Docks. Ken suffered from bronchial asthma, and his daughter would lie awake at night listening to him cough. Dawn inherited his asthma. Dawn's mother, Rose, was born in Balmain. From her, Dawn inherited a good physique and a strong character.

Dawn didn't let her asthma slow her down. She was a tomboy who roamed the streets with a gang of local kids getting into mischief. When she was nine, her three brothers cut off her long hair, put her into football shorts and a jersey, and made her play wing in their football team. Dawn rode her old bike round the streets, climbed factory fences, and even ran through the deserted mine shafts under the harbour. Dawn was a wild one. She smoked, swore, wagged school, and liked to hang around the milk bar.

Another trick of Dawn and her pals was climbing the fence to the Elkington Park Road Swimming Pool so they wouldn't have to pay the entry fee. Dawn had learnt to swim at four when her older brother, Don, threw her into the pool. Don was a good athlete, a footballer and a diver, and his little sister idolised him. Dawn's cousin Ray Miranda, a swimming coach, taught her to race. She won her first race at eight, and joined the local swimming club. Soon nobody could beat her.

Dawn's childhood ended when she was twelve. First, Don died of leukemia, only days after his 21st birthday. Devastated, Dawn ran down to the pool, sat in a corner and cried for hours. Then her father was hospitalised with acute bronchial asthma, and her mother became seriously ill with heart disease. Dawn missed so much school looking after her mother that the truant officer visited. Instead of going back to class, Dawn got special permission to leave school, even though she wasn't yet fourteen, the legal leaving age. To help support the family, she went to work as a machinist in a sportswear factory in Balmain, just as her older sisters had done.

Meanwhile, Dawn was still swimming competitively at the local swimming club — and usually winning. On one of her regular visits to the Elkington Park Road Pool, she had a meeting which would change her life. Dawn and her mates turned up one day to discover a swimming squad in their pool. They were not amused. The swimmers belonged to Harry Gallagher's club, and usually trained at his pool in the nearby suburb of

Drummoyne. Dawn set about showing the interlopers who owned the pool. She dive-bombed the swimmers from the verandah, and upset the girls by telling them there were sharks and eels in the water. When Harry Gallagher came over to see what the fuss was about, Dawn was insolent, then ran off. The next day, when the coach came back, he saw Dawn racing. To his amazement, she almost beat one of his male swimmers in the pool. She was fast.

Gallagher, who'd grown up in an inner-city slum, saw something of himself in thirteen-year-old Dawn. He knew how tough kids had to be to survive in rough neighbourhoods like Balmain. He also saw Dawn's potential as a swimmer. He invited her over to Drummoyne to train. He was astonished when she actually turned up some time later. She'd changed though. A bout of hepatitis had made her thin and sickly looking, and she seemed a bit lost. But she mucked in and helped him clean the pool, and made friends with his mother Gloria, who was working in the kiosk. Mrs Gallagher fed Dawn pies with tomato sauce, and Harry gave her a new swimsuit to replace her tattered old one.

At the time, Gallagher was trying to break into full-time swim coaching. He already had one future star, Jon Henricks, who would win gold for Australia at the 1956 Olympic Games. But since his best female swimmer — Lorraine Crapp — had gone over to another coach, he needed a girl champion. The coach thought Dawn might be that girl, though she would not be easy to tame or train. He took the gamble, and offered to coach her when she turned fifteen — but only if she promised to work hard. He told her she'd have to stop smoking, get well, eat properly, and train most days. Dawn agreed on the condition that she could train with Jon Henricks, not Gallagher's college girls, and would not have to swim breast stroke. There was one other problem: Dawn's father couldn't afford to pay for coaching. Gallagher said she could pay her way by helping out in the kiosk.

Dawn wondered what she'd gotten herself into. At 5.30 every morning, and again in the evening, she had to cycle several kilometres to Drummoyne, do her laps, and ride home again. Gallagher gave her exercises to do which would build up her strength, and made her swim with a tin drum tied to her ankles to develop her arm strokes.

Gallagher's hardest task was getting Dawn to accept discipline. She answered back, wouldn't train in the same lane as the college girls, and refused to do dive starts from the third step of the stand because it bruised her toes. When the Balmain Tigers football team was playing, she would skip training. Gallagher persevered, because Dawn always came back. If he could get this wild girl to take swimming seriously, he thought, he might just have a future Australian champion on his hands.

Dawn had agreed to give Gallagher a year's trial, but she wasn't convinced she needed training. Until now, she'd won easily on natural talent. But Dawn's illusions about winning without doing the hard yards were shattered at her first national titles in Melbourne in

1954. In the freestyle event, she was beaten by her old rival, Lorraine Crapp, after going out too hard and fading at the finish. Third place was not good enough to get her onto the team for the Vancouver Empire Games. Finally, Dawn realised that she was going to have to train seriously if she wanted to be a champion.

She began to knuckle down — and it paid off. At the nationals the following year, she broke the 220-yard Australian record with a swim of 2 minutes 29.5 seconds. Sensing a potential gold medal at the 1956 Olympics, the media made her a celebrity. Then Harry Gallagher dropped a bombshell. He'd bought the Olympic pool in Adelaide and wanted Jon Henricks and Dawn to come with him. Dawn was willing, but her father refused to let her go. The wily Harry Gallagher told Dawn's father that Dawn would not get to the Olympic Games unless she trained with him in Adelaide. Ken Fraser gave in — on the understanding that it was to be a six-month trial, and Mrs Gallagher would look after Dawn.

With some trepidation, Dawn set off for Adelaide, and moved into a flat above the pool kiosk with Gloria Gallagher. She didn't even last the six months, though. When her parents' health deteriorated, Dawn became so worried about them that she insisted on going home. Gallagher was distraught, his hopes of fielding two gold medallists in Melbourne dashed. But victory was so close, and Dawn had put in so much work, that the lure of gold proved too much. Dawn returned to Adelaide.

Before she could get back to serious training, Dawn

had to find a job to support herself. Rules for amateur athletes were very strict in the 1950s. They could not accept money from sponsors, and sporting scholarships did not exist. Harry Gallagher found his protégé a job as a trainee footwear buyer in a department store. Dawn had to do her swim training early in the morning, during her lunch breaks, and after work. She put on weight and became stronger.

Dawn was eighteen now, and turning into a very tough competitor. She discovered she could psych out her more nervous opponents on the blocks, even before the race began. At the 1956 nationals, she distracted her opponents by wearing her trainers and socks on the blocks. She also beat Lorraine Crapp in the 110-yard freestyle race, in a time of 64.5 seconds. This stunning swim smashed a record which had stood for twenty years, and earned Dawn a place on the Australian swimming squad for the 1956 Melbourne Olympics.

Hosting the Melbourne Olympics was a huge boost for Australia's confidence and its international image. Despite our small size, Australia was strong in athletics and swimming, and hopes ran high that we'd win a swag of medals. At the Olympic pool on that hot night in December 1956, all eyes were on the home team. In the women's 100-metre freestyle, the glamour event, Australia had three finalists. The gun went off, and they leapt from the blocks. As the seconds ticked by the audience rose to its feet and cheered the Aussie girls home — Dawn Fraser, gold; Lorraine Crapp, silver; and

Faith Leech, bronze. Dawn's time of 62 seconds set a new world record. 'It was a marvellous feeling. It was like nothing I've ever experienced. I enjoyed many more triumphs, but I cherished that first gold the most. All the family agreed it was Don's medal.' Dawn Fraser would hold the 100-metre freestyle record for sixteen years. The following night, the Australian girls won the 4x100-metre relay, and Dawn Fraser had her second gold medal.

Dawn's parents were able to get to Melbourne to watch Dawn compete, but had to leave after her race to catch the train back to Sydney. They couldn't afford to stay the whole week.

After the Olympic Games, Dawn Fraser and Lorraine Crapp were inducted into the International Swimming Hall of Fame in America. In 1957 they were invited to swim in Honolulu and tour the west coast of America. Dawn helped pay for the trip with money saved from her part-time jobs pumping petrol and working in a coffee shop. It was her first overseas trip, and she lived it up, meeting celebrities like Johnny Weissmuller, who played Tarzan in the movies, and actor Mickey Rooney.

But as Dawn's fame grew, so did her notoriety. She seemed to have a knack for getting into trouble. Her natural inclination was to defy authority, and she sometimes acted without considering the consequences. Dawn seemed determined to provoke the officials in the Australian Swimming Union (ASU). She was convinced that they did not think she was good enough to represent Australia overseas. They would drop her the moment she stopped winning, she believed, and she resented that. Why should she have to keep on proving herself? The only positive aspect of this conflict was that it turned Dawn into a fighter who made sure she won every race.

The media loved Dawn's antics and reported all her confrontations with authority. Swimming officials retaliated by refusing to make Dawn captain of the swimming team for the 1960 Rome Olympics. The word got around that they found her too headstrong. Despite the tension, Dawn excelled herself in the pool, winning her second Olympic gold medal and setting a new world record of 61.2 seconds in the 100-metre freestyle. As part of the freestyle and medley relay teams, she also won two silver medals.

Out of the pool, she continued to irritate officials. When a security guard refused to let Harry Gallagher come to the poolside because he didn't have a pass, Dawn dragged him inside and refused to swim until he was given a seat. That was only the beginning. She also caused a fuss by wearing a white tracksuit on the dais — instead of the regulation green and gold — when she accepted her medal. Caught nightclubbing during the Games, she refused to stop, insisting that it didn't affect her performance. Most damagingly, Dawn fell out with her team-mates on the trip by refusing to swim the butterfly lap in the heats of the medley relay. The girls shunned her for a week.

Dawn was beginning to believe that the officials could not do without the best female swimmer in the country, and this made her overconfident. At an international swimming carnival in Naples following the Games, she finally went too far. She turned up to the meet tipsy after celebrating her birthday with champagne, then she stopped halfway through her race. Her apology fell on deaf ears. The ASU barred her from competing for Australia at overseas meets. A media frenzy erupted.

Dawn was stunned. Overseas trips were an amateur's only reward for the long hours of training, the poor social life and the lack of money. Dawn vented her anger and frustration on some traffic police one night, and was taken into custody. Although the charges were dropped, the incident was all over the papers the next day.

By the time Dawn's father died in 1962, it must have seemed as if the whole world had turned against her. She grew so depressed she considered giving up swimming. 'I thought what the hell's the use of going on?' Ironically, although she was in disgrace at home Dawn was a celebrity abroad. In 1961 the American Holm Foundation named her one of the six best athletes in the world. This helped her decide to stay in the game.

Knowing she had not reached her physical peak, Dawn kept pushing herself in the pool. She set her sights on swimming the 100-metre freestyle in under one minute. Luckily, the ASU lifted their ban in time to let her compete in the 1962 Commonwealth Games in Perth. At the trials for the Games, Dawn broke the one-minute barrier in the 100-metre freestyle with a time of 59.9 seconds. 'Breaking the minute was something that I had set my mind to do and it took me over two years to mentally be prepared. It was probably the hardest week of swimming I'd ever experienced in my life.' At the Games, Dawn also swam the fastest 110 yards and 440 yards in her career. On the basis of these swims, she was given the Babe Zaharias/Associated Press of America Award for the world's most outstanding female athlete. It is one of her most cherished honours.

The lead-up to the 1964 Tokyo Olympics was one of the most difficult periods of Dawn's life. Just before the team was selected, Dawn was driving a car which was involved in a fatal accident. Her mother died in the crash, and Dawn's sister and a family friend were injured. Dawn fractured a number of bones in her spine and was in a neck brace for weeks. She also lost Harry Gallagher as her coach. Gallagher, who was building a sports complex in Melbourne, could not accompany Dawn to Townsville, where the Olympic team was training.

Dawn was facing seemingly insurmountable emotional and physical hurdles. At almost 27, she was nearly twice the age of some of the girls in the team, and grief and guilt over her mother's death had sapped her fighting spirit. With her parents and brother dead, and her coach absent, she no longer had anyone to swim for. To cheer her up, two of her team-mates took her to a pub one night. It changed her life. At the pub she met Gary Ware, a local bookmaker, and fell in love. Dawn's confidence returned, and she vowed to triumph at Tokyo. If she could win the 100-metre freestyle again, it would not just mean another medal. It would mean Dawn Fraser would become the first swimmer in history to win the same event in three consecutive Olympic Games.

Dawn was on the crest of a wave. Nothing could stop her. This mad confidence caused a stir on the very first night of the Tokyo Olympics. Athletes who were competing the next day were forbidden to march in the opening ceremony. But Dawn was not going to miss the best part of the Games. Along with three other swimmers, she sneaked onto the bus at the last minute, and marched — in the front row of the Australian contingent. After the riot act was read, Dawn settled down to the serious work of winning medals. In the 100-metre freestyle, the 27-year-old Australian swimmer left her fifteen-year-old American rival in her wake.

This victory won Dawn her third gold medal, but more importantly, it made her the only swimmer, male or female, to win an Olympic swimming title three times in succession. At the Tokyo Olympics, Dawn also picked up a silver medal in the 4x100-metre freestyle relay. Dawn's performance earned her the privilege of carrying the Australian flag at the closing ceremony, and she was later named Australian of the Year.

When her events were over, Dawn got up to more mischief. This time it backfired. Following the Olympic tradition of souveniring flags, Dawn and two male athletes tried to remove a Japanese flag from a street leading to the Imperial Palace. Police arrested the trio at gunpoint and took them to a police station. The words 'international incident' were bandied about, and the media had a field day. This prank would have a catastrophic effect on Dawn Fraser's swimming career.

In 1988 Dawn revealed the truth about the theft of the flag. Although she had organised the raid, it was hockey player Des Piper, also a triple Olympian, who had liberated the flag. He stood on the shoulders of team doctor Howard Tony to reach it. Dawn stood by, holding their blazers. But far from being outraged, Piper said, the Japanese police had asked for Dawn's autograph when they discovered who she was. Later, the Japanese Emperor presented Dawn with a flag as a gift.

After she returned from Tokyo, Dawn and Gary were married. On her honeymoon, Dawn discovered that she had been banned from competition swimming for ten years. The flag incident had been the last straw for Australian officials. As her career hit rock bottom, so did her personal life. Gary had moved to Sydney to be with Dawn and could not find a job; now, with Dawn's career falling apart, their marriage could not withstand the stress. After only sixteen months — and with Dawn six months pregnant with their daughter, Dawn Lorraine — Gary and Dawn separated. They were divorced in 1968.

The swimming ban was lifted that same year, but the reprieve came too late for Dawn. She did not have time to get fit for the 1970 Mexico City Olympics. As a consolation prize, the Mexican government invited her to the Games as a guest. While there, she gave a demonstration swim. Her time, a fraction outside the

GREAT AUSTRALIAN GIRLS

world record, showed that she could probably have won an Olympic medal had she swum.

Swimming had been the centre of Dawn's life. She was used to the discipline of training, to having a goal, and being in the limelight. Nowadays we recognise that champion athletes go through a period of grieving when their careers end, and try to help them. In Dawn's time, they were left to sort out their emotions and finances by themselves. Dawn's grief was harder to bear because her career was cut short by official decree, not by a loss of physical strength. There was always the regret about what she might have achieved. 'I never felt I reached my ultimate in sprint swimming. When I finished with swimming my world record was 58.9 seconds, but I always felt I could have got down to 56 seconds.'

With a daughter to support, and few skills outside the swimming pool, Dawn found herself back on the job market. She coached swimming, wrote a column for a newspaper, then lived on the supporting mothers' benefit. In 1973 she finally found a job that suited her, as a saleswoman for a company that manufactured pool liners. Her confidence was revived, and after two years she was representing the company at trade fairs and special promotions. Because she travelled so much, Dawn put her daughter into a Sydney boarding school. This also protected Dawn Lorraine from the relentless publicity about her mother.

In 1978 a film about Dawn Fraser's life — *Dawn* — was released. Based on a book by a close friend of

168

Dawn's, it was brutally honest about her impetuous behaviour and drinking. However, it also paid tribute to the way Dawn had transformed herself from a wild girl from Balmain into one of the best athletes this country has ever produced.

Around this time Dawn bought the Riverview Hotel in Balmain. This was the pub where her father used to have a drink on his way home from work every day. At the Riverview, Dawn was back on home territory, and among friends. She ran the Riverview Hotel for four years, until she had a bad fall down the cellar steps. Injuries to her back and neck led to surgery, and Dawn emerged from her long stay in hospital with a huge debt and a paralysed left arm. Dawn Lorraine, now seventeen, stepped in and ran the hotel while her mother convalesced, but it did no good. Dawn eventually had to sell the business to pay off her debts. To get her arm working, she took up swimming again, and realised how much she'd missed it. She started to train seriously again, this time for the Masters Games for older athletes. In 1985, at 47, Dawn went to Canada for her first Masters. True to expectations, she won the 100-metre freestyle, even though her arm was still weak and she'd only had two months to train.

At fifty, Dawn embarked on a new career — in politics. Running as an independent candidate, she contested a seat in the 1988 New South Wales state election. With no party backing, she had to hand out pamphlets on the streets herself. The old-time

Balmainites and the new trendy residents voted for her, and she was elected to Parliament. In the next election in 1991, she lost her seat — but by then she had gained the respect and recognition due to one of our best-ever swimmers.

Dawn Fraser has earned the status of a legend in Australian sport. She marched with the Australian Olympic team in Seoul, and went to Atlanta as a member of the team bidding for the 2000 Olympics for Sydney. As an Olympic elder, she is listened to when she speaks out on controversial issues such as the use of drugs in sport. The pool where she swam as a girl has been re-named the Dawn Fraser Swimming Pool in her honour. With speaking engagements and product endorsements, Dawn is also financially secure for the first time.

Dawn Fraser possessed an extraordinary physique, a fierce will to win and a toughness honed by poverty and hardship. This, and her extraordinary luck in securing Harry Gallagher as a coach, turned a skinny, asthmatic, rebellious Balmain girl into one of the greatest swimmers in the history of the sport. It was a difficult journey. Dawn never learnt to conform, or to accept authority. Her inability to deal with her fame as a champion swimmer often brought her into conflict with sporting authorities. It also ended her swimming career. But after some rocky years, Dawn carved out a new life for herself. She is, most of all, a survivor. Now an elder stateswoman of sport, she is loved, admired, showered with honours and at peace with herself. One thing that has remained

Dawn Fraser at Dawn Fraser Pool
Sandy Edwards

constant through good times and bad is her close relationship with her daughter, who is her most staunch supporter. When Dawn received her Order of Australia in 1998, Dawn Lorraine was there to share her triumph.

PAT O'SHANE 1941 —

Courtesy University of New England

Aboriginal activist, magistrate

As a child, Pat O'Shane wanted to be a doctor. But her teacher told her father she didn't even have the brains to finish high school. Pat was outraged, and decided to prove her teacher wrong. Not only did Pat finish high school, she went on to become a teacher, a barrister, the head of a government department and a magistrate. In all these positions she has been an outspoken champion of her race and sex.

Pat O'Shane was born in Mossman in North Queensland in 1941. She was the oldest of the five children — two girls and three boys — of Gladys Davis, an Aborigine from the western Yalanji-Kunjandji clan, and Paddy O'Shane, a white cane cutter and wharf labourer. Like so many Aborigines, Gladys's family had been moved off their tribal lands by the government. Until the 1970s, the government could move Aborigines off their traditional lands and make them live somewhere else, often a long way from their tribal area. The land would be sold or given to mining companies or graziers. As a child, Pat's grandfather had been 'relocated' from the Palmer River outside Cooktown to Yarrabah, the Church of England mission across the bay from Cairns. Other family members were sent to Palm Island, which was like a gaol.

When Pat was three, her family moved to Cairns. Gladys, who'd been denied an education because she was Aboriginal, wanted her children to have access to decent schools. But racism was rife in Cairns. Pat's father was taunted because he was married to an Aboriginal woman, and the O'Shane family could not find accommodation.

They moved into a tent at San Remo, a little fishing spot in the bush about sixteen kilometres from Cairns. Nowadays it's called Holloways Beach and the houses are expensive, but then it was untouched. There was no transport, no electricity and no running water — the O'Shanes had to carry their water for a mile in buckets made of cut-down kerosene tins.

Pat and her brothers and sister had to walk two miles to the highway to catch the bus into town to go to school. When Pat started at Cairns North State Primary School, there were only nine Aboriginal and Torres Strait Islander children there. Though she loved learning and liked being with other kids, Pat felt like an outsider. 'I was an alien, and that's how I was treated.'

She knew how white people felt about Aborigines. She'd heard them calling her people sly, no good, dishonest and lazy. And how could she forget the old man who walked past their home every day and hurled racist abuse at her mother? When the kids at school teased her, she asked her mother what to do. Fight back, said Gladys. After that, kids who took on Pat O'Shane would find themselves in a fist fight.

'I grew up fighting to show that I was as good as anyone else, and fighting to take my rightful place in society. I wasn't going to accept a status that somebody else wanted to force upon me, so I've always been really fierce, aggressive, independent, and I have always had a healthy self-respect.' Later, she would learn to fight racism in other ways.

It wasn't until Pat was nine that she began to understand what dispossession had done to her people. She and her mother were sitting eating lunch under a tree in Cairns one day, when a group of Aborigines from Yarrabah walked past. Their heads were bowed, and they kept their eyes down, afraid to look white people in the eye. Pat's mother told her that they had lost their pride. Never be like that, she told Pat — always hold your head up.

Though Pat was clever, getting through school was a struggle. The seven O'Shanes continued to live in a tent, with the two girls in one army stretcher, the two boys in another, and the toddler in a cot. The only other furniture was a table, a couple of stools and a kerosene lamp. As her father would not let the kids do homework or study by the light of the kerosene lamp, Pat would do hers at school. Luckily, she had a great memory, and did well in her exams.

All through primary school, Pat wanted to become a doctor when she grew up. In year 8, she had to decide what subjects to do at high school. Her father took her with him when he went to the school to consult Pat's teacher about her studies. When he raised the subject of medical school, the teacher was blunt. No, said the teacher — in front of Pat — she doesn't even have the brains to finish high school. As Pat had been getting good marks, she was stunned. What was even more devastating was that her father accepted the teacher's judgment. 'I felt my father had abandoned me at that point,' says Pat. 'He should have known better. That was my biggest disappointment. After that I felt I was on my own. Anything I did after that would be my own effort. I had nobody to rely on, nobody to thank.'

Instead of crushing her, the injustice made Pat angry. She decided to show them they were wrong. In the Scholarship exam at the end of year 8, she came second in the state in English and performed very well in her other subjects. But with four other children to support and educate, Pat's parents could not afford to keep her at school, let alone send her to university. Fate stepped in when a careers officer came to the school and told the students about teaching scholarships. Not only did these pay for teachers' college, they'd also pay the recipient's way through high school. Pat decided she'd become a teacher. 'I knew we were poor. Poverty was one of the reasons I couldn't go to university. Teaching was a ticket to freedom.' She applied for a scholarship and won it.

When Pat had started secondary school at Cairns High, there were four Aboriginal and Islander kids. By the end of year 10, she was the only one left. Aboriginal families simply could not afford to keep their children at school. Though she was now allowed to study at home until nine o'clock at night, Pat knew she had a much harder life than her classmates. Her mother didn't let her give in to self-pity, though, telling her there was always someone worse off than herself. To inspire her, Gladys told her stories about African American slaves who'd triumphed over adversity and made names for themselves. Her mother's strategy worked. 'I have always thought of myself as being just like anybody else, just as good.' Pat was always grateful for her mother's encouragement.

The American civil rights movement had begun in the United States in the 1950s, and the ideas spread to Australia, where Aborigines began demanding equality. Following her mother's lead, Pat joined the Aboriginal and Torres Strait Islander Advancement League at fifteen. Its secretary, Joe McGinness, became one of her heroes, along with poet and activist Oodgeroo Noonuccal and the tribal Aborigines who were fighting for their rights. 'Even my own mother, I saw her as a hero,' says Pat. 'She was very active.'

One of the greatest obstacles to Aboriginal equality was the *Aboriginal and Torres Strait Islanders Act*. This law dominated the lives of Indigenous Australians until the 1970s. Aborigines living on reserves had to get permission to enter or leave, and they were not allowed to manage their own money. Money earned by state wards — what we now call 'stolen children' — was withheld from them and put into a trust fund run by the Queensland Board of Native Affairs.

Pat's grandfather was lucky enough to get an exemption from the *Act* and live outside the reserves. Other members of the family were not so fortunate. In her teens Pat found out how powerful these laws were. One of her mother's cousins answered back to the manager of the Yarrabah mission. The manager immediately packed him off to Woorabinda, a penal settlement two hours from Rockhampton. People from the Advancement League and the wharfies' union helped him escape, and he fled to the O'Shanes' place. Pat watched in horror as four carloads of police surrounded their home, captured the cousin, and took him back to Woorabinda.

People had been complaining about the *Act* all Pat's life, but few Aborigines understood it. Pat got hold of a copy, read it through, and wrote a simple booklet for people explaining what it was all about. In the early 1960s she went much further, helping Joe McGinness organise a symbolic burning of the *Act* on the lawns in front of Cairns council chambers. 'When I was burning it I felt joy,' Pat remembers. 'We were leaping around like witches. I can remember feeling we were doing something very liberating. I was fighting against this great, big, black mass of racism.'

At seventeen, Pat travelled south to Brisbane to attend teachers' college. She felt she was finally on her way. She was the only Aboriginal woman there, though another Aborigine, Mick Miller, was just finishing the course. When she graduated, she was the first Aboriginal woman teacher in Queensland. Pat was exhilarated by the freedom and power her qualifications gave her — the teaching certificate was her ticket to an income, status in the white world, and the power to change things for her own people. 'It was having the freedom to move in the world that was the object of the exercise. That's what I try to tell Aboriginal students today — it's so important to get that piece of paper.'

Pat's first posting was Cairns Central Primary School. By now, many of the Aborigines from Yarrabah had been allowed to leave and had moved to Bessie's Point, a fringe settlement across the bay from Cairns. The kids came to school by boat. In 1962 Pat married Mick Miller, who was also teaching in Cairns. The couple had two daughters: Lydia in 1963, and Marilyn in 1964.

After eighteen months at the primary school, Pat was transferred to Cairns High School. Instead of four Aboriginal students, as in Pat's day, there were now 165. Though she knew it was crucial for Aborigines to get an education, Pat saw her role as a teacher as being quite broad. So they could take their place in society, her students would need confidence and a sense of self-esteem — they would have to be proud to be black. Pat held lunchtime meetings designed to give her Aboriginal students a sense of self-worth and teach them how to fight back against racism. The Department of Education took a dim view of Pat's activism, and marked her down as a trouble maker.

Besides taking the troubles of the whole world on her shoulders, Pat also made huge demands on herself. Since childhood, her family had regarded her as the one who would succeed in the white world. When she was in her mid twenties, the pressure became too intense. The crisis came when her mother, who had suffered a massive heart attack, died after twelve months in a coma. For a year after Gladys's death, Pat found herself unable to cry or express her grief. To make matters worse, her turbulent marriage to Mick Miller was breaking down. One night she started to cry and couldn't stop. Diagnosed as manic depressive, Pat began a long battle with mental illness, and spent much of the next four years in hospital as a psychiatric patient.

While Pat was in hospital, the campaign to amend the constitution to give Aborigines the right to vote was heating up. In 1967, after years of lobbying, Aborigines and their white supporters finally persuaded the government to hold a referendum on the issue. A resounding 91 per cent of the population voted in favour of the amendment. It also meant that Aborigines could finally become Australian citizens. Pat was overjoyed.

In hospital, Pat was given electro-convulsive therapy, also known as shock therapy. When it didn't work, she was sent to Sydney to undergo brain surgery. When Pat met Dr Harry Bailey, the surgeon who was going to perform the operation, she refused to go through with the procedure. Her instincts were good. Dr Bailey was later brought before a Royal Commission investigating the scandalous number of deaths and injuries among his patients at Chelmsford Private Hospital.

Wanting a second opinion, Pat went to Melbourne and consulted another psychiatrist. He told her she didn't need surgery, that she was simply a square peg in a round hole. Back in Sydney, Pat collected all her prescription drugs, threw them at Dr Bailey and told him he was a charlatan. Though withdrawing from the drugs was painful, Pat persevered. She'd decided she didn't want to be ill any more.

Leaving her daughters with their father in Cairns, Pat enrolled in a law degree at the University of New South Wales in 1973. It was a bold step: there were only two women in her year, and no Aborigines. Law school didn't excite Pat the way teachers' college had. A law degree was simply a means to an end — as a lawyer, Pat could help keep Aborigines out of gaol. At university she became involved in campus politics, the anti-Vietnam War protests and the debates over racism and sexism. She also plunged into Aboriginal politics.

Lydia and Marilyn joined their mother in Sydney in 1975. Studying, working part time and raising two girls was a terrible strain, but they survived, and in 1976 Pat graduated with a law degree. She went to the bar, and became Australia's first Aboriginal barrister.

Pat started working for the Aboriginal Legal Service, but had to give it up when they could not pay her. Her first big career break came when she was employed by the New South Wales Royal Commission into Prisons. As a disproportionate number of Aborigines end up in prison, this was an issue which greatly concerned Pat. From there, she was hired by the Aboriginal Legal Service in Alice Springs. They wanted a woman barrister because traditional women would not talk about their business to men. Alice Springs opened Pat's eyes. She was horrified by the number of Aborigines being sent to prison by the Northern Territory courts.

In 1979, Pat returned to Sydney. After tutoring in law, she went to work for a committee set up by the New

South Wales government to review the *Mental Health Act*. This was an area where Pat had bitter, first-hand experience to draw on. As a result of that review, psychiatric patients were given the right to be represented by a lawyer in their dealings with the health system.

From mental health issues, Pat worked for a New South Wales parliamentary committee on Aboriginal Affairs. The government was so impressed by her performance that it appointed her Director of the Ministry for Aboriginal Affairs in 1981. This made her the first woman to head a government department in Australia.

The job was a political minefield, especially when the government began debating new laws concerning Aboriginal land rights. Pat was often caught in the middle. The Aborigines expected her to take their side, but she also had to answer to the government she served. Because she was black and female, Pat was also watched closely by the media. She found the criticism hurtful and often unfair. In her years at the Ministry, Pat helped guide the New South Wales land rights legislation through parliament.

The alarming state of Aboriginal health and the number of Aborigines in custody are still serious problems, but Pat can see progress. 'When I look back, I can see the changes that we have made. It's only thirty years afterwards and I can see all the Aboriginal kids in school. I can see Aboriginal teachers and Aboriginal lawyers and doctors and administrators. You never used to see anything like that.'

After five years in Aboriginal Affairs, Pat was appointed to the New South Wales Magistrates Court. She was the country's first Aboriginal magistrate. Pat's philosophy was to make gaol a last resort for serious criminals. She believed the laws against offensive language, usually interpreted as swearing at police, were being misused. In 1991 she caused a furore by dismissing a case against an Aboriginal man accused of swearing at two police officers in a cafe in Lismore.

By 1997, Pat O'Shane announced she was retiring from the magistracy. She was sickened by several grisly murder cases she'd heard, and an almost fatal attack on her nephew, Tjandumurra O'Shane, in a Cairns school playground the year before had taken its toll. However, after a cooling-down period, she changed her mind.

Pat has remarried and lives in Sydney's eastern suburbs. Her daughter Lydia became a nurse, then turned to acting in the mid-1980s. She is now studying for an arts/law degree at the University of Sydney. Marilyn is a dancer, and is studying business and marketing at the University of Technology, Sydney.

Pat's daughters grew up in a highly political household, listening to people discussing Aboriginal issues. They continue to fight for her ideals, but in their own way, through the arts.

Pat O'Shane knew from an early age that she had a destiny to fulfil. Her clan expected her to go out into a hostile white world and make it a better place for her own people. She has done that, but at great personal cost.

Being a pioneer is a tough and often lonely job. As an Aboriginal woman, Pat has had to withstand a degree of scrutiny and criticism that whites in similar positions seldom have to bear. And by choosing to fight on white man's terms, which meant living away from her family, she sacrificed some of her Aboriginality. Unlike her siblings, she cannot speak her Aboriginal language, for example.

'My parents would impress on me that it was my duty to change the world, to make the world a better place. So I did it. It didn't take me long to realise that if I changed the world for Aboriginal people, I'd change it for everyone.'

IRENE MOSS / KWONG CHEE WAI LIN
1948 —

Fighter for justice

When Irene Kwong Chee was twelve, another girl in her class was named dux of the school instead of her. Sure that she had higher marks, Irene challenged the decision — and won. It was her first successful battle against injustice, but it would not be her last. When Irene grew up, she became an anti-discrimination lawyer. She also became the first female federal Race Discrimination Commissioner and the first Asian woman magistrate, and is now the New South Wales Ombudsman.

Irene Moss's Chinese ancestors came to Australia in the 1850s to seek their fortune in the gold rushes. They settled in New South Wales. Irene's father, William Kwong Chee, was born in about 1893 in the mining town of Kiandra.

William's first marriage to an Australian woman broke up, and in the 1930s he went to Hong Kong to look for a Chinese wife. There he met and married Poy Kin, known as Ann, and started a business. They had four children — Phyllis, Barbara, Reginald and Lynette. But during World War II the Japanese invaded Hong Kong and immediately commandeered most of the food for their troops. The people of Hong Kong faced starvation. Afraid his children would go hungry, William put away as much rice as he could buy. The Japanese found out and threw him into jail for hoarding food.

When the war ended, William was released, and the family returned to Australia to start a new life. They settled in Sydney's Chinatown, where William started a tomato wholesaling business. People called him 'Willy the Tomato King'. Every morning at 3 a.m., Willy and his three Chinese workers would buy tomatoes at the market. They would bring them back to Dixon Street to be sorted, packed, and sold to wholesalers. The green ones were ripened in Willy's hothouse.

Irene Kwong Chee was born in Chinatown in 1948. Her Chinese name was Wai Lin, Cantonese for 'water lily'. She was delivered in a tomato hothouse by a Chinese midwife because her mother, who could not speak English, was too frightened to go to hospital.

Irene spent her first five years in Chinatown, which had grown up around the fruit and vegetable markets in Hay Street. In those days, the cheap rents in Chinatown attracted family businesses, small Chinese restaurants, and boarding houses for single men. It would be many years before Chinatown became a tourist attraction with huge restaurants, expensive shops and high-rise apartment buildings.

As a little girl, Irene played in the laneways and out the back of small, dark shops. While her mother played mah-jong, a popular gambling game, with her friends, Irene would talk to the old men sitting on the street smoking their pipes. Many of these men lived alone. Some had families in China, but when the Communists took over after the war, they could neither return home nor bring their families to Australia.

When Irene was about five, her father decided it was time for the family to move to the suburbs. He bought a house in Belmore, in Sydney's inner south-west. Irene

Irene Kwong Chee and her mother Ann in Belmore
Courtesy Irene Moss

was sent to live there with her two older sisters, Phyllis and Barbara, who were then in their twenties. Phyllis did not work outside the home, but Barbara studied accounting and worked as a bookkeeper. Irene's mother stayed in Chinatown to cook for the tomato packers and look after the two other children, Lynette and Reggie. Irene grew up speaking Cantonese with her mother, but quickly picked up English in kindergarten. At Belmore Primary School, where she spent the next eight years, she was the only Chinese pupil.

Irene learnt how to stand up for her rights from an early age. When the time came to give out the prizes in the final year of primary school, Irene had expected to be named dux, but discovered that another girl, a friend of hers, had won. The prize for the dux was a handsome black leather briefcase with the dux's initials engraved in gold. 'It was a wonderful prize,' recalls Irene. She was upset and confused: 'I thought, something's wrong. I knew which subjects I'd topped. I'd worked hard for those marks.' After adding up her marks, Irene became convinced she was right. She stewed about it for weeks, then worked up the courage to confront her teacher. In class, she put up her hand and said she thought there had been a mistake. The teacher disagreed. But Irene persisted and asked for the marks to be checked. The teacher came back later and said: 'You're right. You're dux.'

Irene was worried that the friend who'd missed out would be angry at her. 'I felt like such a rotten egg for doing it,' she says. But her friend didn't blame her, and the girl's mother even asked Irene to lunch to show that there were no hard feelings. The ghost of that girl's initials was always visible under Irene's, but that did not spoil the victory. 'I used that briefcase right through high school till it dropped dead.'

Although Irene was doing well at school, life at home was difficult. Irene's father had suffered a stroke when she was seven. He never fully recovered, and wasn't able to work hard again. The money stopped coming in, and the Kwong Chees had to live on their savings. Frustrated, irritable, and used to getting his own way, William was not an easy man to live with. Like most Chinese fathers of his time, he was not close to his children. 'He was a good, honest man, but not a "father" to me,' explains Irene. 'He wasn't someone you could go to for support on an emotional level.'

For emotional support, Irene went to her mother. 'My mother was a real rock in my life. She didn't care what I did, as long as I was happy.' For intellectual support and guidance with the important decisions in her life — such as what subjects to study — Irene learnt to rely on her own judgment from an early age.

Irene did her secondary schooling at Wiley Park Girls' High School, where she ended up as Head Girl. A girls' school could have been expected to encourage its best pupils to excel, but Irene found the school unwilling to go the extra mile. For a start, many subjects were not taught at the honours level. And when Irene and some of her friends requested extra tuition so they could do honours, the school refused. But Irene remembers some excellent teachers who inspired students with their love for their subjects. Her science teacher was one of these.

To finish her schooling, Irene had to stand firm against her father's opposition. He didn't encourage her academic interests. In the Chinese culture, girls got married — you didn't waste money educating them. When Irene was trying to study, he'd do things like use his noisy power tools nearby. Ann would tell him to stop. She hadn't had much schooling, and instinctively understood that education would be her daughter's passport to a better life.

Ann was prepared to mortgage the house to send Irene to university, but in the end that didn't prove to be necessary. Irene won a Commonwealth Scholarship which paid her tuition fees and a living allowance. She enrolled in a science degree at the University of Sydney. With its elegant sandstone buildings and teeming throngs of students, university was a shock to the quiet Chinese girl from Belmore. She didn't know anybody on campus, so she looked about for friends. She found them among the 'westies', kids from the western suburbs. 'I thought, "Who else looks lost?"'

A few months into her first year, Irene realised she'd chosen the wrong course. She was not enjoying her studies, and didn't want to become a scientist. When she heard that there were positions available in the arts/law course, she switched. Though she knew nothing about

Irene Moss, new law graduate, at the University of Sydney
Courtesy Irene Moss

law, she liked the sound of it. 'I wanted to get away from the poverty and drudgery we had all experienced growing up, and felt a profession — no matter what — was the way to go. I wasn't going back to Dixon Street. I wanted to do something better.'

As she gained confidence and learnt her way around, Irene decided there was more to life than study. She wanted to make her mark on campus by becoming involved in what was going on outside the classroom. When her friends suggested she run for the Students Representative Council and promised to campaign for her, she ran for — and won — the position of Arts representative. Through student politics she became involved in the anti-Vietnam War protest movement of the late 1960s.

While Irene was at university, her father had another stroke, and became an invalid. For more than 25 years, Ann Kwong Chee nursed her husband at home. With no English, she was dependent on her children to communicate with the outside world. 'Mum had a miserable life,' says Irene. 'Nursing Dad was very difficult for her. She was never able to break out of it.' Irene loved her mother, but did not want to end up like her.

Getting a law degree was just the first step in Irene's professional career. The next was getting articles — that is, a job with a law firm for a year. Without articles, a law graduate cannot become registered as a solicitor. In the 1960s, only 10 to 14 percent of law graduates were women, and they found it much harder than men to get articled. Irene's marks were good, but she knew it would be an uphill battle. She got out the phone book and started sending out applications to the firms listed. She was not optimistic. As far as she was concerned, she had three strikes against her — she was female, she was Chinese, and she had not attended a 'good' school. She didn't even bother applying to the top firms.

In all, she sent out more than 100 applications to prospective employers. 'I would write "Irene Kwong Chee" on my application so they'd know right from the start they were getting a female and a Chinese,' says Irene. 'The hardest thing was watching all the men get jobs. I had a sense of futility.'

Eventually, one of her applications was successful, and she went to work for a firm which specialised in company law. Irene quickly realised she didn't fit in. She found the work tedious, and wasn't prepared to put in the long hours to prove she was a high-flier. 'The speedy corporate life was not for me. I was happy to go and they were happy to see me go.' Her next job was with a firm which had a branch in Chinatown, where she could use her Cantonese. She did mostly small commercial deals, property conveyancing and wills.

In the meantime, Irene had married Allan Moss. Irene met Allan, a member of a prominent Sydney Jewish family, in her university law lectures. They were married when she was 26, and are still happily married. 'Allan is a compassionate, kind human being,' says Irene. 'He's very supportive of me. We've been married for over twenty years and have never had a harsh word.' Allan, who'd done a postgraduate degree in law, discovered that he wasn't happy practising law either. He applied to Harvard, the eminent American university, to do a Master of Business Administration. He was accepted, and in 1974 the couple set off for the United States.

In Boston, surrounded by excellent universities, Irene decided to continue her legal studies. After sending applications to several universities, she was accepted by Harvard. She enrolled in a Master of Law program, specialising in tax law. She was still planning on a career in law, and company law was the way into the prestigious firms and the big money. In a highly competitive field, Irene got excellent marks. Unfortunately, company law still bored her.

The Mosses returned to Australia in 1977. Allen went into banking, eventually becoming managing director of the Macquarie Bank. Irene looked around for a job. By this time she knew she wasn't suited to commercial law; she wanted to work in a field that captured her imagination, something she believed in. Her timing turned out to be impeccable. While Irene was overseas, the New South Wales government had passed the *Anti-Discrimination Act*, which made it illegal to discriminate against people on the basis of sex, race or religious affiliation. This was a cause Irene could identify with. The New South Wales Anti-Discrimination Board had just been set up, and was advertising for legal staff. Irene landed a job as a conciliator — a lawyer who handles complaints being heard by the Board. In the next nine years, she rose to the position of Senior Conciliation Officer, and was second-in-charge at the organisation.

In 1986 Irene was headhunted for the position of federal Race Discrimination Commissioner in Canberra. She was the first woman to hold the job. 'It was my first big break into the big time,' she says. Sadly, her mother died four days before she was appointed. It is one of the great regrets of Irene's life. 'She would have been so proud.'

As Race Discrimination Commissioner, Irene chaired a national inquiry into racist violence. It made her a target for racists. She received death threats, and racist graffiti appeared over the doors of her garage. After the attack on her home, Irene had a sophisticated alarm system installed. She spent seven and a half years in the job, then in 1994 she moved back to Sydney, where she was appointed a magistrate. She was the first Asian woman magistrate in the country. Irene found the work demanding and a little frightening. A magistrate has to deal face-to-face with people convicted of crimes, and decide whether or not to send them to trial. Some of the people committed for trial are violent criminals with long memories and vengeful friends. She was relieved when the New South Wales government approached her to be the new Ombudsman.

The Ombudsman is the watchdog who tries to keep the government honest. It's an influential job, as well as being interesting and varied. Irene looks into complaints about everything from rude public servants to police corruption. Her staff of eighty investigators handles up to 20 000 written and oral complaints every year.

Irene Moss was profoundly influenced by her childhood. For her, Chinatown, with its poverty and overcrowding, was not picturesque; it was something to escape. She quickly realised that a good education would help her realise her goals of financial security and social status. She worked hard to overcome the obstacles that stood in her way because she was a Chinese girl from a poor background.

There is a Chinese proverb — be careful what you wish for, in case your wish is granted. When Irene got her law degrees from Sydney University and Harvard, she saw the wisdom in this old saying. After working so hard to excel at company law, which caters to the rich and powerful, she found it didn't satisfy her. So she found a way to use her legal training to help people like herself. Irene Moss has made a career in public service, using her hard-won knowledge, skills and talent as a negotiator to protect the interests of the disadvantaged and the powerless.

EVONNE GOOLAGONG CAWLEY 1951 —

From Barellan to Wimbledon

At eleven, Evonne Goolagong was given the chance to leave the tiny outback town of Barellan in New South Wales and train seriously to become a champion tennis player. She grabbed that opportunity, and never looked back. By the time she was in her early twenties, she was one of the top female tennis players in the world.

Evonne Goolagong's parents — Kenny and Linda — were Wiradjuri people from central New South Wales. Linda was born in a shepherd's hut near Warangesda Mission, close to Darlington Point on the Murrumbidgee, in Wiradjuri traditional lands. Kenny was born in Condobolin. His people had moved from their camps to the Condobolin Aboriginal mission. Members of the Goolagong family — the name probably comes from the Wiradjuri word 'galagallang', or 'big mob' — set up camp on a nearby flood plain called the Murie.

Evonne Goolagong was born at Griffith Hospital in 1951, in the middle of a bitterly cold winter. She was the third of eight children. Kenny and Linda were itinerant labourers, moving often in order to find work. But in 1953, they moved to Barellan with their children — six-year-old Barbara, four-year-old Larry, two-year-old Evonne and Kevin, who was only a few months old. About 65 kilometres from Griffith, Barellan was a little wheat town dominated by huge grains silos. Kenny had found regular work as a shearer. A house in Barellan owned by the grazier came as part of Kenny's wage. The

Goolagongs could finally settle down. They were the only Aboriginal family in the town.

It was hard making ends meet on a shearer's wage. The girls slept four to a bed for a time, top to toe, and bathed in a big tub on the verandah-cum-washroom outside. Linda cooked on a wood stove. When money got tight, they lived off the land, shooting rabbits and picking mushrooms. Whenever they could, Kenny and Linda packed the kids into the car and went back to the family camps at Griffith and Condobolin. Evonne's earliest memories are of sitting around campfires at the family camp at the Murie, listening to the grown-ups playing guitars and singing.

At the Barellan State School, the Goolagong children were the only Aborigines among the 150 pupils. When his classmates called Larry racist names, he fought back. As a result, nobody ever called his little sister names or treated her differently because of the colour of her skin. Evonne liked school, but was shy and nervous. Her mother's stories about the 'Welfare Man' had made her wary of white folk. When Linda was a girl, every knock on the door could mean a government official coming to take an Aboriginal child away from her parents to put her in an institution.

The Goolagongs were all good at sport. At her first athletics carnival, Evonne was named the individual champion after winning the long jump, the triple jump and the 100-yard dash. She became a tomboy, competing with the boys at cricket, running and jumping, and often beating them. Even then, she was good at whacking a ball.

In 1955, Bill Kurtzman, a grazier, decided it was time Barellan had some decent tennis courts. He formed a committee, raised money, and four tennis courts were built. In 1956, the same year Evonne started school, the Barellan War Memorial Tennis Club opened. Though she'd never seen a tennis match before, she was soon obsessively hitting a tennis ball up against the wall of the old butcher's shop. Her racquet was home made — a plank taken from the side of a fruit crate, with a wooden handle. But when Linda saw how good she was, she bought Evonne a little wooden racquet from a toy shop in Griffith.

As the caretaker of the tennis courts was a friend of the family, the Goolagong kids had the run of the place outside hours. Soon Barbara, Larry and Evonne were borrowing racquets and the net from the club lockup and trying to play tennis. They all had talent. Evonne was so impressive the club relaxed its rules and let her join at the age of seven.

In the August school holidays of 1960, Bill Kurtzman organised the club's first coaching clinic. Evonne was too young to attend. The following year Kurtzman talked Vic Edwards into running a clinic. Australia's top tennis coach, Edwards also ran VAETS — the Victor A. Edwards Tennis School — in Sydney. This time the tennis club paid for Barbara, Larry and Evonne to attend. One of the coaches, Faith Martin, told Bill that Evonne could go all the way to the top if properly handled. Bill started driving Evonne all over the countryside to compete in bush tournaments to give her practice. She was so good that when she was ten the school headmaster asked her to play doubles with him and the local policeman. Evonne loved these matches. Tennis had given her so much confidence she was no longer afraid of authority figures.

Around that time, Evonne picked up a copy of *Princess* magazine in Smith's general store and read a story. It was about a young unknown tennis player who found fame and fortune at Wimbledon. Though Evonne had no idea where Wimbledon was, she wanted to be that girl. A dream was born.

During the coaching clinic, Bill and the VAETS coaches talked Vic Edwards into driving down to Barellan to take a look at Evonne. Impressed with Evonne's natural grace, her timing and her tennis sense, Vic invited the eleven-year-old to Sydney for the 1963 NSW Lawn Tennis Association age championships. Her parents faced a dilemma. Linda was frightened of losing her child to the white world, but Kenny saw it as an opportunity for Evonne to get ahead. Barbara, who might have become a champion herself if she hadn't had to go out to work, encouraged her little sister to go for it.

Barellan got behind the campaign to send Evonne to Sydney. The local service station donated petrol for her travels to tennis tournaments. People gave money for meals and expenses. The local paper helped drum up support. When Evonne won a string of tournaments that summer, her trip to Sydney was confirmed. In the May school holidays, she set off alone for the big smoke.

She arrived in Sydney starry eyed from her first plane trip. Faith Martin picked her up and took her to the Edwards' big two-storey house at Roseville Chase. There she met Vic's wife Eva, and their two younger daughters — twelve-year-old Jenifer and ten-year-old Trish. That night, Evonne cried herself to sleep. It had been a long and stressful day for a little girl who had never been away from home before. But the next day, when she started training at Vic Edwards' tennis school around the corner, her spirits revived.

After only a week in Sydney, Evonne competed in her first big tournament — the Under-13 Grass Court Championship at White City. She did well enough to convince Edwards to continue training her. Evonne was thrilled. She loved the tough tennis practice sessions, and she felt at home with the Edwards family.

Life was never the same after that trip. From now on Evonne would lead a double life — an ordinary school-girl in Barellan and a budding tennis champion in Sydney. Before she was thirteen, Evonne had won more than eighty singles and doubles age titles. By the time she finished primary school in 1963, her future had been decided. Vic Edwards had convinced Kenny and Linda that only by training in Sydney and competing against the best could their daughter become a champion. They agreed to let Evonne move to Sydney in 1966, when she was fourteen. The Edwards would become her guardians.

For the next two years Evonne travelled between Barellan and Sydney. Her tennis improved enormously, and the media began calling her the next Margaret Smith. At 22, Margaret Smith was the Australian singles champion and reigning Wimbledon champion. While Evonne was busy playing tennis, Bill Kurtzman had been collecting pennies in the street and organising exhibition matches to raise money for her training in Sydney.

As the parting grew near, Kenny Goolagong started to have second thoughts about losing Evonne, but Linda had now decided it was for the best. Confused, Evonne went and asked her headmaster what she should do. He told her to stay in Barellan and finish her schooling. Instead of discouraging Evonne, this galvanised her. She emerged from the meeting determined to stick with tennis and become a champion.

At fourteen, Evonne left home. 'Leaving my home town and my family was very tough, but I was shy and didn't say anything,' she says. 'I figured being homesick and in tears at night-time was the way it was supposed to be. It was the toughest stage of my life, leaving home. But I thought, "If I can get through that, I can get through anything." What helped was that I was doing something I really enjoyed — I didn't want to let the townspeople down, and I didn't want to let Dad down.' Her love of tennis sustained her. 'Even when I went through the tough times, I realised this is the way it is if I'm going to be the best in the world.'

Evonne shared a room with Trish Edwards and

became good friends with Jenifer. Their mother, Eva, became her 'number two mum'. She started school at Willoughby High. The big city school was a shock after Barellan Central. Evonne had never had to wear stockings, a hat and gloves in her life, and she hated the strict rules. But soon she was absorbed into the school's sporting elite, becoming junior house captain, a member of the sprint team and the broad jump champion. In summer she swam for the school. Every other waking moment was spent playing tennis.

Evonne had her first taste of the big time at the Under-19 NSW Open and Junior Grass Court Championship in November 1966. Competing against the best players in the country, she reached the quarter-finals before being knocked out. Vic Edwards was happy with that. She was only fifteen, after all. Soon she would be winning.

In 1968, just sixteen, Evonne was the top-ranked junior female player in New South Wales, and one of the top three in the country. Though she had no ambitions beyond tennis, Vic Edwards insisted she learn some work skills to fall back on. After the School Certificate, Evonne and Trish spent a year at secretarial college. In the meantime, Evonne trained hard to qualify for her first European tour in 1970.

At the time, a tennis revolution was under way which would have a huge impact on Evonne's life. Tired of the artificial distinction between amateurs and professionals, top amateur players began to demand the same fees as the professionals. International tennis authorities buckled under the pressure, making it possible for tennis players to make big money out of the game.

There were important social changes afoot in Australia, too. In the 1960s Aborigines were demanding the right to be citizens, to vote, to have a decent education and proper housing. In Sydney, the Foundation for Aboriginal Affairs was set up as a centre for Aborigines living in the city. In 1968, Evonne, Trish and Jenifer started going to dances there, and Evonne made her first Aboriginal friends. These young Aborigines were politically aware and ready to take to the streets to demand their rights. But at that age Evonne was not interested in racial politics, and they did not push her into joining them.

Up till now, Evonne had been protected from racism. But in 1969 she had a taste of the abuse most Aborigines grew up with when she and Trish beat two women in a doubles match at White City. One of the women said: 'That's the first time I've ever been beaten by a nigger.' Evonne went hot and cold with shock and burst into tears. It was the first and last time she would come up against open racism in tennis, but racially slanted criticisms would dog her career. When her attention lapsed on court, the media liked to accuse her of 'going walkabout'. Insults like this only made Evonne more determined to win.

In March 1970, Evonne left on her first overseas tour to Britain and Europe. At nineteen, she was at the very beginning of her international career. At the British Hard Court Championship she advanced to the semi-finals at Bournemouth before being thrashed by Margaret Court (Margaret Smith's married name). It was on this trip that Evonne met the man she would marry — Roger Cawley, a former tennis player then writing romance stories for women's magazines. When Vic Edwards tried to stop the budding romance, thinking it would take Evonne's mind off tennis, she continued to see Roger in secret. It was on this first overseas tour that Evonne fulfilled her childhood dream: playing tennis at Wimbledon. Though she lasted only 34 minutes in her second match — and her first on the legendary Centre Court — the English media went wild over this new phenomenon, an Aboriginal tennis champion.

On her return, Evonne was selected to play for Australia for the first time in the 1970 Federation Cup in Perth. She stayed with Margaret Court and practised with the champion. Though Australia went into the tournament as the underdogs, they won. The following year, at twenty, Evonne beat Margaret Court for the first time, in the Victorian women's singles at Kooyong. But Evonne's victory was marred by a demonstration by Aboriginal activists. They were shocked that she had agreed to play tennis in South Africa, a country that treated its black population like second-class citizens. Evonne insisted on going. She was determined to show South Africans that a black athlete could play tennis as well as any white person. To this day she remains unrepentant.

When Evonne went to England for the 1971 tour, she discovered that her long-distance romance with Roger had cooled. He'd been scared off by Vic Edwards' opposition and Evonne's growing fame. Evonne was confused and distressed, but not enough to put her off her game. On the European tour she won the French Open, and the French media dubbed her 'La Belle Evonne'.

But the big event was Wimbledon. Evonne made it through to the finals, where she had to face Margaret Court. Could she do it? Back in Barellan, glued to their television screen, the Goolagongs watched with bated breath — then screamed in triumph as their girl won the women's singles title. Evonne returned home to a joyous welcome — a ticker tape parade in Sydney, followed by a welcome-home procession and motorcade in Barellan.

In September 1971 Evonne Goolagong was the number one female tennis player in the world. The money rolled in, and she bought a new water tank, toilet, stove and phone for her family. Later, she paid off their house. In the New Year's Honours List the following year, Evonne was made a Member of the British Empire (MBE). She was also named Australian of the Year on 26 January. Although she was proud to receive a medal from the Queen at Buckingham Palace, the Australian honour meant more to her. Only one other Aboriginal, the boxer Lionel Rose, had ever received it.

At 21, Evonne was at the pinnacle of her tennis career. She had turned professional, and was a one-woman business. To help her with her media, sponsorship and advertising deals, she hired an international management company, IMG. But it was a double-edged sword. She was wealthy and famous and met all sorts of important people, but she toured nine months out of the year, living out of suitcases and eating in restaurants. She had missed out on normal teenage friendships, and at a time when her friends were getting engaged and married, she was still alone. But perhaps not forever. Her relationship with Roger Cawley had heated up again and was beginning to get serious.

Evonne began spending more time in the United States, and in 1973 she signed a million-dollar deal there to play for the new World Team Tennis, along with some of the world's top players. The following year, the owners of the exclusive Hilton Head Racquet Club asked her to be their touring professional, and use the club as her base. Evonne leapt at the chance. Hilton Head, a resort island with small quaint shopping villages, pine forests and protected wetlands, was the perfect retreat. Connected by a bridge to the mainland, the island was situated just north of the border of South Carolina and Georgia.

The next time Evonne was in London for Wimbledon, Roger Cawley proposed. But Evonne needed time to think. They'd had their ups and downs, and she wanted to be sure. With all the excitement in her tennis career and her private life, Barellan seemed like a distant dream — until an accident that made home seem terribly real. In October 1974, Kenny Goolagong was run over in Hillston and killed. Evonne was devastated.

She also felt guilty that she'd seen so little of her family lately. She wanted to go home. Vic Edwards advised against it. He was afraid that if she went home, she would not come back. Kenny Goolagong would want her to go on with her tennis career, he said. Evonne did not return for the funeral. It's a decision she's had to live with, and she sometimes wishes she could go back and relive that time.

Determined to win one for her father, Evonne beat Chris Evert in the final of the Virginia Slims — the new American all-women tour — and took out the richest prize in women's tennis. But when she returned to Australia later that year, she came close to a breakdown. At 22, she was starting to crack under the pressure. When she realised she had to play forty weeks of tennis in 1975, she put her head in her hands and howled. But despite the pain and confusion, she had made one decision. That February, she agreed to marry Roger.

Worried that Roger would want to take over as Evonne's manager, Vic Edwards voiced his opposition to the marriage. Evonne and Roger were married in a registry office in Canterbury, England on 16 June 1975. To prevent the wedding turning into a media circus, only their families and closest friends were invited. Vic Edwards did not show up. After Wimbledon, where she lost badly to the American champion Billie Jean King, Evonne split with her old coach. It was a bitter end to a winning partnership. Whatever their later disagreements, Vic Edwards had turned Evonne

Goolagong from a promising child player into a world tennis champion.

In October, the Cawleys had a second marriage ceremony in Barellan. All Evonne's relatives and the townsfolk turned out to celebrate. The jubilant crowd filled the little Anglican church and spilled over onto the lawns. The singing and dancing went on till dawn.

Back in the US, the Cawleys bought a house at Hilton Head. Later they built their own nightclub and pub complex on the island. With her emotional life under control, and with Roger as her practice and travel partner, Evonne clawed her way back to number one. But when she became pregnant in 1976, she had to give up tennis. In May 1977, with her mother present, she gave birth to a daughter, Kelly Inala. After five months she took up tennis again, and despite the stresses and strains of travelling with a baby, won the NSW and Australian Opens in 1977.

In 1978, injury began to plague Evonne. After several months off, she fought her way back to the quarter-finals at Wimbledon the following year. The English media started calling her Supermum, but it was far from the truth. Emotionally and physically she was depressed. A blood disorder was eventually diagnosed. When it was brought under control with medication, Evonne became determined to compete at Wimbledon in 1980. After her disappointing loss to Chris Evert the previous year, she was going in as the underdog. When the two women finally met on the court, Evonne won the first set and was winning the second when it started to rain. The game was called off and both players had to stew for just over an hour. But Evonne didn't lose her nerve or her concentration. When the game resumed, Chris Evert came out fighting, but Evonne withstood the onslaught and won. Evonne Goolagong really *was* Supermum now. It was the first time in 66 years that a mother had won the women's singles at Wimbledon. At the prize-giving, Evonne wept. No longer the naive girl who'd floated through her first Wimbledon title, she knew how much this win had cost in terms of hard work, tough competition, gruelling travel and injury.

After the euphoria died down, the old injury problem returned. At the same time, her relationship with her people at home deteriorated. Her cousin, the poet Kevin Gilbert, attacked her for not speaking up on behalf of Aborigines. Believing that her prowess at tennis did more for her people than any speeches or demonstrations, Evonne was hurt and angry. 'I didn't like being used by Aboriginal activists to get publicity for their cause,' she says. 'It wasn't fair. I felt that I was representing not only my people, but my country as well.'

In 1981, pregnant again, Evonne pulled out of competitive tennis. Her son, Morgan Kyeema, was born in May that year. Though she played on through 1982, Evonne was constantly nursing injuries. It was time to go. In 1983, she retired from competition tennis. It was easier said than done. After devoting her life to tennis for twenty years, she had to learn to live without the rush of competition, the travel, the fame, the glamour, and the focus the game brought to her life. It took her years to work through her sense of loss. In 1986 the Cawleys sold up at Hilton Head and moved to Naples in Florida. In the company of other tennis legends, Evonne started playing on the over-35 circuit. In 1988 she was inducted into the International Tennis Hall of Fame in the US.

But something was lacking in Evonne's life. She was beginning to wonder who she was, where she belonged. On trips to Australia she would pick up Aboriginal art, and books and tapes about Aboriginal culture. In Adelaide for the first Aboriginal Sports Awards, she saw her first corroboree. Her mother's death in 1991 decided her. It was time to learn her family's stories, to discover what it meant to be a Wiradjuri. In 1992 the Cawleys moved to Noosa Heads in Queensland. After seventeen years in the US, Evonne was home for good. She set about rediscovering her Aboriginal roots and introducing her children to their culture. In 1993 she published her autobiography, *Home!*, in which she traced her physical and emotional journey from the Murie to Hilton Head and back again.

Evonne Goolagong Cawley can look back on an incomparable sporting career. Though she claims she was just doing what came naturally, she is one of the finest athletes this country has produced. She was also the first Indigenous Australian to play international competition tennis. These days Evonne is a consultant to the Indigenous Sports Program, helping to raise money for sporting equipment for Aboriginal communities. 'Sport has given me so much,' she says. 'It was a way out for me, out of the country. And it's been a great education for me — the travel, meeting people — and it gave me confidence and self-esteem. I'd like to give that to kids. It works.'

LORRIE GRAHAM 1954 –

Photojournalist

When Lorrie Graham was fourteen, her father gave her a book of photographs taken by Margaret Bourke White. Captivated by the American photojournalist's work and her glamorous and adventurous life, Lorrie discovered her destiny. After fighting her way into the male stronghold of newspaper photography, she transformed herself into one of Australia's leading photojournalists.

Lorrie Graham was born in 1954 in Windsor, on the north-western outskirts of Sydney. With an older sister and a younger brother, she was the middle child of Joyce, an accountant, and Eric, an engineer. As a child she attended Marsden Park School, which had only thirty pupils then. When she was eight, her father — who was a keen amateur photographer — gave her a camera. She began taking photos of the family and the scenery around Windsor.

Lorrie was fourteen, and a student at Riverstone High, when her father gave her a book of photographs by the American photojournalist Margaret Bourke White. In a time when war photography was dominated by men, Bourke White had photographed Nazi Germany during World War II, had flown over Germany in a US bomber, and had covered the Russian front for leading magazines. It was a revelation to Lorrie, and she decided on the spot to become a photojournalist, and have extraordinary adventures in exotic places. 'I thought it would be a fantastic life, lots of adventure, lots of travel, and looking gorgeous while you were doing it.'

Lorrie was not academically oriented. Instead of going

to university after the HSC, she started looking for a way into a career in photography. At seventeen she left home and moved to Sydney, living on forty dollars a week in a flat in a converted terrace in Paddington. She quickly found a job as a 'runner' in a black and white photo lab in North Sydney, where the owners let her 'play around with chemicals'. She had no idea how to go from there to becoming a real photographer until a friend of the lab's owners told her about newspaper cadetships. He worked for the *Mirror*, a Fairfax newspaper, so it was there that Lorrie tried her luck.

What she hadn't realised was that it was almost impossible for a girl to get a cadetship on a Sydney newspaper. Women had been hired as photographers during the war to take the place of the men who'd enlisted, but when the soldiers came home, they'd all been sacked. They'd never got their foot in the door again. 'When I was applying, there were sixty men and no women in the department,' says Lorrie. 'The reason they gave me was that there were no female toilets on the photographic floor.'

Having run up against a wall of prejudice in the newspaper world, Lorrie tried the magazines. She approached the editor of the rock magazine, *Rolling Stone*, with photos she'd shot at a concert of the American blues singer, Muddy Waters. They made a deal. Lorrie would be given free film for her camera and tickets to concerts in return for getting published, but she would not be paid. In those days, performers didn't have to worry so much about their personal safety, so she could get close to the stars and take lots of photographs. 'It was a good learning experience, taking photographs in extreme conditions,' says Lorrie. For an eighteen-year-old girl who loved music, it was a dream assignment.

Once she had a portfolio — the collection of photographs she'd taken for *Rolling Stone* — Lorrie tried repeatedly to get a cadetship at Fairfax. They fobbed her off. But in 1975, the International Year of Women, the government began pressuring companies to open up jobs to women. Bowing to the pressure, Fairfax decided to offer them cadetships. Lorrie was selected. 'I was particularly persistent,' she says. 'Maybe they got tired of me.' But first she had to pass a trial. 'I had to go in three weekends in a row and "rock the dish". I'd have to stand at a dish of developer, and the guys would come back from the footy or the races and chuck their prints into the dish. I'd have to tell them whether they were underexposed or overexposed and take a lot of abuse.' She got her cadetship.

As a cadet photographer, Lorrie had to learn developing and processing, mixing vats of chemicals and printing photographs. Two nights and one afternoon a week she attended courses at the Institute of Technology. Eventually she was allowed to go out and take photos. Because of her prior experience in the photo lab, she was able to complete the cadetship in three years instead of the usual four.

Lorrie's male colleagues made it clear from the start

that she'd have to fit in with them. They were not going to treat her differently because she was female. 'I got to be very tough. But it stands you in good stead. It prepares you. You have to be tough to do this job. It is no profession for "really nice girls".' She had to learn to swear as well as the men, put up with teasing and hide her feelings.

Like the men, Lorrie had to take whatever assignment she was given by the powerful head of the photography department. She went up in a Macchi jet taking photographs for Navy Week, but also had to take her turn attending grisly car accidents, and once photographed a drowning. In her second year as a cadet, she was sent to Brisbane to photograph the West Indian cricket tour. It was a test. Though Lorrie knew nothing about cricket, she was determined not to fail. For six gruelling days she sat on a hot tin roof taking photographs of cricket matches. It wasn't all hard work and tension. She celebrated her 21st birthday with the West Indian team, and Tony Greig, the cricket commentator, explained what terms like 'LBW' meant and wrote the captions for her photographs.

Meanwhile, Lorrie was trying to become a better photographer. At a course at the Australian Centre for Photography, she studied the work of famous photographers like Diane Arbus and set about improving her technique. Instead of setting up her shots and photographing them as newspaper photographers did, she started waiting for something to happen, then photographed it using available light. This did not go unnoticed in the industry. Max Suich, the editor of the *National Times* — the Fairfax quality weekly paper — gave Lorrie some assignments for his paper. She photographed musicians in their environment for one series, and shot portraits of well-known people to accompany stories about them.

When she'd completed her cadetship, Lorrie tried to get a full-time job on the *National Times*, but the head of Fairfax's photographic department did not approve the proposal. At 23, Lorrie was tired of the obstruction and bloody-mindedness of the local media, and quit to go to London. It was time for some international experience. In London she got a job on the *Sun*, and found it wasn't very different from her old job on the *Sydney Morning Herald*, the *Sun* and the *Sun-Herald*. The *Sun* and the *Sun-Herald* were full of sport and scandal; Lorrie wanted something better. She talked her way into a trial with the *Observer*, a quality newspaper.

To get a contract with the *Observer*, Lorrie had to prove herself. The first test was photographing a factory that made photo optics. The second was shooting a businessman who'd developed a chemical to use with a laser to clean the gargoyles on St Pancras Station. Lorrie lit him with a laser beam, with the shadows of the gargoyles on the back wall. The editor was so impressed, Lorrie's photos were given a huge spread. She was hired.

It was a different world. The *Observer* took its photographers seriously. Journalists and photographers were briefed together on a story, and were expected to help each other. Lorrie was given time to do a good job, and the pages of the paper were laid out around images instead of photos being used to fill gaps. She also found herself welcome in places that had been closed to her when she worked on the *Sun*. 'You didn't have to fight your way into a shoot,' says Lorrie. 'You had some cred.'

In London, Lorrie began calling herself a photojournalist. In some countries this means writing the story as well as taking the photographs. But in Europe and the US, it applies to a particular type of photographer — one who tells a story through an image, or a series of images, rather than just illustrating a story. 'My experience on the *Observer* taught me the worth of images,' says Lorrie. 'It gave me the confidence to fight for photographs to be used properly and for photographers to be taken seriously.' It also made her realise the political power of an image — that it could move people, even influence their attitudes.

After three years in England, Lorrie decided to go home. She wanted to put her new skills and knowledge into practice in her own country. 'A sense of place is important,' she says. When she ran into Max Suich, by then a senior executive at Fairfax, she asked him for a job. He agreed.

Back in Australia at 26, Lorrie began work at the *National Times*. One of her favourite assignments was accompanying a group of Aboriginal stockmen on a journey from the Northern Territory to Canberra to see

Prime Minister Bob Hawke and demand the return of their stock routes. The trip, in broken-down trucks and buses, took six days. Lorrie ate char-grilled kangaroo, collected wood, and slept in a swag on the ground with the older women. In 1983, she worked on her first book, *Australians Today*, in collaboration with writer Suzanne Falkiner. The *National Times* became the *Times on Sunday* in 1987, and Lorrie was made chief photographer — attending news conferences, allocating jobs and briefing and supervising three other photographers.

When the paper folded, Lorrie worked for a time on the weekly news magazine, the *Bulletin*. When the major assignments she'd been promised did not eventuate, she started freelancing in 1989. One of her most dangerous and exciting assignments was a month spent with

A photo of Bob Hawke in 1983, taken by Lorrie Graham
Courtesy Lorrie Graham

Kurdish separatists during the Gulf War of 1991. Driving an old Peugeot, Lorrie and Phil Kier, publisher of *Rolling Stone*, travelled to the camp of the English Royal Marines, who then flew them into the Kurdish camp by helicopter. In the mountains with the Kurds, they lived on American army rations and slept in a two-person tent. When some of the Kurds set off back to Northern Iraq, Lorrie and Phil walked out with them on a nine-hour trek along a goat track through mountains strewn with landmines.

Back at the Royal Marines' camp, Lorrie had her first shower in two weeks, under a water pipe coming out of the mountains. That night, sitting around a campfire under the stars, they played Dire Straits' 'Brothers in Arms' on a ghetto blaster. This had been the marines' theme song in the Falklands War in 1982, and everybody cried. After two nights at the camp, Lorrie and Phil picked up the Peugeot and pushed on to the Iraqi front line before returning to the Turkish capital of Ankara.

Like the great photojournalists who influenced her, Lorrie Graham is committed to telling the stories of people in turmoil. In 1993, she teamed up with writer Robert Milliken to document the decline of the family farm in a book called *On the Edge: The Changing World of Australia's Farmers*.

In 1999 Lorrie received the sort of assignment most photographers only dream about. As part of an Olympic arts festival, she has been asked to photograph the people of Sydney — she hasn't been given any more direction than that. 'It's the biggest commission and the broadest brief I've ever had,' she admits. 'I can do what I like. It will be as raw and real as I can make it.' Of the thousands of images she shoots, fifty will be selected and exhibited at the Museum of Sydney until the end of the Olympic and Paralympic Games in 2000. The museum will then keep the images in its permanent collection.

As a teenager, Lorrie Graham saw photojournalism as a passport to travel, adventure and glamour. And it has been that. But along the way she discovered the power of the image to influence opinion, and that changed her relationship with her art, and her life. 'You have to have something to say,' she says. 'Pictures don't mean very much unless you're trying to communicate something very strongly.'

BEVERLEY BUCKINGHAM 1965 –

Horse racing champion

When her father started training horses, eight-year-old Beverley Buckingham decided she wanted to be a jockey. She became Australia's top female jockey, winning 906 races before a riding accident ended her career in 1998.

Born in England in 1965, Beverley Buckingham immigrated to Western Australia with her parents, Ted and Joan, at the age of two. Beverley was introduced to horses in Perth, when Ted bought himself a thoroughbred horse and taught himself to ride. By the time she was four, she was riding to school on horseback.

When Beverley was six, the Buckinghams decided to move to Tasmania. In a station wagon bursting with luggage and three cocker spaniels, they set off to start a new life. In Hobart, Ted started training horses. He'd never trained before, but he had grown up around horses on a farm. A trainer, he knew, was like an athlete's coach — except you're dealing with horses. Like coaches, trainers get the horses fit and teach them how to behave in a race.

It was in Hobart that Beverley decided to become a jockey. She was very much Daddy's girl. When Ted had played soccer, she wanted to be a soccer player. When he took up training horses, she decided to be a jockey so she could work with him. Ted and Beverley always had a fiercely competitive relationship. When Beverley was ten she became ill after helping her father lay concrete blocks, and was rushed to hospital. Ted and Joan thought it was appendicitis, but in fact she had strained her stomach muscles trying to keep up with her father.

Women were not allowed to ride against men on Australian race tracks in those days. But Beverley wanted to be a jockey so badly, she took the risk and hoped the rules would change. 'It was all I dreamed about. I would have moved heaven and earth for it.' She was a natural rider, with excellent balance. She also had an ability to get the measure of a horse quickly. This is essential for a jockey who might have to ride several strange horses in one race meeting.

When Ted was offered a job as a trainer in Devonport, the family moved north. Eventually the Buckinghams bought themselves a twelve-hectare property at Latrobe, outside Devonport, and called it Brigadoon. They now run about twenty horses there, ten of them in training.

Horses and riding became a passion for Beverley. School came a distant second. After first term in year 9, she asked the Department of Education for permission to leave. As she had turned fourteen, and had a job as an apprentice jockey with her father, her request was granted. The following year, when horse racing was opened up to women jockeys, Beverley was ready for action. At fifteen, she had her first ride, on Bickley Hero. 'I was absolutely terrified,' she remembers. 'I'd wanted to do it for so long.' She came second last, but that didn't worry her. You have to begin somewhere.

It wasn't enough to know you were good — you had to prove it. But how was a girl going to break into such a masculine world? 'It was a really male-dominated sport when I started,' says Beverley. 'It was terrible compared to now. Trainers would say, "Why would I put a girl on?"' Their hostility used to make her cry in the early days, but it didn't deter her. Fortunately another girl, Kim Dixon, took up riding soon after Beverley, so she didn't feel like such a freak. Although the two girls were rivals at first, they soon became friends.

Beverley had her first win in November 1980, and when she started winning, the trainers sat up and took notice. With the shortage of jockeys in Tasmania, they couldn't afford to ignore someone who could make them money. They forgot their old prejudices and gave Beverley rides. As the men got used to her, she became just another jockey.

There was no stopping Beverley Buckingham after that. In 1982, when she was just seventeen, she rode off with the Senior Jockey's Premiership. This prize is given to the apprentice or senior jockey who has won the most races in the previous racing year. She was the first woman in the world to win such an award. In only her second year of professional racing, Beverley had won 65 races. At eighteen, she became the first woman to win the Hobart Cup, riding Dark Intruder, a horse trained by her father. By the age of 25, she had notched up 400 wins.

Meanwhile, in Devonport, Ted Buckingham had established himself as a successful trainer at Brigadoon. Beverley bought into the family business. But as a jockey, she was conscious of being a big fish in a small pond, and longed to make it big on the Australian mainland. In 1989 the Buckinghams moved to Ballarat to try their

The first woman to win the Hobart Cup
Courtesy Beverley Buckingham

luck. Their timing was poor. The economy was in recession and Beverley found it hard to get rides. Without the money from her wins, the family couldn't survive. After two years, they gave up and returned to Tasmania.

In 1994 Beverley met Jason King, who worked at the particle-board mill in Devonport. 'Within a week of meeting Jason I knew we'd be together for the rest of our lives,' says Beverley. 'He was like family.' They married in May 1997 and moved in with Beverley's parents at Brigadoon. Though Jason wasn't a 'horse person', he was quickly absorbed into the Buckingham family business. He now owns a couple of racehorses.

Beverley's life was on track. She was happily married, successful, and well respected in Tasmania, which takes its horse racing seriously. By 1998 she'd notched up 906 wins, and it looked as if nothing could stop her from achieving her goal of 1000. Then it all fell apart. On 30 May, at the Elwick Race Course in Hobart, Beverley was riding a horse called Theutelle in the mile race. She was in a good position to win the race, running fourth or fifth. Suddenly, the horse in front slowed down. Beverley tried to pull up her horse, but it didn't stop quickly enough; its feet clipped the back feet of the horse in front. Horses clip hoofs all the time, but this time the accident had catastrophic results. Beverley was catapulted into the air and landed on the back of her head.

Jockeys get used to falling — it's an occupational hazard. 'If you're frightened, if you lose your nerve, you might as well retire,' says Beverley. She had fallen many times during her racing career, but always got up and walked away. Not this time.

'I was conscious,' she recalls. 'A couple of other riders fell. I could see a horse coming for me. I tried to roll out of its way and realised I couldn't move. It stepped on my leg. I later had forty stitches. The ambulance drivers came rushing over and asked, "Are you all right?" I said, "No, I can't move." My legs had no feeling except pins and needles. I don't remember anything after the ambulance.'

She came around briefly in hospital in Hobart and realised she still couldn't move. Her first reaction was disbelief. The fall hadn't seemed any different from others she'd experienced. She'd just landed wrong. 'I thought I was indestructible. I used to bounce up from falls and get into the next race.'

Beverley is no wimp. In 1997, a week before the Hobart Cup, she dislocated her thumb. She looked down to see the bone sticking out of her skin. Before the pain started, while she was still numb from shock, she pulled the thumb back into place. She was going to need all that toughness for the ordeal that lay ahead.

At first she seemed to be doing well in Hobart, able to talk to the doctors and her horrified family. But then her lungs collapsed and she got pneumonia. Her family and her best friend, Kim Dixon, maintained a vigil by her bed. The response from the media and the public was overwhelming. Beverley Buckingham was Tasmania's sweetheart. Cards and flowers flowed in. 'It shocked me,' says Beverley. 'I had no idea I was so popular.'

Five days after the accident, Beverley was flown to Melbourne to the spinal unit of the Austin Hospital. Her parents and Jason went with her, returning home to Tasmania in shifts to keep the business going. The news from the doctors wasn't good. Vertebrae C3 and 4 had been fractured and C6 had lodged in her spinal cord. Surgeons operated two days later to remove the disc from her spinal cord. During the ten weeks Beverley was in the spinal unit, she had an emergency tracheotomy to allow her to breathe, and was on life support in intensive care for ten days. Then she had to undergo a second operation on the back of her neck to stabilise her spine. Doctors put metal plates on both sides of her spine and fused the bones so that her head would not flop.

Though she was heavily sedated, Beverley was aware of what was happening. She could not talk because of the tube in her throat from the tracheotomy. But even worse were the terrible nightmares she suffered from the morphine prescribed to ease the pain. A week after coming out of intensive care, she insisted on being taken off the morphine.

After the crisis was over, Beverley had to undergo rehabilitation at the Talbot Rehabilitation Centre. Though she had no movement in her legs and arms, she did have some feeling. It turned out she was what is called an 'incomplete' quadriplegic. As the spinal column was not completely severed, some messages get through from the brain to the muscles. Once more Beverley had beaten the odds — only one in fifty quadriplegics ever walks again, but she had a chance.

The doctors wanted Beverley to stay in the rehabilitation centre for four to six months, but she believed she'd recover faster in her own home. To enable her to come home, Beverley's family had to redesign the house. Ramps were built for her wheelchair, the bathroom was redesigned, and a standing frame and massage table were bought. As jockeys do not get any workers' compensation in Tasmania, the Buckinghams had to find the money themselves. The Tasmanian Racing Club came to their aid and launched an appeal which raised $200 000 for Beverley. 'It got me home early,' she says gratefully.

After less than two months in rehabilitation, Beverley went home. The family took over the responsibility for her rehabilitation, and Jason became her official carer. She was confined to a wheelchair at first, and a physiotherapist came in four days a week. Rather than give her false hope, the doctors had told her after the fall that she would never walk again. But three weeks after the accident, Beverley felt a twinge in her legs. At the rehab centre she started using a standing frame, and within a week of coming home took her first steps.

In the year after her accident, Beverley worked hard to build up her strength. She can now walk, slowly, and use her arms and hands. But she tires easily and has reached a plateau in her recovery. She is fit, and she feels strong enough to run, but the message cannot get from her brain to her legs.

Beverley is finding it very difficult to come to terms with the fact that this is as good as she will get. Her hardest battle has been with depression. 'I was full of self-pity. I cried all the time.' Her image of herself as a super-fit sportswoman, a champion, was shattered. She had also lost the great love of her life — the excitement of thundering down the track on a fast horse.

Since the accident, Beverley hasn't been on a horse. 'I don't want to ride if I can't be a champion,' she says. 'I'll never get used to what I can't do any more.' Her old dream of becoming a trainer after she retired from racing has died too. Beverley is a hands-on person, and she no longer has the strength needed to manage horses. 'It's too emotionally difficult as well.'

But Beverley is on the mend. On 21 April 1999 she woke up and decided she was through with being depressed, and agreed to seek counselling. Perhaps a contract with the Tasmanian TAB to do promotions and television ads for horse racing has helped her realise there is life off the track.

Beverley Buckingham blazed the trail for women riders in Tasmania and became the country's leading female jockey. Now, at 34, she has to find a new identity and a new life. The Buckinghams are a tightly knit clan, argumentative but fiercely protective of their own. Their love and support, and Beverley's own toughness and stubborn nature, will pull her through.

HEATHER TETU 1967 —

Ponch Hawkes.

Acrobat and trapeze artist

When the Flying Fruit Fly Circus was recruiting in Albury-Wodonga back in 1979, Heather Tetu was not interested. But at her mother's urging, she auditioned and was accepted. Almost immediately she found herself aloft on a trapeze as well as doing tumbling and acrobatics. After nine years with the Fruit Flies, Heather became a freelance trapeze artist, but then a horrific fall put an end to her career.

The first child of Aileen and Ray Tetu, Heather Tetu was born in 1967 in Bendigo, Victoria. When she was four years old, her family moved to Albury on the border of New South Wales and Victoria. She attended Albury West Public School, then Wodonga High School, and dreamed of becoming a physical education teacher.

But in 1979, the Year of the Child, Australia's only circus for children was established in Albury-Wodonga. It would change Heather's life. Recruiters from the Flying Fruit Fly Circus visited the local schools rounding up 100 children to audition for the circus. Heather, who was away from school at the time, missed out on the auditions. She would have missed out again the following year, if the recruiters had not had to replace some children who dropped out. Heather's mother heard about this at the high school where she taught, and urged her daughter to try out. After all, she excelled at gymnastics and ballet — she should be a natural. Eventually Heather gave in and went to the audition. She was selected.

Because she was strong in the arms and stomach, the

circus coaches put her straight onto the trapeze. She loved it, and her life changed dramatically. Every day after school she practised for two hours, and on Saturdays for three. Now the circus has its own school and teachers, but in those days the performers stayed at their original schools, and had to miss school if the circus went on tour during term time.

The Fruit Flies helped Heather see the world. By the time she'd finished high school, she'd performed in most of Australia's capital cities, as well as in Canada and Hawaii. As both her parents were high school teachers, they were able to accompany the circus on its tours in the long summer vacation. When both Heather's brother Peter and her younger sister Kelly joined the Fruit Flies in turn, the whole family became part of the circus.

Being a circus performer was an exciting and exhilarating experience. It also did wonders for Heather's confidence, self-esteem and maturity. 'It gave you a sense of achievement,' she says. 'You could learn an act and perform it, and people would clap and you'd get a nice feeling. It also taught me how to work with other kids and how to deal with adults, like directors, trainers and set designers. I learnt how to relate to a cross-section of people.'

It also taught her the value of teamwork. 'I performed an act with two other girls, called the Tower of Chairs. We did handstands on top of six chairs standing on four bottles, which sat on a table. We were quite high, and it was a matter of teamwork, strength and balance. One of the girls in the act was Emma George.' Emma George is now a world champion pole vaulter.

When the Fruit Flies offered Heather and three other performers jobs with the circus after finishing high school, she jumped at the chance, abandoning her ambition to become a PE teacher. She continued to perform as well as learning how to run the circus and organise tours. As this was the only time in its history the circus employed performers as administrators, Heather and her three friends shared a unique experience. 'I was really lucky,' she says.

In 1986 Heather was selected to go to China to do further acrobatic training with the Nanjing Acrobatic Troupe, who'd made the offer after touring Australia. At eighteen, not knowing a word of the language, Heather found herself living in China for seven months studying trapeze, handstands and tumbling with the Nanjing and Guangzhou Acrobatic Troupes.

The trip was an eye-opener. In 1986 China had not opened up to mass tourism, and visitors had no choice but to live like the locals. It was a shock to the Australians. They lived in the Foreign Students dormitory at Nanjing University. As there were no showers, they had to boil water and wash in a bucket. The toilet was a pit in the floor. Meals were provided in a hotel restaurant — a western lunch and a Chinese dinner — but it didn't agree with the acrobats. 'It wasn't the right sort of food for athletes,' recalls Heather. After Australia, Heather found the sheer number of people in the streets daunting, and the weather extreme, either very hot or very cold. 'It was hard and harsh,' she says. 'I learnt a lot very quickly. It was sink or swim.' She also learnt to appreciate what she had at home.

The acrobatic training was difficult, but bearable. 'They taught me how to be tough and disciplined, and how to get through the pain,' says Heather. She discovered the value of persistence and hard work. 'If you put in the work, you get the rewards.'

Running the program in Guangzhou was Li Shen, a 56-year-old man. Li Shen took Heather under his wing. 'He had two sons and always wanted a daughter,' she explains. At the end of the course, Li Shen asked Heather to organise a three-month visit with the Guangzhou Acrobatic Troupe for eight young Fruit Flies. Heather decided to do it, although she realised the red tape would be a nightmare and people kept telling her it was impossible.

It was Heather's experience with the Fruit Flies that gave her the confidence to try. She was inspired by the women coaches from Circus Oz who'd taught at the children's circus. 'The Fruit Flies really encouraged girls to take positions of power, to be on the bottom of the pyramid, the role boys traditionally were given. They had a fantastic influence on girls of my generation. There were women riggers and musicians. They drove trucks, they were in the air. They broke down a lot of stereotypes because it wasn't just talk — you could actually see women doing these things.'

Back in Australia, Heather made it happen. It took nine months to steer the project through Chinese and Australian government bodies and line up the funding from private enterprise and the Commonwealth and state governments. The Fruit Flies got behind her, and the Guangzhou Acrobatic Troupe did their bit. The Victorian Department of Education treated the trip as a school excursion and paid for a teacher to accompany the children. 'It was a big achievement,' she says. 'A one-off. No one had ever done it before.' She was only 20.

In 1987, as manager and interpreter for the group, Heather took eight Fruit Flies, their teacher and a parent to China. Li Shen ran the program at the other end. By then the living conditions had improved, and the Australians lived in a village with the Chinese acrobats and had showers, their own dining area and a chef. 'This time the food was fantastic,' says Heather.

The trip was one of the highlights of Heather's life. 'It goes way beyond doing a perfect handstand,' she says. 'It will be a personal experience we'll always have.' The Fruit Flies blossomed. 'They were treated like little kings and queens,' says Heather. 'They were praised for their physical achievements, and there was a celebration when they mastered a new trick.'

With the successful Chinese project under her belt, Heather returned to work at the Fruit Fly Circus in 1988. But she longed to go back to China and spend more time with the people who'd looked after her. She decided to study Chinese properly so she could better communicate with them. In 1989 she moved to Melbourne and started a Bachelor of Arts at Melbourne University, majoring in Chinese language and linguistics. She supported herself during her years at university by performing as a freelance trapeze artist. During the holidays, she even performed overseas in Italy, Japan and Scotland. In 1990 Heather returned to China with her mother and put her language skills to use. This time she did the tourist sights as well as visiting her old friends.

The only options at the end of Heather's degree seemed to be teaching Chinese or becoming an interpreter. She did not want to do either, she realised. Instead, she and Matt Hughes, another former Fruit Fly who was doing a business degree at university, started up a double trapeze act. The act was a hit and the work rolled in. Deciding they belonged together on the ground as well as in the air, Matt and Heather became a couple. When they were offered a contract at Jupiter's Casino, it seemed like the answer to all their prayers — professional recognition, good money, and sunshine. They packed and moved to the Gold Coast.

But just four months into the contract, during a performance of the *Jewel of the Orient Express* show in December 1992, a terrible thing happened. As Heather was being hoisted to her trapeze rig, a cable slipped through swages which had been improperly secured by a technician. In front of an audience of 1000 and her horrified partner, she plummeted nine metres to the floor. Landing on her feet, she smashed both ankles and her knee, and injured her back. Fortunately, she had the presence of mind to roll on impact — which probably saved her from paraplegia or death. She can remember hoping someone would catch her before she hit the ground.

At 25, her body shattered, Heather's career as a trapeze artist was over. 'My career, and everything I'd learnt in my childhood, everything I'd known as a performer, had gone out the window,' says Heather. Her initial reaction was disbelief. 'I didn't believe it when they said I wouldn't walk for a year. I thought "They don't know." They didn't seem to be talking about me. But they were right, and I was in denial. I couldn't cope with the fact that someone else had caused my accident. Through no fault of our own, our future had been destroyed.'

Though it was a struggle to get well and strong enough even to stand up, Heather's toughest battle was in her head. She could not convince herself this was happening to her. 'I thought I'd be back in the show, but the doctors were talking about how long I'd be in a wheelchair.'

Heather was confined to a wheelchair for nine months. She avoided mirrors. Only when she caught sight of herself in a shop window did the reality sink in. 'I'd been physically active and sporty from early on. I wanted to be a PE teacher, and I became a trapeze artist. Now I was in a wheelchair being pushed around by other people every day and I loathed it.'

It took Heather three years to realise she would not perform again. This was after she had an operation to permanently fuse her left ankle. But six years on, she's beginning to accept it. Now she's grateful that she can walk and drive a car. With two badly injured ankles and a bad knee, she still needs a wheelchair for shopping and for moving long distances. Otherwise, she walks with the aid of a stick.

Now in her early thirties, Heather requires constant medical attention and suffers chronic pain. She swims and goes to the gym twice a week to build up muscle, and is treated by an osteopath twice a week. 'It takes a lot of time and energy, but I have to keep doing it,' she says. To deal with the emotional impact of the accident, she sees a psychiatrist, an energy healer and a masseur. 'It was the combination of them, and a huge amount of family support — and in that I include my friends — that helped me through,' she says.

In 1996, on her first trip since the accident, Heather revisited the Guangzhou Acrobatic Troupe. 'I was very apprehensive about going, so Matt went with me,' she says. 'I was worried that the Chinese would see me as a wounded bird returning home to the nest, broken, no longer able to be a performer, stripped of my worth. Instead, the troupe was so excited to see me and I was smothered with love and care. I think they were more worried about me coping in China, because for the time I was there I had my own doctor, driver and personal assistant. Li Shen, my Chinese "father" told me that my body might be broken, but my spirit was still intact.'

Heather is not the only one affected by the accident.

After he saw Heather fall, Matt gave up the trapeze — it was too dangerous. 'He saw me fall and thought I was dead,' says Heather. 'The image stayed with him. And he lived through what it takes to get back on your feet.' Matt now works full time with Circus Oz as programming manager and administrator, and does a trampoline act. Heather accompanies him on overseas tours, doing his music and costumes. 'It's so we can still be part of the same thing,' she says. 'It's hard, though. It's such a little thing compared to what I used to do.'

In January 1999 Matt and Heather were married. The wedding marked the end of six years of grief and uncertainty. 'It celebrated the closing of the last chapter and the beginning of the next, not only for us, but for our families,' says Heather. Their friends rigged up a flying fox trapeze so that Heather could arrive at the ceremony in a spectacular fashion. Her parents then helped her walk to Matt's side. 'It was symbolic. It was the first time I'd been back on a trapeze. Some of my ongoing desire to perform had been satisfied. I was so happy, I was laughing. All the guests started crying.'

Heather and Matt on their wedding day
Glenn McCulloch Photography

SONYA HARTNETT 1968 —

Reluctant writer

A quiet, solitary child in a big family, nine-year-old Sonya Hartnett discovered that she had a talent for making up stories. After writing several novels in school exercise books, she had her first novel published at fifteen and became a literary sensation. She now has many books for young adults to her name, and has won several major literary prizes.

Sonya Hartnett was born in Melbourne in 1968. The second daughter in a family of six — four girls and two boys — she grew up in a small house in Box Hill. Her father, Philip, was a proofreader on a Melbourne newspaper. Her mother, Virginia, was a nurse who gave up work to care for her family.

With one salary and a growing family, money was tight in the Hartnett household. The children were always well dressed and didn't go without, but there were no luxuries. This included books. Sonya would be in agony at school when parcels arrived from the Book Club, knowing they were never for her. She still has an aversion to libraries, too. When the time came to take her overdue books back, she'd lie awake all night worrying because she thought her mother didn't have the money to pay the fine. And she still hates sausages and mashed potatoes, because she ate them so often as a child.

Sonya remembers her childhood as happy. In the 1970s, their corner of Box Hill was wild, with lots of parks and horses and plenty of space for kids to roam. 'We ran wild through those parks. We were the bad influence that kids weren't allowed to mix with.'

Sonya's mother was also independent and adventurous. Every Christmas she would pack the children into the car and drive all the way to Goondiwindi in Queensland to visit relatives. These trips were a highlight of Sonya's life. With its heat and its flatness and the trucks roaring through the main street, Goondiwindi became one of her special places. Sonya stored away memories which she used later in her novels. 'We used to stay in this fantastic old house, which I eventually based the *Sparkle and Nightflower* house on. Mum took us to the farm that I based *Sleeping Dogs* on, and to the place I based the monastery on in *Wilful Blue*.'

Sonya started at the local school in Box Hill, then transferred to the Holy Redeemer Catholic primary school in Surrey Hills. Her new school was run by Indian nuns, who spoke English the way they were taught it at home. Sonya thinks she picked up some of the old-fashioned words she uses in her novels from them.

School was an ordeal for Sonya. Sometimes she would sit on the fence at the edge of the playground hoping that her mother would drive by, see how miserable she was, and take her home. Because she was shy, she didn't make friends easily. In class she was a perfectionist. Though she performed well in most subjects, she was afraid of failing. In secondary school English and art were the only subjects she enjoyed, though she found science interesting.

From the start, Sonya was a homebody, happiest when inside cutting and pasting or playing with dolls. In fifth grade, she dropped out of school altogether for a time. When her best friend changed schools temporarily, Sonya wouldn't face it alone. She stayed home — with her mother's permission. Virginia, who'd had a strict father, decided that her children would be independent and free. They were punished for misbehaviour, but encouraged to make decisions for themselves. 'Mum knew we were bright,' says Sonya. 'She let us make up our own minds about whether we should go to school or not.'

It was fortunate that Sonya did go back to school, because that year the class was taught composition. At nine, she suddenly discovered she could invent her own stories and people would listen. 'I could see what was happening in the story so clearly. I was right there.' The teacher was impressed, and read out her stories in class. At first Sonya was simply glad to find something she was good at. 'I could cease to be a rather quiet child surrounded by large, boisterous siblings and be somebody else, somewhere else. I liked that.' But as she got better at it, she found that writing made her feel powerful. It gave her a sense of control over the imaginary lives she was creating in her stories. Incorporating the writing into her cutting and pasting, Sonya began making her own little books. She'd write the story on pieces of paper, staple them together and paste in pictures. Gradually, her stories became more sophisticated.

Sonya did her secondary schooling at Siena College, a private girls' school in Camberwell. She didn't like it any better than primary school. In private she began writing novels in her school exercise books. Several were thrown away because they did not come up to her standards. Finally, when she was thirteen, she had a story she was satisfied with, about a fourteen-year-old boy whose best friend has just got his first girlfriend. Even so, her writing career might never have got off the ground if her father hadn't brought home a typewriter. She taught herself to type and produced a professional-looking manuscript.

But it was only after a friend read the manuscript and urged her to send it to a publisher that she found the courage to go ahead with it. In the Yellow Pages she found the addresses of two Melbourne-based publishers — she couldn't afford the postage needed to send the manuscript interstate. Then she sat back and waited. To her amazement, Rigby accepted the book. After Sonya spent a year rewriting, it was published in 1984 as *Trouble All the Way*. She was only fifteen.

Because she was so young, the book caused a sensation. Her publishers sent her off on a gruelling publicity tour around the country. The girls at school gave her flowers and chocolates but, with a couple of exceptions, the teachers acted as if nothing had happened. Perhaps they didn't want Sonya to get a swelled head.

It's hard to deal with publicity, especially if you're fifteen and agonisingly shy. Although Sonya became more confident in dealing with the media over time, she never really came to terms with the attention. She particularly hated having to live up to other people's expectations. 'I've tried not to let the expectations get to me too much, but people expect me to be the "writer", to say clever things all the time.' Even her appearance came under scrutiny. 'I have to defend myself against my mother and say, "I'm not a beauty queen. I don't need to have my hair done and my eyebrows waxed to go to the Premier's awards, because I'm not there as a beauty queen, I'm there as a writer."'

Before long, Sonya was doing the HSC, but found that the crowded family home was too small to give her any privacy to study. Her mother bought a caravan and parked it in the garden. As well as studying there, Sonya later used the solitude of the caravan to write *The Glass House*.

Faced with the choice of a career, Sonya chose television production. Being around the media had made her think she might like it. But after completing a Bachelor of Arts in Media Studies at the Royal Melbourne Institute of Technology, she decided television was not for her. It meant relying on other people too much. 'I didn't like the collaborative part of it, or the waiting for other people to do their bit.' At least with books she'd have much more control over the final product.

In 1986 she published *Sparkle and Nightflower*. It was followed by *The Glass House* in 1990 and *Wilful Blue* four years later. In 1996 Sonya received international recognition when *Wilful Blue* won an award from the International Board of Books for Young People. But literary awards didn't mean much to potential employers. Sonya soon discovered that there was little demand for people with her qualifications. Desperate, she took a job with Kew Council as a painter. For nine months she painted street signs and lines on the road. With the money she saved, she took herself on a six-week trip overseas. Back in Melbourne and unemployed, she went on the dole. This was one of the happiest periods of Sonya's life — enough money to live frugally and plenty of time to write.

Occasionally, though, the employment service would send her out to jobs. Sonya's favourite was at Merri Creek Primary School. When she turned up, the teachers had no idea what to do with her, so she made a job for herself. Discovering that they were about to put on a couple of plays, she took over the art room and made all the props. She was in seventh heaven. 'I was back doing my cutting and pasting!'

That year, 1995, also saw the publication of *Sleeping Dogs*, Sonya's most successful book to date. It won the inaugural $12 000 Schaeffer Pen Prize for Young Adult Fiction in the Victorian Premier's Literary Awards, and the Kathleen Mitchell Award for young writers. It was shortlisted for the New South Wales Premier's Literary Awards and was an honour book in the Children's Book Council awards. *Sleeping Dogs* catapulted Sonya into the literary big time. It also increased the pressure on her to excel. 'It is held up as the book I have to do better than,' she says.

Not all the reactions to the book were positive, though. Some readers and reviewers criticised the inclusion of violence, and maintained that its subject matter was too confronting for young adult readers. Even Sonya's publishers had trouble deciding whether her book was for teenagers or adults. Sonya cannot understand what the fuss is about. 'Kids know all about this sort of stuff,' she argues. 'They know the world is not a bright and sparkly place. I've literally defended *Sleeping Dogs* on the phone while the aftermath of the Port Arthur massacre was on the TV behind me, with all the blood soaking out from under the plastic.' She refuses to censor her fiction for teenagers. 'There's nothing I wouldn't broach if I had to.'

The word 'dark' is often used to describe Sonya's books. She does not set out to make them that way. 'I'm not aware of their grimness while I'm writing them. It's just that I'm more interested in dark characters. If I'm not interested in my characters, I can't write.'

Just what is it about Sonya Hartnett's fictional world that makes people so uneasy? 'I write about how frightening real life can be, how twisted and warped and how unsafe, unstable and unreliable it can be,' she says.

Dealing with the critics isn't the hardest part of a writer's life, according to Sonya — making a living is. Even though she has produced many successful books and has won prizes for writing, she doesn't have a lot of money. It's almost impossible to survive on a writer's income in a small country like Australia. To get by, she works in a bookstore, but only part time, as she needs to have time to write. She wishes she had a decent income, a good car, some security. 'If I were given my life over again, I would make a bigger effort to study zoology or entomology,' she says. 'If I'd studied for a proper career, I wouldn't be chained to writing as I am now. I could give it up, or do it as a hobby.'

Sonya Hartnett is regarded as one of our very best young writers. 'A book should be, as much as you can make it, a work of art. There must be art in writing, otherwise it's a waste of trees. If you're going to do it, you have to do it as beautifully as you can. A book should be as compelling to the ear as a painting is to the eye.'

Like many writers, Sonya Hartnett is often ambivalent about writing. As a career, writing has many drawbacks. It pays badly, and if you fail, you fail in front of a big audience. And spending most of your time hunched over a computer can be isolating. Sonya's life is particularly solitary — she lives with her old whippet Zak, and her cat Idaho. 'Writing can be a curse,' she says. 'It has often proved wretched to me, but it has also given me much to be thankful for. It is a ball and chain to me, but not one I've always hated dragging.' So why do it? Sonya says she writes because she doesn't have anything else to do, and because her publishers want her to. 'And if I don't write, what else?'

FIONA COOTE 1970 —

Courtesy Fiona Coote

A great heart

When Fiona Coote was fourteen, a bout of tonsillitis developed into a deadly heart disease. She was chosen for the newly revived heart transplant program. After her first donated heart failed, she was given another. After fifteen years, that second gift heart still beats strongly. Fiona's bravery throughout her ordeal turned the shy country girl into the nation's sweetheart.

In January 1970, Fiona Coote was born in Manilla, a small town near Tamworth in northern New South Wales. Her parents, Terry and Judy Coote, already had two daughters, Kim and Stacey. The Cootes were farmers, and Fiona had a normal country upbringing — horse riding, keeping pets and feeding baby lambs by hand.

Fiona attended St Michael's Catholic School in Manilla for her primary education, then transferred to Our Lady of the Rosary College in Tamworth for high school. School was the centre of Fiona's life. She didn't mind the long bus trip every morning and afternoon.

But Fiona's life changed dramatically when she was in year 9. In April 1984 she came down with tonsillitis, and spent two weeks at home in bed. Worried about falling behind in her work, she returned to school the following week. Instead of bouncing back to health, though, she felt exhausted all the time. On the Friday of that week, she started vomiting at school, and was sent to the sick bay.

Over the weekend, Fiona's condition grew worse. Breathing became difficult. Alarmed, her parents rushed her to the Tamworth Base Hospital. The doctors at the country hospital diagnosed cardiomyopathy, a rare and fatal disease that scars the heart so badly it cannot pump blood. Eventually the whole body shuts down. They told Fiona's parents that their daughter's heart had swollen and was squeezing her lungs. As well, her kidneys and liver had shut down, and her blood pressure was dangerously low.

Fiona was close to death by now, and swam in and out of consciousness. The doctors did all they could for her — gave her medication to ease the pain and monitored her heart — but they knew it was hopeless. Cardiomyopathy is incurable; it was only a matter of time. But rather than watch Fiona die, they decided to take the risk and send her to Sydney by Air Ambulance.

Fiona's only chance for life was a dangerous heart transplant operation. Australian surgeons had begun doing heart transplants in 1968, but had closed down the program six years later. Too many patients were dying because their bodies were rejecting their new hearts. The drugs they were using to stop this rejection were simply not up to the job. But Fiona was lucky. By the time her heart failed, a miracle drug, cyclosporin, had been developed. Heart specialists decided to revive the heart transplant program. Fiona was the second patient to undergo a heart transplant in the new program. The new drug was not 100 percent effective, however. There was still a strong chance a heart transplant would fail.

After some debate about Fiona's chances, the doctors decided to go ahead. After a three-day search, a suitable heart was found. She was transferred to Australia's top heart unit at St Vincent's Hospital in Darlinghurst. Back in Manilla, her schoolmates at Our Lady of the Rosary College prayed hard. Then, with all Australia holding its breath, Fiona was given a new heart in a four-hour operation. It was hailed as a success.

Fiona was probably the only person in the country who didn't know about her heart transplant. She found out about a month after the operation. 'My initial reaction was anger that they had not told me,' she says. 'But they explained that I'd been unconscious before, and so critical after, that it was a couple of weeks before they thought I was physically strong enough and emotionally able to deal with it. It wasn't easy to deal with the shock, though.'

Fiona was never told the heart donor's name, only that it was a young male. 'Emotionally, I felt a really deep sadness that someone else had to die for me to be able to live, particularly because it was someone my age,' she recalls. 'The only person I'd known who'd died was my grandmother. The concept of being saved by a young person was difficult to digest.'

After three months in hospital, Fiona spent four months as an outpatient, visiting the hospital regularly for tests and intensive physiotherapy. Finally, she was allowed to return home to Manilla. Because she'd missed so much school, she repeated year 9, but she only attended two days a week, mainly to see her friends. She felt well enough to swim a kilometre a day after school, and gradually her strength and her breathing improved.

It didn't last. 'I had no energy, and life was a bit of a

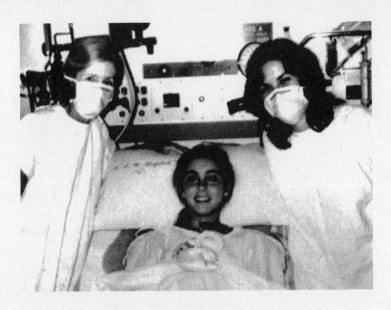

Fiona Coote with her mother Judy and sister Stacey after her first heart transplant
John Fairfax & Co. Courtesy Fiona Coote

struggle. My body was labouring.' By October 1985, seventeen months after the transplant, she was gravely ill again. Her body was rejecting its new heart because it had not been a close enough match to her own tissue. Judy Coote rang the doctors, who put Fiona on the next flight to Sydney. Within a week, the doctors told her she would need another transplant.

'I was shocked,' says Fiona. 'I had never contemplated a second heart. I thought, "No, I can't do this." I was scared. There was so much testing. It was very invasive. And I was worried. It was a difficult time.'

Fiona was in hospital for three months waiting for the

second transplant. Her mother and Stacey moved to Sydney to be with her, and her father and Kim visited on the weekends. The medical staff, many of whom knew her from the first transplant, were supportive, and she made friends with two young men who were also waiting for hearts. Her mother cooked for them, and the three hung out together. When one of them died just before her transplant, Fiona was devastated. Death suddenly became very real.

A heart became available at the end of January. For the second transplant, Fiona underwent three bouts of surgery. The doctors viewed the operation as a success, but Fiona's reaction was much more ambivalent. Not only was the recovery very painful, but she was also upset by the death of her remaining friend shortly after her own operation. 'When people in similar situations to mine died, it was very traumatic,' she explains. 'I felt that life was very temporary. I became very sceptical. I'd seen many people not make it, particularly young people. It really got to me how one person could make it and another didn't. I came to believe that we're all here for however long we're meant to be, and when our time is up, it's up.' She began to question the Catholic faith which had sustained her through her first transplant. Fear and foreboding overcame Fiona. She decided to stay in Sydney to be close to the doctors and the hospital: 'I was terrified something would happen.'

Another worry for Fiona was the strain on her family. The lives of her mother and sister were on hold; her father was trying to keep the farm running alone in Manilla, and the cost of running two households was draining their finances. There was also the publicity to deal with. A shy, pretty country girl thrust into a life-or-death drama, Fiona was besieged by the media throughout her operations and her convalescence. Against all her inclinations, she was turned into a celebrity. She felt hounded, an object of curiosity, and started avoiding the media. But when Fiona was sixteen, a chance remark from a doctor changed her attitude. He told her that when she received publicity, it raised public awareness and increased the number of organ donations. Realising that something positive could come out of her misfortune, Fiona began promoting the Heart Foundation. Her efforts raised over one million dollars for research. She also joined Dr Victor Chang's campaign to raise money for artificial hearts, and supported the Heart and Lung Transplant Unit at St Vincent's Hospital.

Her high profile, good looks and freshness on television also won her some modelling work and a contract to be the face of Willow Valley breakfast foods. While representing Willow Valley, Fiona met Ian Elliot, an advertising executive who handled the breakfast food account. When she was having trouble with her agent, he started managing her affairs as a favour. Fiona found him witty, caring and fun to be with. They married in 1996.

That same year, Fiona gave herself a year off to take stock of her life. She gave up the three children's charities she supported to concentrate on her work on the boards of the Victor Chang Cardiac Research Institute and the Heart and Lung Transplant Unit.

Fiona Coote's second heart has now lasted longer than doctors expected. But once again technology has come to her aid. New drugs are being developed, surgical procedures are improving, and doctors are learning more about how patients' diets can be structured to keep them healthy. Heart recipients in the United States are now living for an average of 23 years from the time of the operation, and Fiona's doctors believe she could live another five to ten years on existing drug therapy. In the meantime, new drugs will become available.

Fiona works hard to keep her heart beating strongly. She keeps to a low-fat diet and avoids stimulants like coffee. For exercise, she walks her dogs for an hour a day, and does yoga twice a week. 'It doesn't rule my life. But most of the time I can't get away with cheating on my diet. I get sick, and have no energy.'

Staying healthy requires discipline — and sacrifice. One thing Fiona has sacrificed is a family of her own. Though the doctors say she might be able to have a child in the future, she has decided against it. She believes it would be unfair to a child, and too hard on her body.

Having twice cheated death, Fiona Coote is determined to get the most out of life. Her philosophy is simple: 'I believe I'm almost obliged to get out there and live life the best I can and enjoy it, so that when my time is up, I'll have no regrets.'

LOUISE SAUVAGE 1973 –

Wheelchair racer

When she was sixteen, Louise Sauvage entered her first international wheelchair racing competition. There she saw the world champion racer, Connie Hansen, in action. At that moment, Louise knew what she wanted to be: the best. Since then, Louise has broken a number of world records and won a swag of gold medals, including seven Paralympic and one Olympic gold. She is now the undisputed world champion of women's wheelchair racing.

Louise Sauvage was born in Perth in 1973. She was the second daughter of Rita, who immigrated to Australia from England in 1963, and Maurice, who arrived the following year from the Seychelles, off the east coast of Africa.

Louise was born with myelodysplasia, an abnormality of the spinal cord which is sometimes called 'incomplete paraplegia'. Although she has muscles to her knees, her legs cannot bear weight. To correct the condition, Louise began undergoing a series of operations, the first at the age of eight weeks. Until she was two, her whole body was encased in plaster. It didn't hold her back — she crawled so fast that she wore holes in the plaster!

Louise was always determined and daring. One day, her mother arrived to pick her up from kindergarten and found her on top of the monkey bars. Louise had clambered up despite her body brace (a hard plastic corset) and leg irons.

Rita Sauvage was protective of Louise at first, but soon began encouraging her daughter to do the things that able-bodied children did — including sport. Louise was mad about sport from the start. She was only three when she followed her older sister Ann into the pool. Before long, she and Ann were swimming in a squad three times a week. Rita ferried the girls back and forth to training sessions.

Louise got her first everyday wheelchair when she was five, and by the age of eight she had a racing chair as well, as she had taken up wheelchair sports, doing track and road training twice a week. On weekends, she played basketball. Training and competing in three sports kept her on a tight schedule, but she loved it. 'I wanted to do it. My parents didn't push me. They thought it was a good thing for me to be active and integrate with the other kids.'

In spite of the wheelchair, Louise never thought of herself as different from other children. 'I've had my disability from birth, so I don't know anything else,' she says. 'My attitude from the beginning was that I wasn't all that different. I was treated just like everybody else and grew up in an able-bodied world.' When people would come up and ask what was wrong with her, she was amazed. 'I'd say, "What do you mean what's wrong with me?"' Louise's outgoing, confident nature helped her fit in at primary school, where she was the only child with a disability. The school was made wheelchair friendly, and her classmates accepted her as she was.

For much of her youth, it looked as if swimming was the sport where Louise would excel. But at fourteen, she had major spinal surgery that made playing sport impossible for two years. When she recovered, Louise discovered that she had lost her edge in the pool. Fortunately, her skills on the track remained unimpaired. The decision to specialise in wheelchair racing had been made for her.

Louise left school after year 10. She could see no point in staying on. 'I hated school,' she explains. 'I wasn't any good at it.' To obtain some work skills to fall back on, she took a secretarial course. As it turned out, she never had to use those skills — wheelchair racing began to take over her life.

At sixteen, Louise got the chance to test her mettle on a larger stage. In 1990 she was selected for the Australian team to compete in the international wheelchair championships in the Netherlands. She was the baby of the team, and still a naive girl from Perth. Travelling overseas opened her eyes. She had never seen so many different races and cultures before, or so many kinds of disabilities. 'In the dining room, I saw people eating with their feet,' she recalls.

It was at this competition that Louise first saw Connie Hansen, who was the world champion. She was too awed to approach the Dutch athlete, but watched her closely. 'She was so strong and so tough. I had seen who I wanted to be. I wanted the respect that Connie Hansen got because she was the fastest in the world.' Indeed, the unknown Australian girl would soon become a threat to her idol.

Although Louise won the 100-metre race, the Netherlands meet was a baptism of fire for her. To her horror, she was disqualified in the 200-metre race for veering out of her lane. Instead of being crushed by the experience, Louise chose to learn from it. 'I decided never to do it again, and I haven't,' she says firmly.

In 1992 Louise went to Barcelona to attend her first Paralympic Games. The people of Barcelona really supported the Paralympic Games and the competing athletes, and during the finals the stadium was packed every night. Louise was nervous about the competition, not knowing what to expect. Since athletes with a disability do not meet as often as their able-bodied counterparts, they have no up-to-date form guide. They never know where the threat might come from.

Louise went in hoping to reach the finals and perhaps win a medal. She exceeded everybody's expectations, including her own. Not only did the eighteen year old win three gold medals and one silver, she also became the first woman to break 30 seconds over the 200-metre distance. 'It was a mad feeling, just being there. Being successful was totally unexpected — but fantastic!'

Up until this point, Louise had been an amateur. Her parents had paid her training and travel costs, and the local swimming club had helped buy her first race chair. But the Australian Institute of Sport had offered her a scholarship on her return from the Netherlands, and Louise decided to turn professional after the Barcelona games. To her knowledge, no one with a disability had ever become a professional athlete in Australia before, and many people were very discouraging — but they hadn't reckoned on Louise's willpower. 'I'm very competitive. I'm headstrong, stubborn and independent. I thought, I'll show you.'

The only positive voice was Rita's. 'Mum told me I could do anything. She encouraged me from the word go.' Louise's father Maurice, a sheet-metal worker, stayed out of the controversy; it was only later that Louise discovered he was taking her press cuttings to work to show his mates. 'He's very proud, but the silent type.'

Encouraged by her success in Barcelona, Louise expanded her training and launched herself into a new field — long-distance road racing. Since then she has won marathons in Japan, Switzerland, Berlin, Los Angeles, Boston and Honolulu.

At the end of 1994, Louise moved to Melbourne to be closer to competition. Emotionally, it was a tough choice. She was lonely, and ran up huge phone bills from calling her family and friends in the west. To help fill the long hours, she studied for year 11 through distance education. After a year, she moved back to Perth to prepare for the 1996 Olympics and Paralympics in Atlanta.

The trip to Atlanta would be an important one for Louise. Instead of being restricted to the Paralympic Games, she was to compete in the Olympics as well. Wheelchair racing was being staged as a demonstration event, which is the route by which new sports get onto the Olympic list. This meant racing in front of 85 000 spectators instead of the smaller Paralympic audience. Louise kept her nerve and won the 800-metre race — and a gold medal. Later, in the Atlanta Paralympics, she set world records in the 1500 and 5000-metre races.

As the only Australian to win gold on the track at the Atlanta Olympic Games, Louise returned home to Australia a celebrity. At the age of 22, she had forced a breakthrough for athletes with a disability. For the first time, a Paralympian received the sort of media coverage and public attention that elite able-bodied athletes took for granted.

Louise recognised an opening when she saw one. If she could be a pioneer on the track, why not blitz the media? Publicity was as necessary for sporting success as oxygen. By making people aware of her triumphs, Louise could attract sponsors for herself, as well as promoting the Paralympic movement. It was also a matter of justice. 'Athletes with a disability don't get the coverage they deserve,' she argues. Louise also took a course in public speaking to equip her for her new role, and has carved out a niche as a public speaker. 'I don't want to be anonymous,' she says. She is now the best known Paralympian in Australia.

In 1997 Louise attended the World Athletics Championships in Athens to compete in the 800-metre wheelchair demonstration race. This was the third time it was being staged at the championships. Louise, who'd won in 1993 and 1995, made it a trifecta and won a gold medal in the event. She and Cathy Freeman, who won the 400-metre race, were the only two Australians to win gold on the track. The Australian Institute of Sport named Louise their athlete of the year, and the Australian Olympic Committee presented her with its International Olympic Committee trophy.

As well as competing in individual events, Louise is a member of the Australian women's relay team. The team started to make its presence felt when it won two gold medals and set a world record at the world championships in Birmingham in 1998. In November of that year, four members of the team — Louise, Christie Skelton, Angie Ballard and Holly Ladmore — staged a wheelchair relay from Byron Bay to Bondi Beach to raise money for the NSW Wheelchair Sports Association. Some of that money will go to the younger team members who have not yet found sponsors. It was a gruelling trip — 845 kilometres over thirteen days, punctuated by speaking engagements and social functions in the towns along the route.

Their progress was covered by the national media, and hundreds of spectators turned out along the route. 'Many of those people would never have seen a race chair before,' says Louise. 'Now they'll support us because they've seen us.'

It was Louise Sauvage's example which attracted these young women to wheelchair racing. 'They've got the potential to beat me. They've got a good attitude, and they're working hard.' However, she's determined to stay ahead of them till the Sydney Paralympics.

It's not only on the athletics track that Louise has made her mark. Since 1993, Louise had competed every year in the wheelchair section of the prestigious Boston Marathon. In 1997, after veteran American champion Jean Driscoll crashed about six kilometres from the finish, Louise had her first victory. She won again the following year, but it was a white-knuckle ride. One hundred metres out, it looked as if Driscoll would clock up her eighth win. Suddenly, with nothing left to lose, Louise found some reserve of strength and resolve, and put on a burst of speed. The two women crossed the finish line together, clocking identical times. But Louise, who'd actually broken the tape, was declared the winner. The media went wild, and the Americans sat up and began to pay attention to the dark horse from Australia. In 1999, Louise again won the Boston Marathon, coming in a chair-length ahead of her rival.

After the 1997 Boston Marathon, Louise relocated to the 'east coast' to be closer to the action. 'Sydney is where it's all going to be happening,' she says. She lives near Homebush, the site of the 2000 Olympics and Paralympics. It was the best option for her career, but it meant starting over in a strange city where she knew only a few fellow athletes. She soon found her feet, however, buying a place of her own and furnishing it, and making new friends. She fiercely guards her independence, and lives alone. Long journeys do not intimidate her. To visit her family, she drove across the Nullarbor Plain from Melbourne three times.

Louise spends six months of the year away from Australia, competing to maintain her world ranking. To stay on top, she has a strenuous training schedule. She swims, boxes and trains in the gym, and does 25 to 35 kilometres of road work six days a week. For fun, she plays wheelchair basketball. She also travels the country regularly, guest speaking, undertaking sponsor appearances and promoting athletes with a disability and the Sydney 2000 Paralympic Games.

This dedication has paid off, but at a price. Being the best requires huge sacrifices. Louise does not go to parties or nightclubs because they make her too tired to train the next morning. Fatigue is a constant problem. 'Feeling tired a lot is hard. It doesn't matter how much sleep I get, I'm still tired.' Is it worth it? 'There are times when it isn't,' Louise admits. 'Like when you see your team-mates going out and having fun. But then I tell myself it's because I don't go out, and because I train hard, that I win.'

Louise Sauvage has come a long way from the inexperienced girl who went to the Netherlands and was awed by the toughness and speed of Connie Hansen. Since Barcelona she has won every track event she's competed in, and holds the 200, 800, 1500 and 5000-metre world records. In international track champion-ships around the world, she has won at least fifteen gold medals and one silver. In road racing, she has won some of the world's top sporting events, including the Los Angeles, Boston and Berlin Marathons. Louise has received an Order of Australia, and has been named Australian Paralympian of the Year four times.

All Louise's energy is currently focused on the year 2000, but she still looks to the future. She'd like to help develop junior wheelchair racing, and perhaps coach. 'I'd like to give them a helping hand and share some of the experiences I've had.'

Her experience will be invaluable for young athletes with a disability coming up through the ranks. Louise's rise to the pinnacle of her sport coincided with the movement to provide people with a disability with access to equal sporting opportunities. Without this surge, there may not have been sporting scholarships for athletes with a disability or respected international competitions. But not all athletes could have grasped the opportunity as forcefully as Louise. She was prepared to do the arduous training required of a champion, as well as becoming the public face of her sport. Louise Sauvage is a sporting pioneer. She led the way for athletes with a disability to become professional and earn a living from their chosen career, and she has created media opportunities that have put wheelchair racing in the public eye.

REBECCA SMART 1976 —

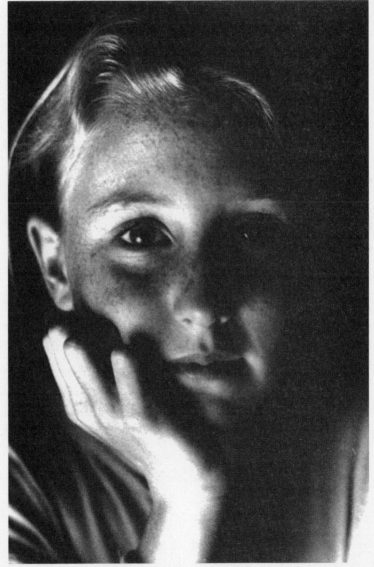

Actor

Rebecca Smart was eight when she was noticed by a film director's wife at an after-school centre in Bondi and given a screen test. She turned out to be a natural actor, and was cast in a film. Since then, she's worked regularly, appearing on television and in a number of films and plays.

Rebecca Smart was born in 1976 to Brenda, who worked in a bookshop, and Paull, a teacher at a business college. When she was three, her younger brother, Aaron, was born. Rebecca's childhood was happy and secure. 'My parents nurtured me and paid me lots of attention,' she says. 'I did what I wanted to do.' She attended Bondi Public School, and spent the weekends at the beach.

When Rebecca was eight, her ordinary life was turned upside down. One afternoon, Bojana Marijan, wife of the film director Dusan Makavejev, turned up at Rebecca's after-school care centre. The director was casting for *The Coca Cola Kid*, a film based on the short stories of Australian writer, Frank Moorhouse. To Bojana, this blonde, blue-eyed, freckle-faced girl looked right for one of the parts. She asked Rebecca to sing 'Mary Had a Little Lamb', and on the strength of that decided to audition her.

But first the project had to win the approval of Rebecca's parents. 'They weren't quite sure till they met the director,' she remembers. He explained what the film was about, and Brenda and Paull read the script. When they realised their daughter wouldn't have to do anything controversial, they gave their approval. In order to land the role, Rebecca then had to make it through two auditions. In one she had to stand with her hands behind her back and eat a chocolate cake placed on top of a stool. Then she had to do a scene with the actor Eric Roberts. That clinched it — she got the part.

Soon Rebecca was on set, playing alongside the glamorous Greta Scacchi. A level-headed young girl, Rebecca knew how to behave, and took this new experience in her stride. 'I wasn't a stupid eight year old,' she says. 'I was smart at school. It didn't confuse me. I accepted it as part of life. I wasn't frightened at all.' For someone so young, she was also highly independent. 'I didn't want my parents to go with me. I wanted to go by myself.'

Landing one film role seemed extraordinary enough, but it was only the beginning. Rebecca soon found herself cast in another. After the director Phil Noyce saw her on the set of *The Coca Cola Kid*, he hired her to play one of three daughters of a farming family in the television miniseries, *The Cowra Breakout*. That meant filming on location in the bush at Windsor for a few days. Shortly after, Rebecca made *Top Kid*, a one-hour television film for the Australian Children's Television Foundation. Still only eight, she had three films under her belt.

But when the whirlwind was over, Rebecca found it hard to return to normal life. She had trouble adjusting to being just one of thirty in her class, instead of being the only child on the film set, spoiled by the country's leading actors and directors. 'I didn't want to be at school. I wanted to be acting. But in fourth class I had a good teacher, who brought me back to earth.'

Rebecca also had plenty of support at home. Until she was twelve, her mother acted as her agent and helped her learn her lines. And when the kids at school started giving her a hard time, her brother would stand up for her. 'They'd say, "You think you're smart because you're in the movies," and I'd get into silly fights.'

The offers continued to roll in, and Rebecca won a small role in *The Empty Beach*, a thriller starring Bryan Brown. In *Spit MacPhee*, she co-starred with legendary English actor John Mills. Then, when she was ten, Rebecca got her big break — she was cast as Buster in the television miniseries *The Shiralee*, playing opposite Noni Hazelhurst and Bryan Brown. 'I can remember being in love with Bryan, and loving him to death,' she says. When *The Shiralee* came out two years later, it was a smash hit, and Rebecca won a Logie for her performance as Buster. She and her mother went to Melbourne for the award ceremony and stayed at a big hotel. 'It was exciting, but overwhelming. The worst part was being too young to go to the party afterwards!'

The success of *The Shiralee* introduced Rebecca to the negative side of stardom. People began to recognise her in the street, and some couldn't resist the temptation to take her down a peg or two, criticising the show and Rebecca's performance. 'Twelve is not a good time to be going through that,' she says. 'At that age you think you're ugly and that nobody loves you. I used to take it seriously. I couldn't see then that people were just jealous.'

Around that time, Rebecca's family moved to Randwick, and she transferred to a nearby school in Waverley. The headmistress and teachers helped her by keeping her up to date with work when she had to miss school, but her schoolmates were not so kind. Though she made a few friends, Rebecca did not feel that she fitted in. 'I was really conscious when I got back from a film shoot that nobody wanted to hear about my life outside school. So I kept my mouth shut. It hurt me at the time, but my career was more important than those people. I'm glad I hung onto it.'

In 1994, eighteen-year-old Rebecca got her first stage part, as Susannah Walcott in Arthur Miller's *The Crucible*. The Sydney Theatre Company play was directed by Richard Wherrett, and toured Australia for school audiences. For Rebecca, who had no formal drama training and knew nothing about backstage rules and stagecraft, there was a lot to learn — including how to apply make-up! In film and television there are teams of people to make up the stars' faces, but in the theatre Rebecca suddenly had to do her own — a new experience.

Being part of a mixed acting troupe was an invaluable experience for a novice. 'The older actors had been doing it for years and years, and the graduates from NIDA — the National Institute of Dramatic Art — helped me. I learnt so much in three months.' The following year, Rebecca was cast as Cherie in *Blackrock*, Nick Enright's confronting play based on the murder of Newcastle teenager Leigh Leigh and the impact it had on a small community. By now, Rebecca knew enough about backstage etiquette and stagecraft to be able to concentrate on her performance in a very demanding role. But she is perfectly happy to be challenged. 'I don't want to be gorgeous or play the romantic lead. I like gutsy roles that get down to the nitty gritty. I'm not the romantic heroine type.' To help her understand the character of the dead girl's best friend, she did some research into the murder and its aftermath. The play ran for two and a half months at the Wharf Theatre in Sydney. 'I had to have a big rest after it.'

When *Blackrock* was made into a film in 1996, Rebecca again played the role of Cherie. A critical and commercial success, the film was a career breakthrough. 'Heaps of people saw it. It was so important, one of the most important films I've made.' In the meantime, she was also playing Melanie Black in *Heartbreak High*, ABC TV's popular teenage drama series.

Then, after years of continual work, Rebecca found herself unemployed after *Heartbreak High*. Realising how insecure her profession was, she began thinking seriously about an alternative career. 'The longer you're not occupied, the less confident you become,' she says. 'You start thinking you're in the wrong business.' She'd always wanted to be a primary school teacher, but her HSC results were not good enough. 'I discovered boys late in life and they started to notice me when I got my braces off,' she explains. 'I got distracted!' To qualify herself for a teaching degree, she started a bridging course in psychology at the University of Sydney. If she passes an exam after completing the course, she can enrol in a degree.

Rebecca is not yet ready to give up the limelight, though. Since *Heartbreak High* she's done a television film, a play and a talking book. She's decided to juggle her academic work and acting jobs rather than abandon either. 'If something really worth it comes up, I'll defer my course,' she says. And later, she intends to combine acting and part-time teaching.

Most people think of acting as a glamorous life — and it can be, with interviews, publicity, and glittering award ceremonies. Rebecca is not interested in that side of it. 'I don't party. I'm not part of the cool Sydney acting set. I couldn't get into the nightclubs they go to!' It can also be a hard life, with financial insecurity and long, anxious waits between professional engagements. By creating a secure private life and working towards her own career goals, Rebecca aims to get the best of both worlds. These days, she likes nothing better than to spend evenings at home with her partner Joe, a film technician she met on the set of *Heartbreak High*, her dog and a video. 'My parents brought me up pretty well, and kept me pretty level-headed. Mum says I was born under a lucky star.'

TAMARA ANNA CISLOWSKA 1977 –

Musical prodigy

*When she was eight, Tamara Anna Cislowska heard a piece of music played
on the piano. Her body tingled, the hair on the back of her neck stood up,
and she wanted to cry. Suddenly, she realised that a good pianist could make
this instrument express any emotion. She is now one of the most acclaimed
and awarded Australian pianists of her generation.*

Tamara Anna Cislowska was born into a musical
world. Her piano teacher mother, Neta Maughan, was
nine months pregnant with Tamara when she
accompanied some of her music students to the ABC
Concerto and Vocal Competition in 1977. Tamara was
born two weeks before the final, and she attended
that, too.

Tamara comes from a long line of musical women.
On her mother's side were piano prodigies, singers and
music teachers. Neta herself studied with Alexander
Sverjensky, who also taught the famous pianist Roger
Woodward. 'I was about two when I started the piano,'
Tamara recalls. 'I was totally fascinated by it, and I
constantly had music around me because of my mother's
students. When I made the connection between the
sound I loved and the piano, I was unstoppable. I tried
to copy what I'd heard, and tried to play incredibly
difficult pieces. My mother decided to teach me.'

Neta encouraged Tamara's interest in music, and
started her on piano finger exercises at three. ' I was so
lucky to have that when I was growing up,' says Tamara.
'There couldn't be any greater influence than your

parents, and having a mother involved in something I was so passionate about was an advantage.'

But most of Tamara's early training came from her surroundings. 'I just seemed to absorb it from the people around me. I would come to pieces in the repertoire and find I already knew them from hearing my mother teaching them.'

Tamara made her public debut when she was three, playing a Bösendorfer piano. It was at the first concert of

Tamara at 3, playing the piano at the Sydney Town Hall
Courtesy Neta Maughan

the United Music Teachers Association, held at the Sydney Town Hall. Tamara was so small her feet did not touch the ground. Roger Woodward adjusted the stool for her. Ten of her piano pieces were recorded for the ABC archives.

Tamara started competing in the Sydney Eisteddfod when she was about four, first in speech and drama, then in singing and piano as well. She can remember rushing from one competition to another and winning lots of first prizes. At ten, she became the youngest ever winner of the Sydney Eisteddfod Open Concerto Competition. It was about this time people started using the word 'prodigy' about her.

Tamara didn't like being called a prodigy. 'I was just doing what I loved. But it didn't affect me much. All the people around me would just laugh.' She enjoyed the opportunity to compete. 'It was a fantastic experience — it's a great way to develop performance skills. It's important because there are no other opportunities to participate in concerts.'

When Tamara was six, she began studying part time at the Sydney Conservatorium of Music. For six hours a week she studied chamber music and theory with her mother. She was one of the youngest students there. That was exciting, but also frustrating. People made a fuss of her, but they didn't take her opinions seriously.

'It was painful as a child. I had the same opinions as I have now. I haven't changed much in fifteen years. But when I was seven, nobody wanted to listen to them.'

As well as piano, violin, singing and later the cello, Tamara also took ten hours a week of speech and drama. It was a big load, but she never felt pressured. 'I thought I'd do it all,' she says. By the age of eleven, she'd obtained her Associate Diploma in Music from the Sydney Conservatorium and graduated with honours from a three-year diploma at the drama school. The following year she obtained her Licentiate Diploma, and at fourteen became the youngest pianist ever to win one of Australia's most prestigious music awards — the ABC Young Performer of the Year.

Tamara attended Del Monte Convent and Santa Sabina College in the Sydney suburb of Strathfield. She did well at school and sport, but it was difficult to fit everything in. 'I had a hard time at school because I felt as if I was trying to be four people at once. Being at school is a full-time job, but I had two careers — the daytime Tamara who went to school, and the night-time Tamara who played music.'

With no time to do school projects, she was always having to ask for extensions, especially if she'd been travelling interstate to perform. 'I started forgetting what we had been doing at school, and I was sleep deprived half the time. There was too much going on.' Tamara solved the conflict by making music her first priority.

Because she moves in musical circles, Tamara has spent most of her life with adults. Inevitably, her school friendships suffered, and she would feel guilty that she didn't have more time to devote to them. 'I got all the ingredients of a full social life. It's just that I got them from different places.' Now she has friends from different parts of her life. Many of them are musical, but not necessarily professional musicians.

In 1992 Tamara was judged Sydney's 'Finest Performer' in the sesquicentennial Sydney Eisteddfod. She became the city's cultural ambassador, travelling to Japan, where she played with a symphony orchestra, and to San Francisco, where she gave a concert at Stanford University.

Before she turned twenty, Tamara had recorded a piano concerto with the London Philharmonic, and Peter Sculthorpe's *Kakadu Concerto* with the Sydney Symphony Orchestra. She had appeared with the six major Australian orchestras and toured the US, Japan and Europe. In 1995 she was the youngest Australian pianist to be awarded the Fellowship of the Australian Music Examinations Board.

All this constant travelling has made a 'normal' life impossible. 'The travelling is hard,' Tamara admits. 'Even travelling interstate becomes exhausting. Travelling from country to country takes a day out of your schedule to recover, but sometimes you just have to go on stage as soon as you arrive.'

Much of the time, she doesn't even see the countries she visits. 'I've done a world tour of concert halls and hotel rooms,' she says. 'I'm always performing, always practising. I've seen pianos all over the world. Being behind a piano is a definition of my life. You forget what's happening outside the window.'

In 1998 Tamara based herself in London to make the travelling less onerous, but simply found she travelled more inside Europe. By this time, she'd been asked by her friend, the violinist Natalie Chee, to join an ensemble — 'a floating foursome' — called Tiramisu. 'I decided I'd go where I was asked. After all, what did I want to do with my life? Playing the piano is what I do.'

Tamara loves giving performances with a conductor and an orchestra. 'By working together, you create something greater than you. You're sharing the stage with a hundred people dedicated to the same goal. It's a collaborative effort.'

But playing the piano can be much more difficult than playing another instrument, she has discovered. 'For a start, you don't have your own instrument. You have a new instrument every day, and every piano is different.' And the same piano can sound different at different times. The piano might sound one way at rehearsals, then totally different after the piano tuner has been in. Or the sound will change with an audience in the room.

'You just have to surf your way through,' says Tamara. 'You have to be flexible and adapt to what's thrown at you. You have to be completely in control of what you can do, like those tennis players who have to adapt to any opponent. You change your game for different sets of circumstances.'

Tamara has already made three CDs, and there are more on the way. She loves being able to come up with an idea, choose the music, and play it as well. It gives her much more control than playing someone else's program in a concert. On her first CD, *Enchanted Isle*, she revived songs learnt by generations of piano students. Unusually, it featured works by Australian composers who were popular in the first half of this century.

'I was very much involved with Australian music as a child. As well as Bach and Mozart, I played Australian composers from an early age. They were my favourite pieces. It was never a conscious thing. It was just that the music I would learn and play and love was Australian. I was fortunate to be born at a time when the cultural cringe was not so strong.'

The CD was a critical and commercial success. 'Other pianists laughed at first, but I did it because I believed in it,' says Tamara. 'And now everybody loves it. When I'm signing albums, old ladies come up to me and say: "That's my life on that album."'

She designed her next CD, *Persian Hours*, for her own age group, and it made the top 20 classical list. Her latest is *The Russian Album*, which is a tribute to the musical tradition in which she was raised. Tamara loves Russian music, and the pianist and composer Sergei Rachmaninov is her favourite pianist. 'He is so elegant, so relaxed and in control of everything.'

Despite her years of success, Tamara acknowledges that she is just starting out on an international career as a concert pianist and recording artist. 'I'm at the bottom of the ladder at the moment.' But she is confident that she has what it takes to get to the top. 'You have to believe in yourself. That's the most important thing. Everyone wants to tell you what to do and how to do it. Everyone's an expert. You have to sift all that and take from it what you need and want.'

She has developed her own ideas about music, which she sees as a mixture of self-expression and sharing. 'In the last few years I've had experiences which have clarified what I don't want to become. I've discarded the trappings, the gimmicks, the commercialism. There's no point in losing the meaning of music.' She refuses to play pop music, and will not promote herself as a sex object on her CD covers.

'I try not to be extreme, to maintain the integrity of what I do. I judge things by their integrity. When I don't like something, it's because it strays from the path of music, it's a distortion.'

Although she loves playing, Tamara doesn't want to spend the rest of her life interpreting other people's music. 'As a performer, you can get bogged down in the official interpretation of things. I want to create as well as recreate, to forge new paths, do new things. I want to be a composer; that's an important part of my musical personality. When you write or improvise, that's coming from inside — it's original.'

Tamara Cislowska's life is exciting and glamorous — the grand concert halls, the bouquets, the praise — but it's also tough and demanding. The travel is exhausting, the hotel rooms depressing, and the critics can be fierce.

At home, there are the lonely hours spent practising. But this is what Tamara wants. It was her goal from childhood, and she has never wavered. She's been in control all the way. 'This is my life,' she says firmly. 'I created it.'

MONIQUE TRUONG 1985 –

Photograph by Greg White, courtesy John Fairfax & Co.

Outwitting the kidnappers

In July 1996, when Monique Truong was eleven, she was kidnapped from her home in western Sydney by a gang of youths and held for ransom. Monique befriended her captors then led the police to the gang's hiding place. She was rescued unhurt, and her kidnappers were rounded up and brought to justice.

Monique Truong's parents immigrated to Australia from Vietnam in 1979. Monique, who was born in 1985, is the second youngest in the family. The Truong family lived in a big house in Canley Vale, halfway between Fairfield and Cabramatta in Sydney's western suburbs. Monique's mother, Thi Be, was a beautician, and her father, Kien Hoa, a businessman. Monique attended Canley Heights Public School.

On the night of Wednesday 3 July 1996, the Truongs were having a family night at home. Monique had made the dinner and fed the dogs. Afterwards, her mother and brothers — Henry and Peter — went out to rent a video. Monique, her father, and her sister-in-law Oanh — the wife of Monique's half-brother Mark — stayed behind.

While Monique was upstairs in her mother's room watching *Who Dares Wins* on the television, six men — three of them armed with pistols — knocked on the front door of the house, pushed their way in and demanded money from Monique's father. After they threatened to kill the family, he handed over more than $2000. Monique was oblivious to the drama unfolding downstairs, until suddenly two boys appeared at the door of her mother's room. One of them was masked and brandishing a gun. He pointed it at her and said: 'Go downstairs or I'll shoot you.' Terrified, Monique jumped up. The second boy grabbed her around the neck, throttling her, and marched her down the stairs, with the gunman following. 'I was panicking inside,' says Monique. 'I was thinking, "What shall I do? What are they going to do to me?"' But she did not try to fight — she was afraid they might panic and hurt her.

Downstairs, the boys had thrown her father to the floor and kicked him. He was still lying there when Monique entered. Oanh was sitting on the floor crying. The masked boy placed his gun against Monique's temple and said to Kien: 'Give us all your money or we'll kill your daughter.' The second boy shoved her into a chair, and the gunman stood guard over her. Then a third boy came into the room. One of the gang went into the kitchen, rifled through the drawers and emerged with a cleaver.

While this was happening, the front door opened and Monique's mother walked in with Henry and Peter. They were told to come in and sit on the floor near Kien Hoa, and a boy with a gun demanded their money. Thi Be handed him her purse, and he pocketed all her banknotes. Meanwhile, another of the boys was dismantling the stereo system and a third was going through the cupboards upstairs looking for valuables. When he came downstairs, someone said: 'Take the girl.'

Monique was pushed towards the front door. Having seen an ad for the film *Ransom*, she knew she was being kidnapped like the child in the movie. But still she tried to appear calm. 'Inside you feel scared, but outside you act like you're not scared,' she says. Wearing pink pyjamas and grey and white socks with no shoes, she was bundled into the front seat of the family's red Suzuki Swift. The driver asked Monique her name, and told her that his name was Pete. Then a man with a shaved head and a moustache got into the back seat of the car. He told Pete to follow a blue car waiting down the street.

The convoy set off, and drove to Fairfield, where they moved Monique into a white car, as the police could be looking for the red Suzuki by now. The driver was one of the masked boys who'd been at the house. When he pulled the mask back like a hat Monique saw his face. Though Monique was frightened, she was still thinking clearly. Worried that her parents' car might get stolen, she talked the boys into turning on the car alarm before they abandoned it.

The kidnappers were obviously not hardened criminals. After they'd driven off, one of the boys insisted on going back to see if the alarm was working. It was. When he got back into the getaway car, the others swore at him for wasting time. He replied that it had been Monique's idea. One of his mates taunted him: 'If the girl told you to jump off the bridge, would you jump off the bridge?'

Back at the house, after agonising about what to do, Monique's family called the police. The kidnappers were by then driving around aimlessly looking for somewhere to sleep. When they reached the outskirts of Parramatta,

Pete called someone for advice. Monique heard a voice tell him to go somewhere far away, like the Blue Mountains, but Pete said they were too tired. He asked Monique if she was sleepy. 'No,' she answered, 'but I am hungry.' She requested a Happy Meal. Pete obligingly went off to McDonald's and came back with the food. When Monique politely offered Pete some of her fries, he declined, but the boy with the mask took some. Later they stopped at a shopping centre and stocked up on lollies, chips and Coke. By this time, Monique had calmed down a little, as the boys had not hurt her and seemed friendly.

When the four boys finally found a secluded spot and went to sleep, Monique stayed awake trying to figure out a way to escape. She considered writing a note with the crayons from her Happy Meal, but decided against it, not sure if the driver was really asleep. When they all woke up, Monique asked if she could have a piece of paper to write things down for her diary. One of the boys was about to give her some, but Pete stopped him. They put a woollen mask on Monique, pulled it right down so she could not see, and set off. She was told to lie down and go to sleep. Obediently, she lay down on the lowered seat, but she had no intention of sleeping.

Eventually Pete decided they'd have to find a hotel to hole up in for the night. They chose the Ramada Hotel at Parramatta because it had no surveillance cameras in the lobby. Two boys stayed with the car, while Pete and another boy went into the hotel with Monique. They told her to say she was their little sister. After checking in, they took the elevator to a room on the fifth floor. Monique looked at the clock — it was about 6 a.m. She'd been gone nine hours, and knew her family would be frantic. Pete grabbed one of the single beds for himself, while Monique and the other boy shared the second one, with a pillow between them.

Monique slept till the alarm on the clock radio went off. It was after eight now. Pete made a phone call in the other room. Monique heard one of the boys whisper that today was the big day and they were going to need a bit of sleep. When the boys nodded off again, Monique lay down and pretended she, too, was asleep — but she was really developing a plan.

'I thought if I wrote a letter, all the boys would get caught,' she says. Quietly, she took some hotel notepaper and a pen from the night stand between the two beds and wrote: 'SOS. Please help me, there are two robbers in this room.' The note also mentioned the two boys outside in the car, and warned the police to wear casual clothes in case the boys saw them. She wrote that she would be in the bathroom waiting for them to arrive.

Monique hid the note in her sleeve, and started writing a letter to 'Dear Diary'. That way, if the boys woke up and caught her writing, she could hide the SOS note underneath it. Then she woke the boy next to her and said she had to go to the toilet. 'I thought that if the police came in and knocked on the door, then the boys couldn't hold me as a shield,' she says. On her way, she slipped the SOS note under the door. She stayed in the bathroom a long time, waiting for the police to come. Finally, afraid the boys would get suspicious, she had to come out. She watched the film *Babe* on television, and waited in suspense for the police to arrive.

'I waited and waited,' recalls Monique. 'When *Babe* was about halfway through, I heard the noise of paper. I looked [under the door] and the note was gone. I thought it wouldn't be long before the police would come and I would be saved.' It was then about 11.30 a.m. A member of the hotel staff had found the note and immediately notified the police. When Monique switched channels on the television set, she received a shock. Her kidnapping was all over the news. According to the report, the gang had demanded $50 000 for her safe return. Shortly after, she sneaked a look out the window to see if anything was happening. There was a police car in front of the hotel! Her heart raced, but she stayed calm and pretended nothing was happening.

Still worried about a shoot-out, Monique decided to get one of the kidnappers out of the way before the police came. Telling Pete she couldn't go around in socks because it looked funny, she asked him to go out and buy her some shoes. Good-natured to the end, Pete took some money and got up to leave. But just as he opened the door, the police charged in. Monique ran to the door and embraced the police officers.

By noon on Thursday 4 July, still in the pink pyjamas she'd been wearing when she was abducted, Monique was reunited with her father. 'I ran up and hugged him and we both started to cry,' she says.

It didn't take the police long to round up the gang. Twenty-four hours after the kidnapping, police raided a house in Bonnyrigg and found a stash of weapons — including a high-powered SKS assault rifle, a loaded pump-action shotgun and 300 rounds of ammunition. They arrested four youths. Of those involved, all but one were under eighteen. Most were high school students — Pete had told Monique he was in year 12. They were charged with robbery while armed, aggravated break and enter, and kidnapping, and were all sent to prison.

Before her ordeal, Monique would not have regarded herself as a brave girl, but she kept her wits about her, made friends with her abductors, and as soon as they dropped their guard she outwitted them. But inside, she was terrified: 'I went with the boys because they forced me to, and I was scared they would hurt me or my family if I didn't do what they said.' She was luckier than many kidnap victims — at least the boys treated her well.

The invasion of their home and Monique's abduction had a profound effect on the lives of everyone in the Truong family. Though not physically harmed, Monique was emotionally scarred by her ordeal. She had trouble sleeping and felt insecure, despite having counselling. And after being just one of the kids at school, she found herself a figure of curiosity after the story hit the news. 'I would hear the kids at school say, "Is that the girl who was kidnapped?"'

Her life changed in other ways, too. Her parents were much more protective and would not let her sleep over at friends' houses any more. Visitors to the Truong house had to get past a huge guard dog which dwarfed tiny Monique. On the positive side, Monique's bravery attracted the attention of a film producer, and she was hired to act in *Your Move*, a film about first aid. Now she's hooked and wants to be an actor.

Since the Truongs no longer felt safe in Canley Vale, at the end of 1997 Monique's mother and brothers moved to the Gold Coast. Monique stayed behind with her father to finish the school year while he sold the house. The following year, they too moved north.

Today, Monique still wakes up sweating with fear from nightmares and has to take medication to get back to sleep. The Truongs are still very security conscious. They never forget to lock the doors and windows, and the children do not go out by themselves. But away from the scene of the crime, Monique has started to heal. She loves the Gold Coast with its open-air lifestyle and its fabulous beaches, and has started a new life at a new school. Most importantly, she is finally starting to feel safe.

Sources

Louisa Atkinson

Atkinson, Louisa & Gilbert, Lionel (1980) *Excursions from Berrima and a Trip to Monaro and Molonglo in the 1870s*, Mulini Press, Canberra.

Atkinson, Louisa (1983) *Tom Hellicar's Children*, Mulini Press, Canberra.

Birkett, Winifred (1988) 'Some Pioneer Australian Women Writers' in *The Peaceful Army*, ed Flora Eldershaw, Penguin, Melbourne.

Clarke, Patricia (1990) *Pioneer Writer. The Life of Louisa Atkinson: Novelist, Journalist, Naturalist*, Allen & Unwin, Sydney.

Muir, Marcie (1980) *Charlotte Burton: Australia's First Children's Author*, Wentworth Books, Sydney.

Alice Betteridge

Thompson, Valerie (1990) *A Girl Like Alice: The Story of the Australian Helen Keller*, North Rocks Press, Sydney.

Interview with Valerie Thompson

Nancy Bird

Bird, Nancy (1961) *Born to Fly*, Angus & Robertson, Sydney.

— (1990) *My God! It's a Woman*, Angus & Robertson, Sydney.

Lomax, Judy (1986) 'Nancy Bird: Australian Mercy Pilot', in *Women of the Air*, John Murray, London.

Interviews with Nancy Bird Walton

Beverley Buckingham

Interviews with Beverley, Joan and Ted Buckingham, and Jason King

Newspaper reports

Evonne Goolagong Cawley

Cawley, Evonne Goolagong & Jarratt, Phil (1993) *Home! The Evonne Goolagong Story*, Simon & Schuster, Sydney.

Wade, Virginia with Jean Rafferty (1984) *Ladies of the Court: A Century of Women at Wimbledon*, Pavilion, London.

Interview with Evonne Goolagong Cawley

Tamara Anna Cislowska

'Tamara Anna Cislowska', in *Soundscapes*, April–May, 1997.

Interviews with Tamara Anna Cislowska and Neta Maughan

Fiona Coote

Interviews with Fiona Coote

Newspaper reports

Dawn Fraser

Fraser, Dawn & Murdoch, Lesley Howard (1991) *Our Dawn: A Pictorial Biography*, Sally Milner Publishing, Sydney.

Gallagher, Harry (1998) *Memories of a Fox*, Wakefield Press, Adelaide.

Newspaper reports

May Gibbs

Holden, Robert (1992) *Visions of Fantasy. Australia's Fantasy Illustrators: Their Lives and Works*, Angus & Robertson, Sydney.

Lees, Stella & Macintyre, Pamela (eds) (1993) *The Oxford Companion to Australian Children's Literature*, Oxford University Press, Melbourne.

Walsh, Maureen (1985) *May Gibbs: Mother of the Gumnuts*, Angus & Robertson, Sydney.

Vida Goldstein

Bomford Janette M. (1993) *That Dangerous and Persuasive Woman Vida Goldstein*, Melbourne University Press, Melbourne.

Henderson, Leslie (1973) *The Goldstein Story*, Stockland Press, North Melbourne.

Women's Political Association, Victorian Central Committee (1912) *The Life and Work of Miss Vida Goldstein*, Australasian Authors' Agency, Victoria.

Lorrie Graham

Milliken, Robert & Graham, Lorrie (1995) *On the Edge: The Changing World of Australia's Farmers*, Simon & Schuster, Sydney.

Interviews with Lorrie Graham

Sonya Hartnett

Hartnett, Sonya (1995) *Sleeping Dogs*, Viking, Ringwood.

— (1997) *Black Foxes*, Penguin, Ringwood.

— (1998) *The Devil Latch*, Penguin, Ringwood.

Interviews with Sonya Hartnett

Marjorie Lawrence

Lawrence, Marjorie (1949) *Interrupted Melody*, Invincible Press, Sydney.

Mary MacKillop

Dunne, Claire (1994) *Mary MacKillop: No Plaster Saint*, ABC Books, Sydney.

Foale RSJ, Marie Therese (1989) *The Josephite Story: Mary MacKillop and the Sisters of St Joseph 1866–1893*, St Joseph's Generalate, Sydney.

Lyne, Daniel (1983) *Mary MacKillop: Spirituality and Charisma*, St Joseph's Generalate, Sydney.

Modystack, William (1982) *Mary MacKillop: A Woman Before Her Time*, Rigby, Adelaide.

MacKillop, Mother Mary of the Cross (1981) 'Life of Rev. J E T Woods', *Resource Material from the Archives of the Sisters of St Joseph of the Sacred Heart, Sydney*, Issue No. 6, August.

O'Brien, Lesley (1994) *Mary MacKillop Unveiled*, CollinsDove, Melbourne.

Gardiner SJ, Paul (1994) *Mary MacKillop: An Extraordinary Australian*, EJ Dwyer/David Ell Press, Sydney.

Interview with Claire Dunne

Linda Tritton McLean

McLean, Linda (1981) *Pumpkin Pie & Faded Sandshoes*, Apcol, Sydney.

Interviews with Linda Tritton McLean and Harold Tritton

Irene Moss

Interview with Irene Moss

Newspaper reports

Pat O'Shane

Rintoul, Stuart (ed) (1993) *The Wailing: A National Black Oral History*, William Heinemann Australia, Melbourne.

Sykes, Roberta & Edwards, Sandy (1993) *Murawina: Australian Women of High Achievement*, Doubleday, Sydney.

Interview with Pat O'Shane

Newspaper reports

Mary Haydock Reibey

Applin, Graeme (ed) (1988) *A Difficult Infant: Sydney before Macquarie*, UNSW Press, Sydney.

Irvine, Nance (1982) *Mary Reibey — Molly Incognita*, Library of Australian History, North Sydney.

— (1995) *Dear Cousin*, Hale & Iremonger, Sydney.

Powell, Jocelyn & Banks, Lorraine (eds) (1990) *Hawkesbury History: Governor Phillip, Exploration and Early Settlement*, Dharug & Lower Hawkesbury Historical Society.

Sydney Cove Authority (1997) *Anchored in a Small Cove: A History and Archaeology of the Rocks, Sydney*, Sydney Cove Authority, Sydney.

Henry Handel Richardson

Clark, Axel (1990) *Henry Handel Richardson: Fiction in the Making*, Simon & Schuster, Sydney.

Green, Dorothy (1986) *Henry Handel Richardson & Her Fiction*, Allen & Unwin, Sydney.

Richardson, Henry Handel (1981) *The Getting of Wisdom*, The Dial Press, New York.

— (1948) *Myself When Young*, William Heinemann Ltd, London.

Louise Sauvage

Interviews with Louise and Rita Sauvage

Rebecca Smart
  Interviews with Rebecca Smart
  Newspaper reports
Heather Tetu
  Interviews with Heather Tetu
  Newspaper reports
Monique Truong
  Interviews with Monique Truong
  Interview with detectives at Cabramatta Police Station
  Monique Truong's statement to police
  Newspaper reports

Index

Susan Geason was born in Tasmania and grew up in Queensland. She has a BA in History and Politics from the University of Queensland, and an MA (Hons) in Political Philosophy from the University of Toronto. She has worked as a Cabinet Adviser in the NSW Premier's Department and as Literary Editor of the *Sun-Herald*, and now writes and edits for a living.

Her five mystery novels and a collection of short stories have been published in Australia, France and Germany, and she has had short stories published in Australia, Europe and North America. *Great Australian Girls* is her second non-fiction book; the first was *Regarding Jane Eyre*, a collection of stories and essays on Charlotte Brönte's novel, which she edited.

Susan Geason lives in Sydney.
You can contact Susan Geason at sgeason@ozemail.com.au